Mistress Devon

A NOVEL BY

Virginia Coffman

ARBOR HOUSE

NEW YORK

Although the Dantine Troupe itself is fictional, I wish to thank my various directors who contributed much to my knowledge. I especially want to thank my sister, Donnie Coffman Micciche, who inspired so much of the theatre background and with whom I shared, at one time, those great nights that began with the nerve-wracking:

"PLACES! CURTAIN!"

Dedication:

> **To Jay Garon, my agent, with many thanks. Moving editorial mountains is his specialty**

The Dantine Players

DEVON HOWARD
MICHAEL DANTINE, *the Director*
DENIS VARNEY, *the Leading Man*
KATE MERILEE, *the Leading Woman*
BOB TRAVER, *the Juvenile Lead*
GERARD DE GUICHE, *the Character Man*
FLOSS ROY, *the Soubrette*

OTHELLO (*He kisses the sleeping Desdemona*)
One more,   One more:
Be thus when thou art dead,
and I will kill thee,
And love thee after.

ACT FIVE, SCENE ii

Chapter One

QUITE SUDDENLY Devon Howard arrived at the place. The playbill was enormous, posted against a red-brick wall, the ends of the bill fluttering in the late afternoon breeze. She had run at least half the way, and was relieved to set her bandbox down and take a long, deep breath. Then she stood back, far enough away from the wall to get the playbill's full effect:

MICHAEL DANTINE
PRESENTS
THE DANTINE PLAYERS
in
the moral dialogues of
William Shakespeare
from
December Third, 1774,
including
King Lear, The Taming of the Shrew
and
As You Like It
at the South Market Theatre

From the size of the playbill, the Dantine Players must think themselves the most important visitors to Boston in a decade, but Devon, remembering the shocking content of Shakespeare's plays, thought that if the Dantine Troupe was to bring "moral dialogues" to Massachusetts, they had chosen an odd assortment of moral teachings for their purpose. However, their morals were not really her affair.

Then she looked closer, holding her breath with anticipation, for it was just as the ostler of the Tremount Coffee House had promised; a post was offered for a young lady of Devon's qualifications. Tucked into a corner of the great playbill was the magic promise on a white placard:

> WANTED: Genteel young female to act as seamstress and tirewoman. Must be able to play small parts upon demand. Apply the South Market Theatre before six of an evening, or at any hour after noon on Sunday.

Shifting her bandbox with its bright but weathered blue ribbons, Devon reread the placard. There was that line about playing parts upon demand, which was a terrifying if titillating thought; for her mother had been an actress. But more important, the fat innkeeper at Tremount House had made it perfectly plain there was to be "neither food nor lodging extended" until he saw the color of his young lodger's money. A single half crown was hardly dazzling enough to move him, he made clear, unless Devon found him as personally dazzling as he found himself.

What did the placard say? *Genteel young woman.* . . . But was she truly genteel? Lean, morose Joshua Howard, her father, had accused her of being her mother's daughter, lacking only her mother's beauty. He had never really warmed to Devon, even during the long months when she nursed him in his final illness. His last days bled him of his hard-accumulated little competence, and what remained after Devon paid his debts was barely enough to take her from Concord into Boston where for these three weeks she had managed to stave off the more acute pangs of starvation while she searched for a post she could fill.

But the big world of Boston had thus far proved immune to whatever hopes she could still muster for a post among the very few for which she was equipped. It was not enough that hard times should have come upon the port at this moment. The entire city was virtually under arrest in the name of the Crown. It was the outside of enough, even for a good Tory like Devon!

While considering the placard, Devon remembered with a flicker of amusement her single experience of employment as a governess, abruptly terminated when her employer, Mrs. Leonidas Carey, found her reading Mister Defoe's romance, *Moll Flanders*, to the palpitating Carey girls in her attic bedchamber. But it was such an amusing book, and Moll Flanders herself was so very odd! Did females of low station really do all those nasty but rather funny things? "Not but what I'd have more sense," she reminded herself quickly. Still and all, it was exciting to read, and one never quite knew what was ahead in these hard times.

Someone crowded against her, pushing her away from the wall. Another young female was looking for work. Devon would like to have hidden the advertisement, spread her cloak across the playbill and guarded the precious little WANTED placard. But the girl was shoving her aside without ceremony. She had a companion, a redhead about the same age.

"Nell, they'd pay a girl to dress the actresses. Let's try it."

"What? Mam would skin me alive if I was to go near them players!"

"The pay wouldn't be worse than Mulligan's Ordinary. I've half a mind to try it. Mulligan! A body with my talents goes all to pieces in this horrid town."

Devon glanced out from under the blue hood of her cloak to see what the girl's talents might be. They were evident in the neighborhood of the tight-laced bodice and the generous hips. Devon picked up her bandbox by the gay, wide ribbons that had grown a trifle soiled from much handling, and she turned away hurriedly. With such competition as this, there was no time to be lost. The December sun had already gone from the now quiet street, and afternoon shadows were swallowed in dusk.

The blonde looked after her and discovered in a clearly audible voice, "Lud, Nell, the little whey-face was after the job, too!"

Deeply mortified by the casual insult, Devon turned and looked back at her. She wished she had her mother's beauty and great presence with which to answer these insufferable wenches. In her lengthy and disastrously straight black hair, the blue-glass ear bobs that had belonged to her mother tinkled as she flashed the girls a look she hoped was devastating. But they failed to read the strength in that delicate, triangular face with its stubborn chin. They laughed in an irritating way that made Devon's fingers itch to box their ears. The blonde, seeing she had aroused her prey, became more impudent. "Don't try your claws against me, Little Miss Innocence."

Devon could think of nothing but the rather crude and unladylike retort which would have shocked her father: "No one's likely to take a fat, vulgar wench like you for genteel."

With what she hoped was a sinuous sway of skirts, including the sight of two frayed petticoats, she hurried down the street toward the South Market Theatre, thinking as she went that if anyone else had heard her speech, Mistress Devon Howard was not like to be thought genteel either.

It was a long way to South Market. Over the clattering cobblestones which became noisier as she hurried along, the evening traffic caught her in a labyrinth of hawkers closing their wares, professional men making their way home to dinner, and of redcoated soldiers, the constant reminder of the rebellious city's occupation by the Crown forces. For all their problems, these good people were secure. They knew where they slept. They knew where to find a hot supper. They jostled her on the street arguing taxes, India tea, the king, and the outrageous price of beef. They disagreed on everything—even the Redcoats disagreed—on the best boot-maker's shop and the place to procure a doxy for the night. Yet they were all united against strangers and loneliness.

Once, to avoid a nest of carts and wagoners, she lost her bearings and had to retrace some steps before she saw the steeple of South Church looming a few squares to the right. At the same time disembodied hands were setting lamps in the window or doorway of every seventh house, in imitation of the New York Lamp Laws. It must be after six.

She began to run, remembering the time limit on the plac-ard. When she thought of the chance to eat a genuine meal again, to know where she would sleep of nights, and to be a part of her mother's precious Theatre, she thought her heart would burst with her speed.

It was too much to hope she might one day equal her dead mother's chameleon charm before the footlight candles. But she would never make her mother's mistake of marrying a stern, overbearing man. Seared into Devon's memory was her father's slow chipping away of the confidence and talent, and last, in his jealousy, even the charm of the great actress until the lung sickness took what was left of her. One thing Devon had determined three weeks ago, sitting in the November sun upon her father's new-turned grave and staring at the grassy plot under which her mother lay: she would never let passion betray her into her mother's mistake—she would have no master but herself.

A sailor caught at her flying cloak as she ran along the street and called a friendly invitation, but she heard it only faintly as she heard the shout of a crab seller and the chimes of South Church. At the cross street she saw the front doors of South Market Theatre, already swarming with disap-pointed seekers after "moral teachings" who had failed to obtain seats, despite the hard times which had followed upon the closing of the port by the royal order. She went around to the back to the stage entrance. A crude lettered sign in red paint ordered TRESPASSERS BEWARE.

She stood there in the gutter of the refuse-cluttered alley, wondering what do next, wrinkling her nose at the stench and careful not to step into the drying sewage. She sucked at the neatly darned knuckle of her last pair of gloves. Unfastening the purse strings from the lining of her cape, she counted up the bright silver half crown, a worn shilling, three coppers. Reason enough to knock where a sign forbade her. She put out her hand to rap on the stage door but caught a glimpse of a new hole beside the darned place in her glove and hastily recalled that hand.

After a moment of fumbling—the other glove looked quite as bad—she put her left hand out and knocked with a resolute sound which produced no immediate result. She heard inside a bustling, shouting angry noise. Many people were doing many things in too small a space. Once, she heard a clear speech and realized the sounds came from the stage within. Just as she was summoning up courage to attack the door again, it was flung outward and would have smacked her in the face if she hadn't ducked around it and hurried inside while she had the chance.

A lithe, tawny-haired young man pulled her into a black passage and closed the door behind her. "We'll do business when the scene is done," he said.

She stood in a narrow, shadowed passage that led directly to the wings of the improvised stage and tried to ignore the lightheadedness that came from so much running and so little eating lately.

The young man, whose hair hung close and unconfined about his lively face, had begun to read his Whig newspaper again by the reflection of the footlight candles. Devon turned her attention to the stage. It was *The Taming of the Shrew*, and Katharina was just announcing that she would see Petruchio hanged before she would marry him.

She was a beauty, very well curved, with long plaits of her own jewel-braided brown hair halfway down her back. Her gestures were superbly theatrical. Nothing subtle about this Katharina. The audience of staid Bostonians, defiant of the city's scruples against playacting, was uproariously in favor of the lovely Shrew.

From what Devon could see of Petruchio, the actor was not so fortunate. In spite of an extremely handsome face and luminous dark eyes, there was a quiet, intellectual look about him, totally unsuited to the dashing Petruchio.

In another moment Katharina stormed offstage in the wings opposite Devon and the ensuing dialogue was interrupted by a burst of applause for the departed Shrew.

When the curtains closed upon the act, and coffee and ale were served to those of the audience who paid roundly, Devon's male companion hustled her across the stage. This area was now cluttered with scene shifters who were mostly out-of-work dockmen and did their work with understandable confusion. Devon found herself in a little room beyond the company office, which also served as a greenroom after the performance. This was formed, like the dressing rooms, by a series of movable screens.

The sounds from the dressing rooms were deafening, but still the untidy young man, busy lighting a candle, cautioned Devon to speak in a low tone. "That monster we call an audience can hear too damned easily in these drafty market theatres."

She was picking the words to explain her mission when he went on. "You seem a funny sort for the job. Rather young, aren't you? How long have you been at it?"

"Quite some time," she lied quickly.

"Well, I'd never have guessed it. Have you any portraits, so I can pick one?"

This astounding request gave her a bad moment. Could she pass off her mother's Drury Lane portrait as her own? She opened her bandbox and handed him the picture.

"Good Lord! Who's this?"

She said nervously, "Oh, won't it do?" and tried her charm on him. "It's all I've got."

"All you've got! But that's impossible. I want a big, buxom wench, a fine, heavily curved doxy."

"But it said in the advertisement . . ."

"Advertisement? What advertisement? Look here. Aren't you Milly Fancher, who keeps girls for the use of us travelling people?"

She was sure she turned fire red all over as she belatedly understood. "No sir, I'm not. I should think you might have guessed. Please give me my picture."

The young man grinned as he returned her property and moved the candle closer to get his first real look at her. "Gad! My error, and what an error! Don't tell me this is your portrait! No. I can see that it isn't. What a beauty she is! Not at all your style, my child. I'm afraid you're much too inexperienced for what I had in mind tonight."

"We seem to be at cross purposes. It is about the advertisement for a seamstress. My name is Devon Howard."

"Devon. Fresh from the West Country? But your accent's damnably colonial."

"I am named for my mother's native county. She was born at Exeter. I came to see the manager of your company."

The sardonic twist to his features was heightened by the flicker of the candle flame. "The manager? You refer, of course, to Our Lord and Master, Michael Dantine. I did not realize it for a second. We always salaam three times before uttering the sacred name. But you will have to be content with his brother. Dantine is gone for the moment. Would I could say—forever!"

This did not sound promising. Michael Dantine must be a dragon. "When may I see Mr. Dantine's brother?"

"Confidentially, Ma'am, the gentleman in question is myself. Denis Varney."

With an effort she recovered from her surprise. He forestalled her half-expressed hope by a theatrical gesture. "Shall we resume after the next curtain? We've been playing down in New York which is reasonably broadminded. But here, we are going counter to the laws. And audience reaction tonight will be important."

"It seems in your favor, to judge by the applause out there."

"They are warming up, thanks to our Fair Kate."

"She is exceedingly good." Devon hesitated. "And your Petruchio, of course."

"No 'of course' about it! That's Bob Traver. Frankly, *I* am the best Petruchio you'll ever see, Ma'am. Ask anyone in New York or Paris. Or in Italy—how they loved me! But I was a bad boy and decamped before our last performance in New York, so I am relegated to a bit part until Master Dantine is satisfied that I have reformed. Here I must wait, like any common rogue, looking as unwashed as my audience, to play a bit part. But I'm doing Petruchio our next performance of this play. You may lay your cards to that."

Devon thought this young man who called himself Denis Varney would make a spectacular Petruchio, with just the right grace and mockery for the tamer of the Shrew.

"Well, here is my cue. I am Biondello. Hardly a part for my capabilities, but then—what is?" And he bounded away from her, almost before she was aware that the third-act curtains had parted. She waited uncertainly for a few minutes and then ventured out to the darkest part of the wings and stood among the props to watch the action. The beautiful Kate's appearance she noticed impersonally, but it was not until her lively friend leaped into the scene with news of Petruchio's coming that she felt a real interest in the principals.

He had a sly tongue and a malicious way of playing his speeches upstage, so that the rest of the cast were seen by the audience in half lights and indistinct profiles. His lines were soon over, but throughout the rest of the scene he kept up a careless, shifting movement, punctuated by an occasional flip of a lace handkerchief and a gentle dab at his lips. Scene-stealing tricks that even an amateur like Devon recognized. Something in his last gesture reminded her that she hadn't eaten all day.

There was no sound from the men's tiring room. Devon went to the opening among the screens and looked in. A whale oil lamp burned smokily on the makeup table among an assortment of paints, powders, greases and patches. Several recently snuffed candles still sent up forlorn little twists of smoke to the ceiling, and among the candles lay a half-eaten loaf of fresh bread. Someone had rubbed a streak of red pomade across the coarse brown surface

She took the bread and began to pinch out the red streak, but not for long. She could not resist the temptation of that bread, soiled or not. She took a bite, and then another. At first, the taste lingered, delicious and satisfying in her mouth. To her long enduring stomach, however, the shock of solid food was almost too much. She sat down suddenly on a three-legged stool, wondering if she was going to be sick. Her stomach seemed to turn over inside and then, slowly, to right itself. It would have been too awful to contemplate, to be sick in front of that sardonic Denis Varney. She grinned feebly in her relief.

The voice of her prospective employer recalled her to the present. "Now, Mistress, to business." Denis Varney stood off and studied her. "Turn around. Not much to you, and that's a fact. Are you handy with a needle?"

"Tolerably so."

"Slide back your hood. Gad's life! A pair of feline eyes! Are they both yours?" She didn't think this in the least funny but he was not intimidated by her scowl. "Let me see what sort of a profile you carry around with you. . . ."

Devon's fingers had hesitated over the pleated blue border of the hood, for the lining of watered silk was badly frayed,

24

but she obeyed him and found herself waiting anxiously for his verdict.

"What's that young nose turned up in the air about?" She thought for a terrible moment he was going to tweak her nose, but instead, he twisted a tendril of her hair over one finger. "These Boston breezes have played with you a bit, I see. No. Don't touch it. Leave those wisps above your brows. They give you a certain charm and deny that sober young forehead of yours. How old are you?"

"Sev- eighteen."

"Yes. About that, I'd say. Well, perhaps you will answer the purpose. I can't abide an ugly woman." Even now, having settled on hiring her, he hesitated. "There is one thing. The job has many facets. There is the sewing, dressing the players, mending . . . Can you act? No stage fright?"

"Oh, no! No stage fright." It was not precisely a lie. She had never appeared on a stage. "I am sure I could fill the duties."

"Possibly. But to get on. We lodge at the Green George. Have your trunks moved there as soon as possible."

"My trunks?" She glanced at her blue-ribboned bandbox. "Of course. My trunks."

"The place is crowded, what with this influx of Red-bellies on the town since the port was closed. But we can find you some cubbyhole. Your work begins tomorrow morning. Someone will instruct you. Probably de Guiche, our character man. Would you care to see the rest of the play?"

"No, thank you. I'll just go and have a cup of . . ." She couldn't have tea. That would shock the staunch Boston rebels. "A cup of chocolate, perhaps. I—I had an early dinner."

Denis Varney snapped his fingers against his satin cuffs to liven them and picked a bit of lint off his hose while he gave her the facts of her appointment. "The salary is three

25

guineas the quarter, plus lodgings and meals. Only the actors are paid by shares. And I might repeat a friendly warning. The last girl was a meddler. Prying into my beloved brother's affairs. He hates it. And I—" although he smiled, his peculiar golden eyes flashed,"—and I too, I hate it." He added after he saw her startled look, "We had to get rid of your predecessor; so keep to your own affairs, and all will be well." Abruptly, he waved her away.

Devon stared after him until the darkness of the wings intervened. She understood very little of the interview except that she was to earn the not inconsiderable sum of three guineas the quarter and that she should not ask questions.

Still, the position was odd. There was something odd about the whole business. About Denis Varney. About the master of the company who was so formidable that his own brother rejoiced to see him gone. They bore different names, too. And then, there was the seamstress who had been dismissed—"gotten rid of," Denis Varney had said.

But Devon did not care. She was going to hire a sedan chair in front of the theatre and ride in style to the Green George. At the tavern she was going to order the biggest meal in the history of Boston.

Chapter Two

SHE DID not eat the biggest supper in Boston, after all. In the private dining parlour of the Green George, she was reminded by the waiter that the port was closed and therefore, in answer to this insult from London, the patriot barricades had gone up at Boston Neck.

"If His High and Mighty Majesty means to bring Boston to her knees before rebellion breaks out in very truth," said the waiter knowledgeably, "he goes about it like an ass, pardon the liberty, Mistress."

Devon was surprised at his frankness, for a placard below the Green George's swinging sign stated that the hostelry was an honest, loyalist house and God Save His Majesty. She mentioned this.

"Ah well, that's as may be, seeing as how old Gamaliel Mather be the owner, and as stubborn a Tory as you'll meet, but truth is truth. And as for food, well now, these an't normal times, Mistress. One takes what one can get, and one gets salt pork."

Oddly enough, she found that the salt pork tasted as good as savory roast of beef. It was amazing what hunger would do to sharpen one's appetite. She left a neat wedge of meat on her plate so that the waiter might not guess she was a glutton and drank her Madeira wine with a warm glow of content. But the longer she stared at the wedge of pork, the sillier it seemed to impress the waiter. Besides, she had left one of the most succulent pieces. She ate it, a nibble at a time. Who cared what the waiter thought?

When he came to clear away she was asleep, with her head on her arms and her arms on the tablecloth. The elbow of her blue worsted gown barely missed her wine glass and one of her frilled white cuffs rested against the dirty plate. She woke while he cleared the table, rescued the bottle of Madeira from his clutches and poured herself another glass. She was studying the dregs of the wine in the candlelight when the door burst open and Katharina, the lovely shrew, swept into the room with a noisy rustling of silver-filigreed brocade under a squirrel-edged pelisse. "Are you the new seamstress?"

Devon admitted that she was.

Kate made an impatient, sweeping gesture with one hand, upon whose fingers sparkled a cluster of diamonds and a single, smouldering ruby. There was a superbly careless grace about her that needed few arts to improve, despite her buxom figure of that type so much admired by Denis Varney.

"Well, come then, Sweet. Don't just stand there. You share my bed. Come along."

The waiter who lighted them to their room could scarcely take his eyes from the Shrew long enough to give her a taper when they reached the room. Kate closed the door firmly upon the boy and leaned against it, laughing. He had been about to blunder after her into the bedchamber.

"Poor beggar. How he'd love to crawl between the blankets with me! I could see that calf look. But his kind won't pay the board bills. Gad's life, but I'm tired!" She stripped off the pelisse and threw it into the corner on top of a worn travelling trunk. "Here, Sweet, help me with these damned stays." She went on with her one-sided conversation while Devon played ladies' maid.

"Do you think you will like it here with us, Devon? That is your name; isn't it? How that takes me back! My first lover was a Devonshireman who jumped ship in New Orleans. But that's another tale. Did you see the play tonight? I vow I could have murdered that insufferable Varney. Upstaging me every chance he got, and him in that tiny Biondello part, too. Of course, he's an attractive beast. Poor Bob Traver, the handsomest fellow I've ever seen, can't hold up a candle to him as Petruchio. Ouch! It's my flesh you are pinching so freely. There! That's better. But go on. Undress yourself, child." Her brocade slipper came into contact with something unexpected on the worn drugget carpet. "This bandbox is part of your baggage, I suppose. That fool porter should have brought up the rest."

Devon looked at the box and said evenly, "That *is* the rest."

Kate glanced once again at it as if seeing something very special about it that she had not noticed before.

"At your size, my lass, you've probably got a whole wardrobe tucked away in there. You might wear decent clothes tolerably well. How do you keep your figure? I'll soon be a fat old . . . Ah, well, let's not anticipate."

Devon unfastened her own cloth cape and laid it with the bright blue silk lining out to attract Kate who examined Devon's wardrobe while unbraiding her hair. She was wrapped in an ugly plaid robe over her faded wool nightrail, and seeing Devon's surprised look, shrugged. "Can't help myself. Your New England is so damned breezy. I remember the first time Dantine saw this robe, he said it was enough to dampen a man's ardor. I was born to hot blood and sultry nights. Up the river out of New Orleans."

It was Kate's turn to stare when Devon was dressed for bed. She had long since worn into holes her store of bedgowns and wore, in the current style, a dressing sacque over a petticoat. The dressing sacque was of blue shag, too revealing in the bodice, and the petticoat had countless ruffles over the fustian base. She was rather pleased with the figure she cut in it and did not fail to observe Kate's glance. Devon brushed and combed her hair, remembering Denis Varney's unenthusiastic comment on her looks, and smiling wryly.

Kate said, "Are you ready, Devon? How I hate to leave this fire! I must make use of it while I may, because it's actually Michael Dantine's room which I've appropriated until his return. He's funny. If he tires of you in his bed, you may as well get out before he throws you out of it. You take the side nearest the shutters. You're used to Boston drafts."

Devon sank into the feather mattress and the pleasant haven left by the warming pan, and sighed with content.

For a long time after Kate was fast asleep, Devon lay with her body aching from the soft comfort after a straw mattress. She watched the fire die into embers, smiling to herself at the sudden loveliness of life. Without looking at them, she was aware of the fine white tester over the bed and the thick luxury of the blankets. If Mama could only know! It was almost like having her alive now, in the darkness just beyond the bed posts, waiting for the footlight candles to revive her laughter that was light as wind bells from China, and her voice, and her scent, fresh with flowers, warm with a hint of summer.

Still pleased with the world and her new situation, Devon closed her eyes at last.

A long time after, it seemed, she began to dream. She was struggling in murky black waters, and a hand rested upon her face from somewhere above her. As she looked up, a face stared down into hers, so close that she was able to see the eyes, intensely black, fettering her with their power. She tried to scream but heard no sound, and the effort tore at her whole body. When she forced her eyes open, the dark face was still there, staring down at her, a foot from her own. She lay perfectly silent, wondering how much of this was phantom and how much reality. In the ensuing stillness she closed her eyes, beginning to shiver.

She awoke to her surroundings with a start. The door had closed softly. Someone was leaving the room. The great dark phantom had been real, then. It was not yet dawn, and the coals in the fireplace were still faintly glowing. She looked at the sleeping Kate.

The rapping of sharp knuckles on the door aroused every nerve in her body. She sat straight up in bed, followed by Kate in short order. It was Kate who cried out, "Gad's life, you idiot! People are sleeping. Go away."

An apologetic male voice announced that he was the landlord. "Master Michael Dantine tells me, Mistress, that he found someone in his room. And I can find him no other vacancy. He's sleeping in the taproom. Would you let me take a blanket off the foot of your bed?"

"Why not?" Kate yawned and crawled under the sheets.

As the landlord came tiptoeing in, he raised his light to get a look at Devon and grinned. "Mrs. Kate, you're losing money tonight. A gentleman in that lady's spot would pay . . ."

Kate roused herself. "Get out, you filthy little pimp!"

"No offense, Mistress. No offense." He retreated with the blanket, ducking the slipper she hurled at him.

"Damned idiot!" Kate muttered and puffing up her pillow again, prepared to go back to sleep.

Devon said in the darkness, "I think I saw Mr. Dantine when he came in a few minutes ago. He seems a trifle—overpowering."

Kate laughed shortly. "So is a thunderstorm. Just as elemental, just as heartless. All the Varneys are heartless. Denis, the way he pays our soubrette, Floss Roy, out and in as he chooses. And Dantine."

"Has he always been an actor?"

"Of sorts, I suspect. But you might say he played different roles. When you know him well, you'll hear about the blackbirding, the smuggling, piracy. He learned his Shakespeare from our character man who was his supercargo in his blackbirding days. I've heard Dantine talk about it when he's drunk. Imagine his voice battling the elements—Lear against a gale, Macbeth against the waves. I'll wager he'd outshout the sea, too."

Devon thought about this and began to understand Denis Varney's warning.

Kate turned over in bed and looked at Devon intently, as if she could see her in the dark. "Bear something in mind for your own welfare, my dear. I couldn't hold Dantine. No one can. I was as young as you, once on a time, and quite as sure of my charms. . . . One bit of advice: don't let him work on your pity. It's fatal. At first, you think he must have a secret sorrow gnawing at his heart, as they say in some bad plays I've done." She laughed with a raw edge to the sound. "And that is very funny. Because he has no heart. . . . But why should I warn you? You will go through it all. They always do. Even now, you are thinking that you are different. *You* are the one woman!"

"Those women who loved him," persisted Devon, after a struggle with herself to keep quiet on the subject. "Were they shocked to find the truth?"

"They think he is the devil. And if it comes to that, so do I. He owns us all. Every human being in his troupe dances to his tune because of this obsession of his to own things. I've seen even irrepressible Denis lose his nerve when he tries standing up to his brother. Dantine cares for human beings the way a gale at sea cares for the ships it drives on the shoals. If I may be permitted a taste of his own melodrama."

Like my father, thought Devon with a jolt. . . . *Like the way he destroyed Mama.* She said sharply, "How I do hate men who fancy that all females are their slaves!"

Kate's voice was suddenly pleasant. "Excellent, my lass. Just keep away from Michael Dantine and you will be a happy little girl."

Chapter

Three

AT BREAKFAST, which the players took at eight in the private room of the Green George, the character man, Gerard de Guiche, announced that the Master —as he termed Michael Dantine—was gone for the day, to complete his search for occasional actors. No one was in the least disturbed that their landlord, old Tory Gamaliel Mather, still unseen in his upper-story parlour, had been the object of catcalls since dawn, the street before the inn being crowded with students from Harvard looking for excitement, with out-of-work dockmen adding to the din and rebels hired (Papa always said) by smugglers and troublemakers like John Hancock and Sam Adams.

At the table Devon found herself between aristocratic de Guiche and the quiet, good-looking young supporting lead of the company, Bob Traver.

She soon found in the course of the Frenchman's conversation that he was a rabid Whig, obsessed with his mission in life, to convert the world to communal life. He heartily endorsed the noisy throng out-of-doors. For a few minutes, hearing de Guiche's treasonable talk, Devon supposed he had suffered at the hands of some royalist in the past. But his lean, hawk-face showed no suffering, only a fanatic's gleam. She wondered what vicissitudes had driven him to a slave-trading vessel captained by Michael Dantine. He was that figure commonplace enough, but still inexplicable, she thought; an aristocrat who desired to suppress his own caste, to remake the universe in the image of a philosopher's dream world.

Bob Traver was a different matter. He did not look so youthfully naive as she had supposed and was, as Kate said, the handsomest man she had ever seen, with his dark, curly hair which he wore a trifle too short for a queue, his poignant brown eyes, and that tall, slender fencer's grace. He disarmed her at once by asking if she had seen last night's play, adding with his warm smile, "The play was better than its hero, I fear."

Devon thought it a little odd, this self-effacing quality of Traver's, almost as if he willed it so, perhaps to preserve the small privacy left him in a group that lived so intimately, or perhaps for some secret reason of his own. Briefly, she wondered if he had affiliations with one of the radical and terrorist groups called the Sons of Liberty, fighting, they claimed, to unite the colonies against the Crown. But the idea seemed absurd. He was so very kind, so gentlemanly, and Papa's friends said no real gentleman was ever a rebel.

The long table was dominated by Kate Merilee. Nothing escaped her, even Bob Traver's innocent remark that he was not a good Petruchio. "But we love our Bob," she said, "for all his shortcomings. There, Bob, don't be shy. Speak up and thank me."

Devon, seeing the red creep over the young man's face, suspected it was more than shyness. He was in love with the beautiful Kate and Kate did not care.

Devon turned her fascinated attention to the others of the Company, to flaxen-haired Floss Roy, the soubrette, in whom she found, close to the surface, a coarse quality that lacked the friendly, bawdy wit of Kate Merilee. She sat at de Guiche's left, rivaling Kate in her noisy command of the Company's attention, but differing from Kate in a number of respects and in none more than her voice, which had the elision of Cheapside London and a tendency to be uncertain on her "h" sounds. She had a native shrewdness and a biting tongue that aroused anger where Kate's raillery was laughed at. Judging from her conversation, the chief bond between the blonde soubrette and the aristocratic de Guiche was a common interest in the downfall of the Tory Party at Whitehall; but her eyes wandered in Denis Varney's direction more than once, in a very impolitic way.

Listening to the furious imprecations of de Guiche and Floss against the party in power, Devon wanted to answer them a dozen times but bit her tongue and remained meekly agreeable to everything. No need to antagonize them so soon, but she would like to have told them that they had more freedom under the Tory ministry in London than they would have under a local government in Philadelphia. She had heard it said, and thought it rather clever, that the further away the government was, the better. When de Guiche talked of the starving people, she remembered that she herself had risen above starvation, and that de Guiche enjoyed extremely full meals himself.

Momentarily proud of herself for her own achievement, she wondered suddenly what did happen when people starved. Did no one help them? No one at all?

As they were leaving the table, Devon came face to face with Denis Varney and after a slight hesitation, waiting vainly for recognition, she smiled at him. He looked at her indifferently and then, as she was passing him with the full dignity of her nearly eighteen years, he winked at her, and she could not be angry with him. He insisted on escorting her to the theatre for rehearsal, although it was obvious Floss had hoped he would come along with her and de Guiche.

During the rehearsal of *As You Like It* Devon found him as charming as an irresponsible baby. He forgot his lines half a dozen times that day while trying to show off before the Company's new seamstress. With Gerard de Guiche's stern eye upon her, she pretended not to notice him, but it was a hard struggle. Like a spoiled child, Denis was bound and determined to be noticed.

Devon worked until after dark that first day in an attempt to patch an ivory satin robe which Kate had torn climbing over a prop staircase to meet a good-looking admirer. The jagged tear was located a foot above the back hem and in plain view. Devon suggested finally that they mend the tear and sew on an overskirt of ivory lace. But there was no ivory lace left; Denis had insisted on the last for his cuffs.

Kate, who never hesitated to use her best friends, put aside the drapes to look out at the dark and rainy street. "My Sweet, I hate to ask you, but if you really want the lace, there are yards of it, and just the right shade, over at the theatre."

Devon hesitated, thinking of her thin-soled shoes, and looked down at them. Kate followed the glance and offered generously, "I'd loan you mine, but your feet would be lost in them, most likely."

"It doesn't matter," Devon lied as she got up and took her blue cloak from the wardrobe. "It will have to be done some time. As well now as later."

When she stepped out on the street with the cowl of her cloak pulled far over her face, a gust of wind and rain met her and momentarily imprisoned her under the eaves. Then, as the storm slackened a bit, she hurried down the street, trying not to let the quick, noisy patter of her own footsteps frighten her. It was a dark night. The few lanterns hanging in front of doorways flickered dangerously in the wind. In another ten minutes they would all have blown out. The return trip did not bear thinking of. She hurried on.

She reached the back door of the theatre without encountering any living thing except a drenched puppy who went trotting along at her heels for two squares and then turned off to his home.

The inside of the building was like a huge mouth opened wide and waiting for her. There was a candle on a table near the door, and, fumbling for a minute, she found a flint fire-maker nearby. After several failures, she got a flickering light started, held the candle high, and ventured across the plank floor of the stage.

Things seemed to move in the darkness beyond her light. She paused before the women's tiring room to stare out into the dark theatre auditorium. A footstep sounded among the benches at the back of the hall. She flashed the candle in that direction. Whatever had been there was swallowed in long shadows. Shivering, she scuttled across the stage to find the brassbound chest where odds and ends were stored. It was in one far corner. Wandering around between the backdrops, squeezing through a space a few inches wide, she found the chest lying on its end, wedged in among an assortment of properties. She pulled and hauled at it vainly. The tight little place made her cough, and the cobwebs over her head hinted of moving creatures. She stood it as long as she could, finally giving up when she saw something black dangle down in front of her from the dark rafters. She did not stay to see whether the many-legged thing was alive but hurriedly pushed her way out of the dusty passage.

In the tiring room she set the candle on King Lear's taboret and began to examine the damage done by storm and dust to all that was left of her wardrobe. It was wrinkled and damp, but a good pressing would see it in shape again. She smoothed out the full worsted skirts and, pulling her hood forward again, hurried across the stage, intending to run back to the tavern with such speed there would be no time for fright.

Then a thing happened so oddly that, halfway across the stage, she stopped with dizzying suddenness. A man in the shadow of the opposite wings was watching her, had been watching her, apparently, for some time. He was so much in shadow that it was difficult to distinguish him from the darkness around him. But his low-pitched laugh as she stared at him dismissed her more immediate fear that he was not human.

"I trust I give you amusement, Sir."

He stepped further into the faint circle of light and held out a large, muscular hand toward her candlestick. She drew back instinctively, and he reached around behind her to take the candle. For a moment she thought he must be intending violence and twisted to elude him. When he took her wrist and forcibly began to loosen her grasp, she struggled in panic.

He pushed her away as soon as he had wrested the candle from her and looked down at her with a curious smile. "What the devil ails you? May I not have a light in my own theatre?"

She paused in the act of caressing the reddened flesh of her wrist. Michael Dantine, of course. When she looked up, he seemed the most overpowering creature she had ever seen. In his broad, mobile face were none of the elegancies that distinguished his brother. And in every other way he lacked Denis Varney's good looks. He had the build of a bo'sun's mate, with heavy-muscled shoulders and body and a great length of limb to set off this imposing height. He did not belong in drawing rooms or on stages, but on slave decks. Perhaps it was these dimensions that had given him his reputation with women.

No. There were other qualifications within the frame of his unruly black hair: the eyes of a man of quick passions, and a full, too-sensual mouth that disturbed some emotion deep within her, a high-bridged, heavy nose that gave to the face a little dignity. But above all these questionable assets, she felt at once the strangeness that made her think of lava rock, blackened by many fires, still having within its core a searing, destroying flame.

It was his eyes. She returned to them in spite of herself. The pupils were black as onyx, and in their depths, shadowed by thick lashes, they had a light that seemed to her evil because it was hypnotic. She looked away from him nervously, asking the unnecessary question, "Are you Master Dantine?"

"I am. And you? You are either a very inept little thief or . . . but of course! That sewing case swinging from your waist. You are the seamstress my brother made hire of the other night. You see, I've heard about you, Devon Howard. What are you doing wandering around alone after dark? Don't you know the town is full of restless Redcoats who eat tasty little morsels like you?"

"I saw no one but a lonesome puppy on my way to the theatre. I have been looking for some ivory lace to cover Miss Merilee's death gown in *Othello*."

Michael Dantine's somber face broke into a smile that took years from his normal appearance. In order to examine her better, he held the candle over her, so close that she had to duck her head to avoid the smoke. "I'm glad to hear that, Devon. A few minutes ago there was such a banging behind the drops that I was afraid our mice had grown to prodigious size."

"Perhaps you could help me then." She explained about the brassbound chest and led him around to the little passageway, and then watched him reach his free hand over her head and pull the chest toward him. Ducking under his arm, she got out of his way. While he lifted the chest out, she noted that his travelling coat, with its three-caped collar and flared skirt, was flattering to his tall figure, though it was unfashionably long, its hem inches below his boot tops.

"Here you are, Devon. Now, find your ivory lace and we will be off for home."

She rummaged through the chest under his interested gaze, wondering what he thought of her, whether he was criticizing her careless fingers as they uncovered tarnished brocades and tossed them aside. She went quickly through her task, wishing he would fix his dark eyes upon something less sensitive to his nearness than Devon Howard. She found the lace at last, and he shoved the lid down with his boot and reached for his hat which hung jauntily on the corner of the dressing screen.

"Let's be off. Leave the stuff where it is. I am tired. It has been a long day. And not over for me yet."

She folded the lace into as small a bundle as she could, reflecting that Michael Dantine would take a conveyance of some kind back to the tavern. He quickly shattered that illusion when they stepped out of the stage door and onto the wet street. "I think it is clearing. Here, give me your precious lace, and we will walk. A good, brisk walk in the night will do me good."

She was disappointed but found herself saying, to her own astonishment, "Yes, it is clean and sharp after a storm."

He went so quickly along she had difficulty matching her stride to his. The rain had stopped and there was a little clear spot overhead. Devon thought her companion ought to make an effort at conversation. Her own feet were wet and her skirts depressingly damp. When her introduction of the weather brought no response, she had nothing more to say. After some time, he asked her opinion of the players.

He seemed the kind of employer who expected flattery and probably would not understand anything else. "I thought they were excellent. I enjoyed Miss Merilee's acting more than I can say."

He grunted. "Yes. She is easy to enjoy. That is her contribution to the world. Careful there. You are stepping in a puddle. Damn these twisted little streets! Don't pull away. Give me your arm. I'm not going to hurt you. There." He boosted her over a puddle of filth and rainwater with an ease that impressed her.

When they reached the Green George, she was surprised at how short the return walk had been. He left her in the doorway with the bundle of lace.

"I'm off to see the Lobsterbacks about a travel permit for

the Troupe." He turned to leave but had a belated thought. "By the by, Devon, will you give my brother a message from me?"

"I shall be happy to, Sir."

"Then say that I commend his taste, and I think he had better do all my hiring. Good night."

She stared after him, and just before he disappeared into the darkness it came to her that from this distance, he looked very much like her father, the same tall, black-clad figure, the same big stride, the way his arms swung free.

As it began to mist again, she went into the tavern and up the stairs. She smiled at Kate's picture of the mysterious and aloof Michael Dantine. It was evident that the actress did not really understand him. That hardness seemed to be only superficial. Actually, he had been very kind. She thought with satisfaction and a certain smugness that she might be the one woman who did understand him.

Chapter
Four

BEFORE DEVON and Kate had finished gulping down their breakfast in bed next morning, the door opened with a violence that shook the windows, and Michael Dantine stormed into the room. There was nothing of last night's gentleman about him. His hair was loosely queued, revealing scattered gray in the black mane, and the sleeves of his white cambric shirt were rolled untidily above his elbows, so that Devon saw the muscular arms of a peasant and a laborer.

"Kate, what in God's name are you doing here in your petticoats at ten in the morning?" He picked up the purple grosgrain gown lying over a chair and threw it at her. It struck her in the face and she called him something vile that Devon did not understand, but laughed immediately after, and began to get into the dress with haste.

He turned to Devon. With a piece of toast in her mouth, she had her head under the bed, where she was shoving her tray out of sight. Her plight struck him as odd, and he stepped over to the bed, pulling her head up by the chin.

"What are you looking for under there?"

"Nothing."

"Well, swallow whatever it is you are eating, and get dressed. I need you down at the theatre to hold script." He studied her face for a short time, while she swallowed hard. "You look pale. Are you well?"

She nodded, trying to clear her throat.

Kate put in, "She got her feet wet last night in the rain, poor lamb."

"Why the devil didn't you say so last night?" he asked Devon. "We might have taken a carriage." He looked over his shoulder at Kate. "Why couldn't you have gone after the confounded lace? Heaven knows you are big enough to brave a storm."

"Now, Dantine, don't be any more rude than you were born to be. You will make Devon think you don't love me."

"Love you!" His black eyes flashed heavenward in astonishment at such a notion.

After a pause, during which Devon made no move, he urged her impatiently, "Dress, child, dress! We haven't all day. We give a performance tonight, you know."

She was embarrassed, and angry because she was embarrassed. "I am waiting for you to leave . . . Sir."

"What?" He seemed not to understand at first. Then a smile slowly lighted his face. "So that's it. You will find it impractical to spend your time looking for a lonely spot in which to dress. By the week's end you won't even notice my presence."

Something in his voice made her look up suddenly to catch his alarming eyes fixed on her uncovered throat and low-necked dressing sacque. She hurriedly covered the hollow of her breasts with her hand.

Kate called out, "Don't tease her, Dantine. Come and fasten my stays and then leave us like a good boy. We will be along in five minutes."

While Dantine was busy with Kate's stays, Devon got out

of bed, wrapped herself in Kate's discarded robe and put her dress and petticoats onto the bed, though she did not begin to dress until he was gone with a parting threat to drag them both out in five minutes.

South Market Theatre was not as confused and noisy as it had been under de Guiche's direction. The domination of Michael Dantine seemed to frighten the Company, and there was very little by-play when Devon entered. She had made up her mind firmly not to be cowed the way the others were. He was only a man, after all, a bully who exerted all this incredible authority because of his strength. He was another Joshua Howard, she reminded herself, and she was disappointed that he was none of the things she had supposed him last night when he complimented her so nicely.

Nevertheless, as his voice rumbled through the theatre, she shivered a little. When he shouted to her from the stage, she jumped to obey. "Devon, sit in my chair and open the manuscript to the first scene. And remember, don't prompt too quickly. Give the actor a chance."

She found Dantine's chair a huge monstrosity in which she almost disappeared. They were doing *As You Like It* which they had rehearsed yesterday for de Guiche, and she was surprised to find how much the whole cast blossomed in the presence of the director.

Devon wondered at this phenomenon and turned her attention directly to Dantine, whom she had been watching, more or less in spite of herself, all through the rehearsal. He was everywhere and saw everything. The dropping of a cue, the least faltering in a line evoked a deadly glance from him. It seldom happened that a player made two such mechanical mistakes.

During the course of the morning he became all the major characters in the play at least once. It was difficult to evaluate his acting ability. He was every adjective known to the theatre: ridiculous, fascinating, awe-inspiring, a dozen people in one. He was not a man at all but many pieces of a man, and

45

when all these pieces were fitted together, they formed a big, rude, gypsy-dark creature whose glance filled a woman with uneasiness and a man with fear.

She saw fear on their faces that day. Even the princely de Guiche, the proud and sensitive Bob Traver. All except Denis Varney. Denis followed every order, every suggestion of his brother, and for quite a long time Devon was fooled into thinking that he shared the common respect for him. Then she noticed how, behind Michael's back, Denis capered and danced and imitated him grotesquely like a well-trained monkey. She had thought it accidental, the exuberance he couldn't control because he liked to show off. But it was more than that. There was a dreadful malevolence about his capering. Everyone felt it.

Noon came and went without any sign of food, and nothing was said publicly among the company, although the audible asides reached clear into the pit where Devon sat. At two o'clock Kate finally broached the subject to Michael Dantine.

The great man frowned. The notion was absurd, but he was dealing with mere mortals and must humor them. He shrugged contemptuously and sent a carpenter off to the Green George to order something in the nature of a meal to be brought steaming hot through the streets to South Market Theatre. "Tell them to make hire of a coach if necessary," he added in the voice of one who is obeyed, come feast, famine or blockade.

Devon watched the proceedings with awe. His high-handedness passed belief. She was in the midst of these treacherous thoughts when Dantine came to the apron candles and pointed one long arm in her direction while addressing the Company.

"This little wench could do with a bite of bread, and has she complained?" Devon tried to look as innocent as he painted her. "No! It is only you fat sluggards who must be

46

chewing something all the time. Listen to Mistress Howard on the subject. Devon, what do you say?"

"I am too hungry to say very much, Sir."

There was a moment of complete silence. Then there was a sputter of laughter, everyone taking advantage of this chance for revenge against him. Dantine said "Humph," and turned his back on Devon. But when the three waiters came in loaded down with trays, Dantine motioned them to give Devon her share immediately after the two leading women had been served.

He leaped down from the stage a moment later and slumped into the straight chair beside her, stealing a piece of bread from her tray and chewing it as he watched her. He sprawled his long legs across the floor in front of him and she found herself staring at his dusty boots, embarrassed by his gaze.

"Well, Devon, your opinion now. In all honesty, what do you think of our little Forest of Arden?"

Between sips of cherry-bark tea, she took courage and said smoothly, "The scenery is excellent. And the play, too. But being your play, it would not dare to be otherwise; would it?"

"Your compliments have a double edge. I don't think I want you for a critic, Devon."

She looked at him over the rim of her cup. He was smiling, and she smiled too. She felt very satisfied with the world.

She was conscious then of a change in Dantine's expression, as his attention was caught by something beyond her. She looked over her shoulder. Denis Varney stood grinning at his brother, with a plate in his hand, his fork buried in a bite of lukewarm cod.

His tawny queued hair kept escaping the confinement of his dark ribbon, hiding a part of his face as he ate. But nothing hid the high sardonic curve of his eyebrows. She was greatly flattered at his proximity, as well as pleased that he found her with his brother. She hoped he would be stimulated by the competition.

"Am I interrupting a tête-à-tête? How clumsy of me!" Denis apologized. "Shall I remove my objectionable self?"

Michael Dantine thrust himself out of his chair and leaped onto the stage without another glance at either Devon or his brother. Denis moved around to take the vacant chair. "Are you as sick of this damned Shakespeare as I am, Devon?"

Before she could answer, Dantine's voice roared through the theatre, calling the cast to the business at hand. Denis sighed as he scraped his plate clean.

"A lovely character, the Master. Well, Devon, be good." He set his plate down and took a leisurely stroll to the stage. For all his almost exaggerated care, he managed to meet disaster. As he stepped into place and made a sweeping obeisance toward Michael, his right shoulder seam ripped noisily. He examined the damage with one roving hand.

Dantine exploded. "Oh, my God! What now?"

"I'm frightfully sorry, dear fellow, but I've split open. Now, just go on as if I were here. I'll get the little seamstress to fix it, and I'll be back in a trice or two. Or are two trices actually a trose?"

Devon got up and amusedly followed him to the back of the theatre. Just as she was threading her needle, he pocketed the spindle of thread. "Forget it, Devon. You can't work every hour of the day. You are going out with me to get a breath of real out-of-doors air."

She could not help laughing at his preposterous notion of defying Michael Dantine. "No. I couldn't."

"And we are going now. Instantly." He took her hand and pulled her toward the door. She was still protesting, but in whispers, when they reached the deserted vestibule.

"Mr. Varney, I swear I shall lose my job. Please, I must go back. And you can't go out in the streets with that costume on."

He was already in action. "I can remedy both objections.

Number One: we need a seamstress, and even if we did not, Dantine wouldn't let *you* go. I saw that right off. Number Two: if I remove this ruff and put on this coat, who is to know my breeches are not those of a normal Boston stroller walking with his sweetheart?"

"I think you are . . ."

"You think too much." He hurried her out the front door.

On the street they paused to decide what they would do with their freedom.

"Shall we start for the Common? Meanwhile, that will give me time to find out all about you."

Devon reflected, And perhaps I shall find out a little about you, my friend!

They strolled along looking like any pair of lovers taking the air together. He glanced at her now and then in speculation. She caught him at it. "Well, Sir, what is your decision?"

He grinned, and his frankness overwhelmed her. "I was wondering that my loving brother should be captivated by a fruit so unripe as you."

There was a small deadly hush for an instant, while she wished fiercely that she might prick his fine arrogance with a sharp dagger. "Thank you, Mr. Varney. If you have quite made up your mind that I am too green for plucking, I shall return to Mr. Dantine and ask him myself. Pray enjoy your walk."

He laughed so loudly two passing Redcoats turned and stared at him, and then, more lingeringly at Devon, who scowled back at them. They strolled on, one of them making a side remark to the other, and they both roared with laughter.

"Now, Devon," Denis said, rubbing the salt in. "Don't be bitter. There are many men, doubtless, who would find you attractive despite your limitations."

She recovered with an effort and pursued the matter vigorously. "What, may I ask, are my limitations?"

He appeared to be very serious, stood off and surveyed her carefully, in an attitude of thought. "In the first place, your figure is to your disadvantage. Everyone knows what a proper form is like. A woman should be big and warm with good honest fat in all the right places. Now, take Kate Merilee. . . ."

"Of course, I have not Kate's natural assets," Devon interrupted in a spirit of desperate bravado. "Any more than you have any of your brother's natural assets."

He had stopped by a coffeehouse but looked at her in surprise. "Honestly, Devon, what natural assets can my brother have? He is the most thoroughly crude, repulsive and ridiculous character I have ever seen on a stage. I would have been mortally offended if you had found us alike."

As she was trying to think of something bad enough to say to him, he ushered her into the coffeehouse whose habitués were in the midst of a heated political discussion. Denis, ignoring the apoplectic patriots, squeezed in among them, closely followed by Devon, to a table in a dark corner. He ordered chocolate and cakes for both of them.

"So you think I am different," he said, hearkening back to his favorite subject, when he had soaked his cake in the chocolate. "We are not really brothers, you know, Devon. Only half brothers. We share the same father. Our chief distinction is that I was born within the wedding ring. He was born without. Simple, isn't it?"

"Very simple. Is that why you hate him?"

He seemed shocked at the direct question. "Hate him? Why on earth should I hate him? He is too ridiculous to inspire such lofty feelings."

"If you don't hate him and are not interested in revenge, and you think him ridiculous, why in heaven's name do you remain in his Company?"

Across the little table his face was in half light. She could see very clearly his cynical eyes, but the rest of his face she could not read, nor the emotions that were masked behind his careless answer.

"Now, there you are, Devon, asking questions as our last seamstress did. My brother and I are bound together in a peculiar way. I prefer the theatre to any other mode of life. At present. Besides, it's a good job, the only one of its kind in the colonies at present. Some day, perhaps, I will seek my fortune through my unwilling brother. If he were no longer at the head of the Dantine Company ... Yes, there's a notion. It appeals to me." He laughed at her face. "A pleasant notion."

"You aren't making yourself very clear, you know, Mr. Varney."

"I did not intend to, Miss Howard."

She was rebuffed and finished her chocolate in silence, wishing she had not been fool enough to come with the heartless gallant. She had not pleased him by accepting this invitation. Now she was going to be given a few pennies for her three days' work and shown the door by the angry Michael Dantine, and Denis would never think of her again. She meant nothing to him. She arose quickly, spilling the dregs of chocolate on the tip of her cloak.

"I must go back now. If you have other things to do, I shall return alone."

"No. I'll go with you. It would be highly indecorous if you were caught returning to the theatre alone."

"On the contrary. I prefer to. It will look better if they do not know we were together. Mr. Dantine will think..."

"Yes." He smiled at her as he stood up. "He will, of course."

She consoled herself that he was transparent about it, anyway, but that did not prevent her from feeling a bit sick over the whole fiasco. For a few minutes today she had been rather sure that Denis Varney was interested in her.

"Still," she persisted as they started walking. "I should

think you would be afraid of your brother. He may be dangerous."

"It's all a sport, Devon. You just don't understand. If I could drive him mad, for instance, it would pay him in kind for what he has done. What a lovely end for that big, indestructible Michael Dantine! And he has not far to go along that path."

She started to speak, cleared her throat, and began again. "You are joking, of course."

"Of course."

When she looked at him, he was smiling boyishly. "It is a delight to tease you, Little Sober Face. You must learn not to be so serious."

Was it only that? Out of the corner of her eyes she watched the ease of his stride, the grace of his fingers as he raised them against the breeze to brush back his tawny hair. After a few minutes, aware of her eyes upon him, he grinned without looking at her. When she least expected it, he reached for her hand and brought it to his lips. She was so astonished, she lost her stride and tried to pull away from him.

"Still angry?" he asked.

"Not in the least."

"Forgive me?"

"Certainly not!"

He kissed her fingertips. "I was rude. It's my damned flip tongue. Please forgive me, like a good little girl." He peered directly into her face. "Please . . . ?"

Chapter
Five

SHE DID not return to the theatre in Varney's company after all. It was late enough for supper by that time, and Denis went alone to the Green George. Devon preferred to face Michael Dantine's wrath in the confusion that must go on before curtain time, and she was industriously sewing one of Floss Roy's petticoats when the Company poured into the cramped dressing space backstage and began to prepare for *As You Like It*.

It was not long before the call went out to Devon from the men's dressing room where Bob Traver was having difficulties with his short cape. She was aware without looking in that direction that Michael Dantine had stopped cutting de Guiche's crepe beard and had turned to look at her when she entered the drafty little room with its dressing-screen walls. Her fingers faltered on the collar of Bob's cape and the young actor chided her in a friendly way. "Your fingers are cold, Miss Howard."

"Oh no. Perhaps I'm nervous about the first curtain."

53

Bob touched one of her hands at his collar and covered it momentarily with his own. "Have a care how you wander through these Boston streets. There is illness about. And the winter sun deceives you."

A sudden hush had fallen over the assembled actors and he and Devon drew quickly apart, while Dantine's voice cut into the silence acidly. "Mr. Traver, will you keep your hands from the servants? Or must we dispense with the girl's services?"

Devon bit her lip to keep from answering him as she finished arranging Bob's cape and went on to one of the minor players whose wig was askew. Well! That was certainly worse than anything his brother had said to her. Calling her a servant, and giving himself airs about who should touch her! She knew that though Michael Dantine had turned away from her, he was still aware of all her movements. She felt nervous and unsure of herself, wondering when he was going to pay her off and send her away. It would be like him to choose the most public and humiliating way of doing so. What would she do then? She had wondered during the past weeks how a woman lived alone where there was no work for her, no sanctuary.

The first-act curtain came at its usual time and nothing had been said to her. After his outburst Dantine had not made another audible sign that he recognized her presence, except to watch her when he thought she did not observe him. But she had other things to occupy her attention as the evening progressed. The theatre was jammed with an assortment of combustibles: lovers of the drama, adventurers into the sinful art of the theatre, patriots who had heard that the British disapproved, and Loyalists who had heard from the governor that the Company was pro-Tory.

The pace of the play was swift—Shakespeare having been edited by Michael Dantine—and delightfully romantic, thanks to the tempo of the playing. The playing was tighter, flowing without a single jagged spot, as if Dantine still stood in the midst of his cast, insulting them, haranguing them, dragging them up to peaks far beyond their individual powers.

They came offstage half dead with fatigue, stumbling into the dressing room and searching blindly for their costume changes. When Kate spoke to Devon it was difficult to recognize the radiant Rosalind who had captivated the throng beyond the candled footlights. She looked haggard and old, devitalized. So did they all, even the sardonic Denis Varney. Life far beyond their capabilities had been breathed into them. Onstage, they were not Floss and Kate and Bob playing parts. They were projections of Michael Dantine, unable to think or feel or react except in his image. Devon looked at each of them in amazement as she imagined she saw the same phenomenon repeated over and over. She thought it unhealthy. Frightening.

As the play progressed the tempers of the stars grew shorter. There was bickering between Kate and de Guiche, and Denis and Floss were fighting as usual. Michael Dantine's appearance on the scene silenced them for the time, though no one felt safe amid so many artistic temperaments.

Floss was late to the dressing room after the fourth act and had to renew her makeup in the wings while Devon laced her into the tiny waistline of Celia's last-act costume. It was a nerve-wracking business. Floss was trying to apply scarlet pomade at the outer curves of her already over-generous mouth, while scene shifters, carpenters and actors brushed by her in the confusion of the last-act curtain.

Devon, nervous and licking her lips, pulled away from her with all her strength and could not get the small bodice closed around Floss Roy's waistline. Every new twist at her waist made Floss lose the pattern of her mouth, and a last frantic heave swung her clear around to face Devon. A smear of red pomade scarred the actress's face, and Denis Varney laughed as he crossed to the further wings. That laugh was the end of Floss Roy's uneasy patience. With the flat of her mirror she struck Devon across the side of the head.

Thrown off balance, Devon staggered and groped for her opponent, too stunned to understand clearly just what had happened or to see Michael Dantine's broad hand suddenly materialize from nowhere to fetch Floss a noisy crack across the cheek.

Floss burst into a stream of Billingsgate filth that was cut short by another slap from Dantine, and someone with great presence of mind called "Curtain!" Panic seized the company, and there was a wild rush for places.

Kate asked Devon if she was all right and being assured, went on her way with the others. Devon looked up after a few seconds but Michael Dantine had his back to her as he rearranged Bob Traver's cape. He did not look her way, nor did Denis, who was in the upper wing awaiting his cue. She went slowly to the dressing room, mentally promising dire things to Floss next time they met.

A sick-sweet nausea passed over her and she fought the easy, pleasant desire to faint. When she closed her eyes, darkness was inviting. She could not quite reach the dressing table. As she fell, she heard her name called sharply. A hand went under her knees and another under her arms. She was swung off the floor as if she had no weight at all, and her head sank against the breast of a man's white cambric shirt. Never in her life had she been so comforted and so secure.

There was a faint glow of firelight in the room when she awoke again, and she was conscious of a dull, heavy pain over her eyes. She frowned and studied the embers in the fireplace, wondering how she had come to be back in Kate's room at the Green George. As she stirred and raised up on her elbows to look around the room, Kate moved from the bedpost where she had been on watch.

"Well, Sweet, you've had a long nap. How are you feeling?"

"Fine, except for a headache. How silly for me to do that! Did I faint?"

"Faint! You've been flat on your back for two hours. It's

nearly one o'clock." She fastened the neck of her nightrobe and swung her thick, dark hair back over her shoulders.

Devon sat up, rubbing her forehead with her fingers, ashamed at having allowed herself to be beaten by that flaxen-haired Floss. "Where are you going, Kate?"

"To Dantine. He won't go to bed until he finds out how you are."

Devon's fingers hesitated. "What on earth has he to do with it?"

"He found you, of course, saw you when you fell and carried you here. The rest of us were too stupid to guess anything was wrong with you until the show was over, when we found no Dantine and no seamstress."

It was amazing! How had he known? Did he have eyes in the back of his head? Devon sank under the covers and sighed. She was ungrateful enough to wish Denis Varney had been as observant.

Chapter
Six

DEVON STAYED in bed the next morning, against her own inclinations and at Kate's insistence, but when the waiter knocked on the door with her breakfast, she was ready to jump out of bed and begin dressing. She was certain that the unpredictable Michael Dantine's mellow mood had passed as his other moods passed, leaving him more masterful and demanding than ever. She reminded herself that this was exactly like Joshua Howard on one of his crabbed days.

During breakfast several visitors appeared at Kate's door to pay their respects to the seamstress, and Devon found the business more than a little embarrassing, especially since Floss was one of the few who did not call, and she had to assume that they were still in a state of active warfare. No one mentioned Floss, but they were all painfully solicitous of Devon and she wished they would stop avoiding the subject.

Bob Traver asked her a dozen times if her head still

ached and if she could use another pillow. To oblige him she would have agreed, except that she was already propped up on a nest of pillows and wished someone would speak to her in a tone that was not solicitous.

Suiting her thoughts to the word, Denis came in, sat on the bed and told tales of other backstage battles, acting them out until Devon's sides ached with her laughter and he was chased out by the indignant Kate, whose latest fight with Floss he had enacted too realistically. Denis went, vowing to sneak back in when the she-dragon was gone.

Before noon, even Floss strolled in, to say that she had heard Devon was feeling poorly. It must be the New England climate. Awful stuff, the Boston cold. And she went on her way rather ill at ease, as if she had wanted to say something and been fearful of a rebuff. In that moment Devon found it useless to harbor her dark plots for vengeance. She had lost her own temper often enough to know the humiliation of an apology hours after the temper had worn off.

Presently, there was a lull and Devon rolled under the blankets to recover from her well-wishers, wondering why Michael Dantine had made no effort to see her, since he had been so concerned over her last night.

The room was radiant with sunlight. It was the loveliest day of the winter, and now that she could sleep, she did not want to. The devil with her headache! A sound in the hall disturbed her. She hurriedly rearranged the bed covers and settled herself as becomingly as possible, wondering if Denis might have returned to finish his ridiculous impersonations.

The door opened without the customary knock, and she felt a twinge of excitement as Michael Dantine moved into the center of the room. She closed her eyes quickly, nervously. He stood at the foot of the bed studying her until she was sure each uneven breath she took was carefully counted, and she tried with poor success to keep from breathing. But she could not control the curiosity that made her study him from under her eyelashes. How big he was, and how grim! But now he was beginning to smile, that special, rare and beautiful smile. She opened her eyes innocently and looked at him.

"Oh. I didn't expect you."

"How are you feeling, Devon?"

"Quite well, thank you. I really intended to get up." She shifted and propped herself on her elbows. "It is dreadfully late, I know."

"You little rogue, you know I don't intend you shall go to work after that crack on the head." He came and sat down on the edge of her bed. She moved away a little, wishing he had not sat on her dressing robe and made her feel so unclothed.

"We are all sorry about Floss last night. I have let her understand the consequences if she ever molests you in any way again."

"Thank you very much, but I can take care of myself."

He shrugged, just hiding a smile. "As you were able to last night? At any rate, you are the most satisfactory in a long line of tiring women, and we are all aware of your difficulties with the Company. My brother has been out in the hall threatening to annoy you for the last hour, but I kept him out of here while you slept." He noted her sudden glance at the door, and frowned. "But that is beside the point. Kate tells me you have only one gown and that you spend half the night refurbishing it for the next day. She says also that she gave you one of her dressing robes here. You hadn't even that of your own. Obviously, something must be done about you."

She was indignant. "Surely, Sir, that is between Miss Merilee and myself! I never imagined she would gossip to you—that is, to a man—about such things."

He dismissed her pride with a wave of the hand. "She tells me, too, that you sold several items of yours to a mercer on Tremount Street. Are you well enough to ride up there and redeem them?"

"Now?"

"Certainly, now."

"But I couldn't let you—"

"Call it a Christmas remembrance. The holiday is not a fortnight away. Or let us make it a Colonial New Year's gift. I believe that is customary over here."

"No. I'm sorry."

"All right, then. An advance on your salary. You will pay me back in installments; say, tuppence the quarter."

She had to smile then, but insisted, "It isn't in the least amusing. It's most shocking, as you are perfectly well aware." She had been very strictly reared on the subject of accepting gifts—more especially clothing—from a man who was not her husband. Michael Dantine was the last man in the world to whom a decent girl should be obligated.

"Now, see here!" He leaned toward her, fast losing his slippery patience. "I am responsible for this Company, and I cannot afford, for business reasons, to have my troupe dress like paupers. Either you redeem your clothes, or you take your pride and your empty purse to your next employer." He got up and went quickly to the door.

She was still too dumbfounded to answer him, and in the doorway he reminded her, "I shall call for you in fifteen minutes, Devon. Be a good girl, and don't waste time in a fit of the sulks."

She sat thinking the matter over indignantly after he had gone. He might very well give her notice to quit the Company if she refused his offer. And the crimson velveteen that she had left a month ago with the mercer, her favorite gown, would be a wonderful addition to her meager wardrobe. Once more, she would have two gowns, and not have to wash the collar and cuffs of this blue worsted every night as she did her stockings and shift. Perhaps it was best to silence her suspicion of his motives and let him loan her the money for the velveteen.

She got out of bed. Five minutes were gone already. As she laced her blue worsted gown, she was angry all over again. She did not want Michael's pity. She wanted nothing to do with him. He would not break her to his will as he had the others last night in front of her eyes, made them into creatures that went through motions onstage, but the motions were Michael Dantine's, not theirs. She would not let a man destroy her individual self as her mother had been beaten down by Joshua Howard.

She was still assuring herself that her defenses were impregnable when she heard him rap on the door, and she scrambled to get her cape on with the bright lining exposed around her face. He was so prompt she wondered if he had been waiting in the hall for the last fifteen minutes.

She wished he did not attract her so violently. She knew it was a wicked attraction, that it appealed to all that was base and carnal in her, but she could not deny it. He looked almost like a gentleman in his well-fitted travelling coat with his distinguished sugarloaf hat in his hand. But as they stepped into the noon sunlight and he put his hat on, she noticed that neither the fine hat nor the romantic fit of his coat entirely disguised his strong, heavy features. They were as unreadable as they had been that first night when he emerged from the shadows to terrify her.

He had ordered a carriage for her, and she was pleased at the elegance of such a service. When he took her hand as she mounted, her fingers were lost in his, and she felt a warmth in their contact that she found as disturbing as always.

The coachman jigged the reins and they were on their way. She asked if there was time enough before she would be needed for the players' packing and other preparations for departure on the morrow.

He sat studying his fingers while he said coolly, "Let them

need you. Kate tells me you have worked very hard these past few days."

That was generous of Kate. "The work is extremely interesting."

"The natural view of an amateur."

"I am hardly that, Sir," she reminded him with some feeling. "My mother was..." She saw that he had stopped listening. He was staring in a preoccupied way at the dirty red wall of a printer's shop as he pursued a subject that, from his tone, had no interest for him. She wondered why he bothered to talk at all.

"What had you been doing before you paid that call Friday night at South Market?"

As if she would tell him, a stranger, about those days when there was nothing to eat and she had lied a dozen times to the landlord about the remittance that never came.

"I was governess to two young ladies, and I wrote letters for their father who used to know my own father. He was a merchant in the Indies trade."

Michael Dantine's eyes finally left the view out the carriage window and turned upon her casually. "Yours is a name of some memories in England, Miss Howard."

"Yes, Sir. I am named for my mother's birthplace. And then too, one of my father's ancestors was Catherine Howard, though I daresay that is no credit."

This seemed to amuse him. "I take it you don't approve young queens who take lovers."

"I don't approve young *women* who take lovers." That ought to set him in his place.

He argued with her as if the foolish question of Queen Catherine mattered in some way to them on this day over two hundred years after her execution.

"Come now, Devon. Wait until the lightning strikes you and all that lovely virgin pallor yields to some fellow's violence and passion. I should like to be present at the metamorphosis."

"You are not likely to be present, Mr. Dantine." What a conversation! It reminded her of things she and the other girls used to whisper in the woods outside Concord, while they gazed at the pale sky and distantly heard the summer sounds.

"Why not? I've been told I have a certain repulsive attraction for women. You would not be the first virgin to yield to me."

She could not forebear interpolating, "Nor the last."

He looked at her and she looked quickly away, leaning forward to catch sight of the mercer's shop where she had parted with her velveteen dress. His manner might be annoying, but it also made her pulse beat in a way she hoped he did not notice.

Dantine gave orders to the coachman to stop, helped her out of the carriage and dismissed the heavy coach. He was very polite with her, entirely overlooking her rebuffs. Apparently, he was not going to be discouraged by anything she might say or do.

The mercer did not help matters by his assumption that Michael Dantine was redeeming her clothes for tawdry reasons of his own. The crimson velveteen was brushed and cared for so that Devon was proud to see it, as if it were a shabby friend who had blossomed during her absence.

Michael looked it over, examined the many generous folds of the skirt and the buff lace top of the bodice which daringly outlined breasts and shoulders. He held the gown against her, and she looked up pertly at him, feeling gay and mature and sure of herself. She saw how pleased he was when she accepted the dress without haggling. He joked about the décolletage of the lace and then about the size of her waistline. "We must fatten you up. My fingers join around your waist. Look at that."

It was not quite true, but she laughed with the mercer's wife, though his touch made her nervous and ill at ease. The mercer, seizing his opportunity, brought out an exquisite dressing gown of finest royal-blue velvet, nipped in at the waist with fancy tucks and seams and trailing its many folds on the floor. Miraculously, it fitted her. She could see that at a glance as the mercer's wife held it before her. With great difficulty Devon found the courage to refuse it. One simply did not receive undergarments f om one's employer. It was too much. Next, he would be suggesting that he have her petticoats made for her. But the mercer and the mercer's plump, knowing wife were insistent.

"Only try it on, Mistress. Only that. Then we will put it by and a less charming patron will buy it."

While she was being firm and dignified, Michael Dantine took the blue-velvet folds from the woman and roughly began to force her arms into the long, full sleeves, with a man's innocent disregard for folds and seams. The mercer unfastened her cape at the throat and slipped it off over the robe, while Dantine stood back to admire the dressing gown and then swung her around to the mirror.

She was fascinated. The image that returned her stare accentuated all the contours of a finely moulded face, and the body of the robe was a perfect fit, giving her height and a certain maturity. She turned from the mirror, undoing the heavy tassels at her waist and beginning to draw the full sleeves off over her own worsted gown.

"Yes. It is vastly becoming," she said, taking off the robe and giving it to the woman, thinking privately that Kate Merilee had never given such a portrayal of calm indifference.

Michael Dantine made a sign with his hand. "Wrap the robe with the gown. We will take them both." As Devon opened her mouth to protest, he explained coolly, "It was a display robe of Mistress Babcock's here. I came round at dawn and had her alter it to your measure. It is yours and no mistake."

Devon looked from the robe to her precious crimson gown and could not give them away. Let people think what they would. She pictured herself suddenly in her crimson velveteen, standing before the astonished gaze of Denis Varney. Would even this development open his eyes, arouse his heartbeat to a flattering speed? In many ways his admiration was much more desirable. He did not make her think constantly of her body, of her excitement at his touch. He lifted her thoughts to higher planes. His influence on her was quite unlike that of his brother.

As if reading her thoughts, Michael Dantine suddenly snatched the robe out of her hands and said roughly, "We had best be gone. We have missed dinner already."

Devon allowed the gay, becoming gown and robe to be laid reverently among silver tissue, and watched the mercer's wife wrap them.

Out on the street, Devon felt that she owed Dantine at least her good nature and threw all her enthusiasm and beguilement into her manner, hoping he had not guessed her quick thought for his brother a moment since. "You have been more than generous, Sir. I shall always be very grateful to you."

His forbidding expression did not soften during her polite little speech, and he said gravely, "Of course, I'll have your tuppence every quarter. That will keep you busy with my troupe for a considerable time."

She hastened to assure him that she would pay him back and be free of debt at her first opportunity.

"Your first opportunity being a rise in your salary, I make no doubt."

"Oh, no! I didn't mean . . ."

He cut her protest short and, taking her arm, forced her through the afternoon crowd. She tried not to resent his control, but her whole nature, even her flesh, stiffened at the way he forced her along the street, and yet, she was confusingly aware that if he had not behaved in this way to remind her of her father's forcefulness, she would have been suffused with an unaccustomed heat at the powerful physical attraction he exerted over her.

They arrived at the Green George shortly after the much-postponed dinner had begun. The silence which fell over the Company at their entrance told Devon that she and Dantine were the subjects of the table talk. She was flattered but guilty too, remembering that a few hours ago, the Company had supposed her half dead.

Dantine stayed a few minutes with his players. She did not hear what they said, but as she went up the stairs, pausing a moment on the landing to eavesdrop, a burst of laughter came from the players' dining room. Were they laughing at her? Then she heard Michael Dantine's deep voice. "Gentlemen, you are warned about this one. As to the others, you may take your choice of vintage casks which, I'll wager, have been pretty well tapped before you."

Devon went on up the stairs in disgust at Michael Dantine's low, coarse disregard for women. She turned into Kate's room, dropped her cape and rushed to get ready for dinner. She washed her face, shivering at the touch of icy water, then brushed her hair until it was smooth and gleaming and pinned back the strands closest to her face with hair bodkins, while the rest, disgustingly straight and dark, hung down her back. She examined her face in Kate's hand mirror. In spite of its washed and scrubbed appearance, the bone structure was not bad.

She changed into the crimson gown. Its waist was a trifle loose for her after her recent hunger period, and it was necessary to take a pleat in it with a pin. Remembering Michael's fingers around her waist, she wanted to frown but somehow flushed warmly at his boldness.

Pinching more color into her cheeks and rubbing her lips with a touch of Kate's pomade, she looked at her reflection in the mirror. Under the influence of the crimson gown her sallow complexion had improved. The color flattered her.

Feeling a trifle giddy, she went down to dinner.

Chapter Seven

ALL THE Company adjourned to the back parlour after dinner for dancing except Dantine and de Guiche who had work to do on the script of *Othello*. Devon, pretending to be busy with Bob and Kate, felt a surge of excitement and triumph, when Denis Varney came around the table and took her by the wrist.

"Come, Mistress, shall we show them how a reel should properly be danced?"

Devon scarcely knew how to make conversation to entertain him, but as long as Denis talked about Denis, both amusingly and lightly, she had no worries on that score. As they entered the back parlour she saw, over her shoulder, Bob Traver escorting Kate Merilee, and the look in his brown eyes was something he could not hide from the careless eyes of the players; yet, beside him, Kate laughed and flirted and behaved altogether as if she wanted to torment him. Devon thought her very cruel.

The music was provided by violin, tambour, and, after Bob came in, by harpsichord; for he was an expert player and Kate had promised to stand by him during one of the dances.

That was to be his reward for entertaining the rest of the Company throughout the evening.

Devon soon found the old exciting turns coming back to her. It was easy to dance with Varney, and when they were whirling through a frontier jig she thought she had never been in the company of anyone so easy, so congenial to her tastes. No terrible, upsetting passions here. No fear that she would betray herself, behave like a wanton! So she felt free to flirt with him. When he was close to her in the turn, she felt his cheek brush hers, and once his lips touched and lingered a moment on hers. A triumph indeed, after his insults to her. She felt her face glow with pride under the brief touch. When she paused for breath, Kate came up and fanned her and then asked if Devon would pin up the lowest flounce on her top petticoat which had been torn in the excitement of the dance.

While Denis and Bob poured brandy for the Company, Kate whispered behind her fan, "By Gad, Devon my sweet, you've captivated Denis. And small wonder. You're looking very well. All the lads are fainting to dance with you."

Devon laughed away the compliment but she longed to take a look at herself in a mirror. One of the Company came to stand up with her in the next set, but before Devon could answer, Denis had slipped one arm around her waist and drawn her to him. "Find Floss or one of the others. Devon has promised this set. Haven't you, Devon?"

She gave the young player her best smile. "Alas, Sir, if it were left to me—but you see I have no choice in the matter."

Denis pulled her away, out of the hearing of the players. "Where have you been hiding this new Devon Howard? Damme, I have been missing something!"

She raised an eyebrow and gave him a cool look. "What, Master Varney? You forget. I am the woman whose 'green' qualities you enumerated at some length yesterday."

"Oh, yesterday. Hang yesterday! That was another woman, a child. Not you."

She laughed and they joined the line for the dance.

It was nearing ten when she became aware that Michael Dantine had been standing in the doorway some time, watching her. She was excited by the knowledge of his presence, as always, but annoyed, too. He was forever playing the skeleton at the feast. As he caught her eye he motioned to her, but she pretended she had not seen him. She felt Denis Varney's arm around her waist and she was aware that her full crimson skirts flew out to reveal her petticoats as she passed Michael Dantine, but she was too busy completing the figure of the dance to care what he thought.

Suddenly, her body was twisted half around as a heavy hand seized her arm in the middle of the turn, and she was swung out of the line. Michael Dantine caught her to him to prevent her falling and made a sign with his free hand for another actress to take her place in the dance.

As soon as she regained her equilibrium, which was not until he had half dragged her out into the hall, she loosened her frantic hold on his shirt. "I suppose you think this is very strong and courageous of you, to humiliate me before my friends."

He had been drinking. His breath as he looked down at her had the odd and frightening smell of gin, like a branded bondservant who had once worked for her father. But more than that, his somber eyes blazed with fury. "I motioned for you to come to me almost ten minutes ago. But you were so engrossed with my charming little brother that you deliberately ignored me."

"I didn't see you."

"You see me now. Come along! Gerard and I need you for some copy work." He pushed her before him, and she felt the indignity of her position, and, most of all, the disappointment of having her lovely evening ruined.

At the staircase she tried to be superior but only succeeded in being petty when she said, "I am afraid, Mr. Dantine, that you drink more than is good for you. I thought gin was reserved for slaves and servants, not for free men." She did not know what prompted her to make such a dangerous criticism, except that she wanted to see him hurt.

"Really?" He looked at her with the sardonic humor that reminded her slightly of his brother. "Then let me give *you* a bit of advice, my dear. Brandy is not a plaything, either."

She stopped in the middle of the staircase, openmouthed at such an unchivalrous remark. "I? Do you imply that I am foxed?"

"I imply, my child, that a quart of Blue Ruin has affected me less than your thimbleful of brandy tonight."

She walked on without a word to say for herself. Any man who drank a quart of strong spirits in a matter of hours was not sober enough to argue with. When they entered Michael Dantine's quarters, she looked in vain for Gerard de Guiche. The room, lighted by a candelabrum with four candles on the center table, left each corner of the darkly panelled room in shadows. She glanced at Dantine. He shrugged and did not seem surprised that they were alone.

"You could not expect de Guiche to wait all night while you pranced about below stairs with your gallant beaux."

"My gallant beaux, as you call them, engaged me so closely I could not see you. Perhaps if you had spoken politely . . ."

He was standing so near she could not see beyond the barrier of his body, and when she moved to avoid him, he put his hands on either side of her throat, pushing away the neckline until her shoulders were bared. She felt the warmth of his fingers on her flesh and wondered confusedly why she made no resistance. His voice held a hoarse intensity unlike his clear stage tones. "If I chose, I could make you forget Denis Varney had ever been born."

Suddenly, dangerously, she retorted, "I doubt it. You can not even make yourself forget he was ever born."

He stared at her as if she had struck him, and the muscles

of his face seemed to flincn. Just as she feared he would stanq there all evening, he laughed. "By God, Devon, you've a few tricks you can teach Kate about bedeviling a man."

Slowly, she freed herself, covering her shoulders again as she said quietly, "Shall we get on, Sir?"

"Get on?" He looked at her in amazement.

"Yes, certainly, get on—our work with *Othello*."

At last he began to understand. "Oh. *Othello*. Yes. Let me see. I . . . the devil! I've forgotten what I did want." He went over to the table and found a dozen handwritten copies of the play. "I want you to strike out certain lines or put in bits of business as I give them to you. Do you understand? Here. Take this armchair. Is the light satisfactory?"

"Quite satisfactory." She seated herself, shakily took the quill he offered, and was ready for his dictation, with the inkstand close by and her work propped upon her knees.

He paced the floor for a few minutes, trying to pull his thoughts into some kind of coherent order. When he finally began to speak, she was surprised to discover that he knew every role in *Othello* and could quote the lines with a high degree of accuracy. His object at the moment was to adapt the text of the play to the numerical limitations of his cast. Several of the minor roles had to be duplicated and a couple removed entirely. All the time that he was giving her his reading of the play, she was struck by the power and beauty of his voice which lifted the most trivial lines to a new, high realm of art. Here was a master of the language, this black-birder, pirate, and who-knew-what besides? She listened, enthralled.

In the middle of the second act Devon enquired how the play was cast. "I should think," she ventured, "that the leading roles would be ideal with Miss Merilee as Desdemona, yourself as the Moor, and . . ."

He turned on her suddenly as he was pouring himself a drink from the decanter. She had never seen a gentleman drink raw gin before and could not stop staring at him. She saw that he was smiling, the terrible smile that had in it no lightness or humor.

"And, you would say, Denis Varney to play Iago, the most frightful villain in all stage history. A natural casting choice. You are right. You are more right than you guess." He paused in the act of drinking to study her face in the candlelight. "Devon, you give me an idea. Some day, you shall play Desdemona. A far more convincing one than our voluptuous Kate."

"And have you strangle me, Sir? No, I thank you. You are much too convincing a performer." The instant she had spoken, she was astonished to find that she really did fear him. But her words put him in a better humor. He finished the gin in his glass and resumed his thoughtful pacing, while he argued this new idea with himself. "I see you in a number of roles. Your voice. It has good timbre, quiet, but perfectly audible, and with a little training, you might develop grace of movement. We'll consider the matter when there is more time."

She was prey to a conflict of feelings. She would like to follow in her mother's tradition, but she was by no means certain that she had those theatrical qualities Michael found in her.

As the moments sped under his spasmodic dictation, she could not get her thoughts away from the odd relationship between the two brothers. Because she was interested in both of them, she tried to work out leading questions, feeling confident that Michael would be easier to break down than his brother, who seemed so frank and yet remained so devious.

After midnight they finished the last lines of the last act, and Dantine took up the decanter, motioning her to get herself a glass from the cupboard behind her. She refused politely, having no taste for the undiluted stuff, and when she had gathered up the scattered copies of the play, tried to end the evening on a congenial note. "It seems to me, Sir, that you have accomplished a great deal in your own life. It might have made a worthwhile play."

"Hardly worthwhile. It is a dismal story, I'm afraid."

Too late, she realized her praise had opened up ancient wounds. She wondered what he was recalling as he leaned with his back against the table and stared at her, seeing beyond her into what seemed to be a sordid and terrible past. He roused himself. "But I once knew a child whose story would have had a maudlin interest for a woman."

"Please tell me."

"It would probably bore you."

She looked at him without speaking but resumed her seat, and he began to talk, very much the actor, without quite realizing it.

"That boy I speak of—I knew him in my sailing days, before I picked up de Guiche in that French harbor twenty years ago. Can't say I was overly fond of the boy, but as a prospective dramatist I saw in him certain dramatic qualities. His mother was a kitchen drab who had yielded to a gentleman with an evening to spare. Three years after the birth of her brat, she died in Newgate Prison of jail fever. Why she was in Newgate, I've no idea. But God knows, it's easy enough to get there. The boy, of course, was placed in a workhouse."

His eyes were as black as well water in starlight, and she could not turn her fascinated gaze from him.

"You must remember, Devon, all this happened almost forty years ago. An aeon ago to anyone your age. Until he was thirteen this boy knew nothing but the workhouse. He was forever longing to possess something of his own. Something that no other person could share. The toys belonged in the fine shops, stared at and coveted. He found a starving kitten once and they drowned it because it got under foot."

She felt that his need for sympathy and perhaps understanding made him strain to arouse her emotions, but in spite of this knowledge, she was deeply moved. She cleared her throat, tried to speak unemotionally. "Couldn't he share some of his feelings with the other children?"

"Why? He was too strong for the poor brats of the workhouse. Had a boy stood up to him, our hero might have been his devoted friend. But none did. Starvation, bad gin and the workmaster's knout—they destroy, or they strengthen that iron vein in man. He was not a pretty character, this urchin of ours."

"No," she agreed. "But he was human."

Michael gazed at her for a long moment. Her heart beat fast. It was hot in the room. Stifling.

He said finally, "Thank you for that look in your eyes, Little One."

"And then?" she prompted him huskily, unable to control her voice.

"Then—he was thirteen, and saw his father for the first time. His mother's story was well known to him, of course. And now, the only person in the world bound to him by ties of blood was coming as a person of some consequence to inspect the public institutions. Here at last was something that belonged to him, something fine and great, bigger than he. His father!

"But spare your tears, Devon, from here to its finish, it is a comedy. . . . The grubby inmates worked eighteen hours a day in that place, and most of them were dazed and stupid enough when the great man came through. But not our hero. He had been awake all night, picturing the meeting and grinning at the discomfiture of the brats who feared him.

"The great man was accompanied by a son—his legitimate son—a little dandy ten years old. As his father passed, the workhouse brat grabbed at one of his taffeta sleeves, half expecting to be embraced publicly. The great man freed himself with the observation that he had no doubt there were other urchins who might also make claims upon him. He was no ecclesiast. The workhouse master laughed too, and was still laughing when he kicked the brat out of the way. Not a gentle kick, I can tell you, Devon." He grimaced. "God! I can feel it yet."

She started at the comment and culled her brain for something to say, while Dantine shrugged at himself or the world, and drained his glass. Full of self-pity or not, she found his story impossible to forget. He was pouring from the decanter again as he spoke.

"Don't be so big-eyed, Little One. I'd almost forgotten the story until tonight. I think I am talking too much. It is a habit I indulge rather too frequently."

"Did he . . . what did your friend do then?"

"As I recall it, he was too choked with fury and tears to do anything. But the tears vanished, as tears do vanish. He did not weep again. And one spring night when the brat's back was not quite so raw, he got away to Liverpool and shipped out for Africa in an old barque. She was a blackbirder."

Devon said nothing.

He smiled. "Ah, Devon, you begin to like him less, my hero. He is no longer the beaten little waif of the London streets."

"It isn't that. But I should think, after his own tragic experiences, that he would have been reluctant to send other human beings into slavery." She had seen a slaver once, with its dehumanized cargo emerging from the hold . . . the rattle of chains, and the smell of death thick on the air.

He made a quick, angry motion, spilling a drop of liquor upon her head. She ran her fingers absently over her hair, still staring at him as he talked.

"What the devil! Should I suddenly recall the world's humanity when I myself have the whip hand? No, my child. The world is a dingy little workhouse, inhabited by two kinds of creatures—the evil who lead, and the weak who follow. Let us take ourselves, for example. I daresay a Barbados worker in the cane brakes would say I am evil. You are certainly weak. You are at my mercy this moment, if I choose. Is it better to be weak than to be evil? What do you think?"

With an effort she smiled. "I think you are drunk, Mr. Dantine."

His harsh laugh answered her. "I try. But I never quite reach that happy state."

This excuse failing, she dismissed his words lightly. "It is growing late. Another time, perhaps, we will discuss my weakness and your evil tendencies. I don't think you seriously want to tell me that you are proud to be evil—as you call yourself. And to lash out at humanity as you do."

He set his glass down and leaned toward her, putting one hand on each arm of her chair, imprisoning her. "Shall I tell you something, Devon? When the whip is in my hand, I satisfy an urge that has been in my soul since I first cringed at the workmaster's knout. Those days I used to ask only one thing of the strange little gods that watch over us: Give *me* the whip for one moment! *Give me the whip!* Now when you pronounce that fat word 'humanity,' you strike in me a hollow sound. Doesn't that make me an evil man in your eyes?"

There was a little, dead hush. The wind outside the shuttered windows rattled in noisy panic, to fill the silence. Was he a liar? Was he a melodramatic liar and hypocrite?

Devon felt her heart beating in fear, so that even in her head she heard the beat. She thought she knew why. It was not the warmth of his nearness, or her own uncertainty, but the shadow cast over her face as he stood between her and the light. It was his eyes, and his long fingers that had come so naturally to wield the whip. It was his voice. The throbbing anguish and power of the man made her long to comfort him, to kiss him and soothe him. In the silence that engulfed the room, she flicked her tongue nervously over her lips to stifle the impulse.

Suddenly he backed from her. The passionate hatred was

77

gone, leaving only mockery, and the candlelight flashed into view again.

"So the little girl could be frightened, though she said she couldn't! Run along, child. Run along and climb into bed with Kate and tell her all about your narrow escape from that wicked man. I won't hurt you . . . not tonight."

She needed no second chance. When her skirts were rustling and swaying down the drafty corridor as she ran, she could hear his laughter behind her.

Chapter Eight

DEVON WAS relieved that Dantine did not appear at breakfast. As soon as the meal was over, she and Denis went up to his room to pack his clothes for travel. Watching Denis as they ascended the staircase to his chamber, Devon caught his glance, held it, and knew that he really liked her, and yet, in his usual way, was toying with the sensation, like a connoisseur who must savor before drinking the potion. His attitude amused her. She felt no alarm, no sensation of danger in his presence. She was comfortable and a little self-satisfied that he had conquered his original insulting aversion to her.

When she entered his sunny, elegantly furnished room, she knew it could belong to no one else. There were several fine sketches on the wall, three of them of nude aborigines, but done in what she hastily told herself was excellent taste. It was the first personal work of his that she had seen, though she was familiar with the fine backdrops and flats he made for the stage. One of the women, a curvacious blonde, was a younger Floss Roy, attractive in a poignant way. She wondered if there was more to Floss than she herself had noticed, a sadness, a hopeless desire to be something else, rather than what she was.

Denis, wasting no time on social amenities, went to his wardrobe and began to take his clothes out; first the neat, stylish breeches, one pair at a time, then the coats and capes, followed by his waistcoats, his linen, and last, the shirts. These were all flawlessly ironed; the ruffles were so stiffly white they could almost stand alone beside the spotless neck-cloths.

Devon tore herself away from the paintings to take charge of the packing. She saw at once that there was no nonsense about Denis Varney's care of his clothes. The way he laid them in her lap gave her the sensation that the Bank of England stood back of them, and each finely clocked stocking was carefully placed in one or the other of his trunks under his watchful eye. He was very silent. She could not understand him and began to wonder what she had done to displease him.

The morning sun moved away from the windowsill but the bright sky beyond the window had never been more blue. When Devon stood up after an hour to stretch her cramped muscles, Denis went to the window and looked out, frowning. In an effort to drum up conversation, Devon said pleasantly, "Isn't it a nice day for winter?"

"I hadn't noticed."

She looked at him in surprise and saw then that he was studying not the beautiful, cloudless sky but the dirty roof-tops as they huddled close below his eyes.

"God! How long must a man follow doggedly along in servitude for lack of a handful of guineas? How long must a gentleman go bowing and scraping to a nameless beggar?"

She moved a little, wondering if he wanted her to leave. He drummed his well-kept, artistic fingers on the window and Devon, watching him anxiously, saw him grin. What was he thinking about? She wondered if he knew she was still there.

He looked over his shoulder at her, still smiling, and, turning in a quick, impulsive movement, shook her gently.

"Do you like me a little, Devon? Do you? Would you come away from the Company with me if I needed you? No. Don't answer yet. Understand me first. If it came to a test of loyalty, who would it be—for you? My brother? Or me?" Bowing gallantly over her hands, he kissed the palm of one, then the other. When he broke away from her and returned to the problem of packing, she was disappointed.

"Here," he said. "Let me give you a hand up on this trunk. I want you to stand here while I buckle it down."

As she obeyed him, he began to force the buckle tight, glancing at her as he did so. "What I really need up there is a buxom wench like Kate."

She smiled but her voice had an edge as she reminded him, "I think you told me that the first time you saw me."

"That's true. I hired you; didn't I? Are you glad you came to work for us?"

"It was better than starving."

He laughed. "Devon, you surprise me. There is a wicked core beneath that deceptive young face of yours. I think you are surprising my brother, too. He undoubtedly looked to see you an easy conquest, like the others. Tell me, Devon . . ." He stepped nearer, lowering his voice to a whisper, still indulging his twisted sense of humor. "How much of a struggle did you offer him last night?"

She said tartly, "Why don't you ask him that?" She was sure he knew the truth and wanted only to anger her, and she was resolved not to let him succeed.

Denis whistled. "How sharp the claws are this morning! And my honored brother isn't talking today either; so, of course, I can only assume, from the scowl on his dark and noble brow, that he failed last night. . . . Come, let me tease you. Perhaps I like you better than I want to like anyone. It is bad to like anyone. You lose your identity if you do. All right, now. You can come down. I've a great deal of work, and some errands to see to."

She jumped down, switched her heavy skirts off the trunk and hurried across the room, indignant at the dismissal, but as she was leaving, she could not avoid staring at the very nude and shameless sketch of a pink-skinned female beside the door. Denis came up beside her.

"Well?"

She said quickly, "It is very well drawn."

"You mean that in your vast experience of nudes, it meets all specifications."

She ignored the sarcasm. "Yes. It—the shading is exceptional. The Spanish shawl seems so beautiful, and her hand, too, very well drawn. I never could draw hands and feet."

"I'm glad that you like them. No one else gives them more than a glance. Even the women who have seen them. Art means nothing to them, only the identity of the subjects." For one of the few times in his life, he seemed sincere. She turned and looked with new appreciation at the sketches that relieved the white severity of his room. The women did not look so shameless now. There was a certain insouciant grace in each of them that was a part of their creator. They were unusual, and remarkably well done, increasing her admiration for him. She wondered jealously if the women had all been his mistresses.

"Which is your favorite?" he asked suddenly. "Kate Merilee over in that corner? Or the other brunette, perhaps? Damme, what was her name? Too bad. I've forgotten. And she had the most beautiful thigh I've ever seen."

She was uncertain. "Which do you yourself prefer?"

"The portraits I have not yet done. They are always my favorites."

She opened the door to leave. For an instant his hand covered hers, and they looked at each other without speaking. Then he bowed her out and stood in the doorway as she left him.

It still lacked half an hour of noon when Devon departed for the theatre where the coach and prop wagons would pick up the Company. She felt a warm satisfaction in the contrast between her departure this fine morning and her approach to the Green George a few nights ago, sick with hunger, dragging an almost empty bandbox and wanting nothing so much as a bite to eat and a bed in which to sleep.

It was so early she walked up the street, crossed to a mantua-maker's shop and spent her long-hoarded half crown upon the materials for a new petticoat and new violet sachets, feeling herself prosperous in the acquisitions, in despite of her flat purse.

There was an air of excitement in the streets as she came out of the shop, but after looking up and down and seeing nothing likely to cause such a tension among the little knotted groups arguing on the street corners, Devon went on her way, stopping every few minutes to reverse the bandbox from one hand to the other. It was at one of these stops, almost within sight of the Old South Market, that she was jostled off into the gutter by a pair of hurrying men with coattails flying. Her purse was torn from her fingers and swept into the street. She was just about to rush after it when a red-coated soldier picked it up and handed it to her with a flip little bow and salute.

"Your parcel, Mistress?"

She thanked him and hung the cords again from her wrist beneath her spreading cape, preparing to go on, but he seemed likeable and so anxious to speak that she asked if he knew what the disturbance was.

"Looks like some excitement, Ma'am. Just now, some Indians left a notice in blood on the doors of Mr. Gamaliel Mather's Ordinary, the Green George."

"You are joking! Indians in Boston? And writing in blood?"

"That's right." He grinned then. "Only you see, they're

the same kind of Indians that threw the tea in the harbor last year. And the blood they used is probably good red barn paint. They're members of the Sons of Liberty, out to get old Mather's scalp in a friendly way. He's been warned before about importing from the East India Company's agents, but he still does a deal of under-the-counter business with Boston's confirmed tea drinkers."

She started to run, to warn the Troupe, in the remote possibility that they weren't out of the George by this time. She hoped someone had saved the contents of her baggage, and especially her red velveteen gown, but she recognized the selfishness of the thought when the inn itself was threatened.

The Redcoat's voice pursued her and she stopped in surprise. "Now, he'll be getting a dozen of the lads from my regiment down there to protect his precious property. The grenadiers are already off to save his hide."

Devon was confused. "Forgive me, but surely these sentiments are strange in a man who wears your uniform."

"Mistress, if you were as lonesome as me in this hellish town, you'd be careful how you offended the natives, too. Not that a sweet little lady like you could ever be offending anybody. But, there's another reason. I don't like under-the-counter havey-cavey, no more nor I like treason. The way I see it, a man has to do his duty and serve his king, but that don't mean he'll be standing up for skinflints. These be our own people when all's said. It's not like we're at war with Frenchies, or some-ut." He saw that she was moving politely but firmly away and saluted her.

"Well, Mistress, I hope our paths may cross so pleasurably again sometime. Maybe you—well, good day to you, Ma'am."

She cried a quick "Good day" and hurried down the street, retracing her steps to the Green George. But foot traffic in that direction had become so heavy during the past few minutes that she found it difficult to push her way through the noisy throng. It was not an affair for women, and those

few who passed Devon on their way to see the excitement
had their overskirts hiked up a foot above their petticoats
and were prancing along with a fine display of ankles. There
were clubs in the crowd, and now and then the dull blade
of an old hunting knife. And the crowd grew larger at
every corner.

Devon, coming to the cross street that led past the Old
South Market, tried vainly to push against the current. She
could see the Long Wharf where only yesterday a regiment
of His Majesty's seasick grenadiers had landed in full force
from one of the Men-of-war that still rode at anchor in the
choppy waters of the harbor. It was long past noon by this
time. She was suddenly afraid that the incipient riot at the
Green George would cause the Company to go off without
her, and she would be back where she had been last Friday
night, only worse—for she had not then known Dantine. Or
Denis. Life without the two brothers seemed inconceivable
now.

As she stepped out of the crowd and into the dirty gutter,
her elbow struck a resistant object, and she saw that she
had run into Floss Roy, her blond hair disheveled and her
pert, green-feathered hat hanging by a thread, halfway down
her back. Her angry face did not brighten as she recognized Devon.

"Lud, what may you be doing in these parts, Miss
Mettlesome?"

Devon suggested that they both bend their efforts toward
returning in the direction of the Green George, there to
warn the Troupe and rescue their belongings. They hurried
over the cobblestones, retracing their steps.

They did not get far. Around the corner came the even
tread of perfectly trained British soldiery. Floss and Devon
barely made the safety of the gutter in time to avoid the
heel of the nearest grenadier.

"Gawd, I hate 'em, Lousy Lobsterbacks!" muttered Floss,
shaking a fist at them.

85

"Take care. Here come some more," and Devon pulled the flaxen-haired patriot out of danger. She, too, resented the soldiers for their careless contempt toward the populace, but she remembered the lonesome Redcoat and could not condemn them all. The grin of that friendly soldier had in it a certain poignance that lingered when he had gone.

Breathless, the girls were pushed along with the mob, not at all sure when they would come out of the nightmare labyrinth. After a minute or so, Floss asked her if she thought Michael Dantine would take the trouble to go searching for them if they failed to reach the inn. Devon did not hear her and she had to shout the question.

Devon yelled back, "What's more important is that they get out safely. Anyway, you know Master Dantine better than I do," and Floss laughed.

"Oh, don't be modest. You had him last night."

Devon pretended she had not heard.

With a kind of nasty, uncontrollable interest on her face, Floss came close to her ear and asked, "What kind of lover was he, Devon? Cruel devil, I make no doubt."

"He was very drunk," said Devon firmly.

There was no escaping the sweep of the mob. The girls came upon the little street in front of the Green George. A landmark of the city, it stood curiously dark, ancient, and deserted, against the winter sun.

Almost dreading the answer Devon asked the nearest by-stander, "Did they all escape? The—the Players? Master Dantine? Master Varney and the others?"

The man shrugged. He was a ship's chandler, out of work and surly toward mankind. "The Players? Why not? They can escape. Ay. They are at their foul theatre now. And they call it Moral Teachings!"

Heavy wooden clubs were being bound with rags and dipped in buckets of oil. Muscular arms waved the rags before the high, shuttered windows of the attic story, behind which the George's owner, Gamaliel Mather, the proud, penny-pinching old Tory, had dealt in the condemned tea trade. There was a great deal of laughing and horseplay.

"But they may kill someone."

At Devon's anxious cry, a blond young student looked around, laughing. "Not so, Mistress. We've come to put the fear of God into the old Tory."

A down-at-heels dock worker, more bold than the rest, threw a heavy stone that crashed against the loft shutters, and a sudden silence fell upon the mob; for the dusty shutters were painfully opened by a pair of gnarled hands, and Gamaliel Mather's face peered out at them, a sere autumn leaf that a breath of wind would vanquish. Many in the crowd tried to back away. They swirled around Devon and Floss who likewise tried, but vainly, to escape. And even among the violent ones there were few whose fathers had not been this old man's cronies against the French at Quebec on the Plains of Abraham, or against the redmen of the North.

Someone in the crowd shouted up at the shaking old man, "Go home, Grandpa. Go home where you can't meddle with politics." And the crowd laughed goodnaturedly, a few cat-calling, crying "Home, Granny, home!" and stamping in unison.

The old man leaned far out of the narrow loft window. His thin voice wavered on the wind. "Go home yourself, Jamie Adams. I know you, I laid on with a will to your pa's breeches when he had no more sense than you've got now."

A roar of laughter went up and was broken crisply by a girl beside the disgruntled Jamie. She found an empty rum jug and, scattering those nearest her with her gesture, hurled it at the loft window. It cracked against the open shutter, the heavy crockery spattering upon the old Tory's hand, drawing blood. He withdrew his hand hastily, looked at it as if he could not believe what he saw and then stared down at the upturned faces and yelled in a creaking voice, "Rebel scum!"

In a moment other missiles went hurtling up to the loft window. Even from her place in the midst of the rioters, Devon could see Gamaliel Mather's watery eyes, and turned red with helpless fury.

"How can they do it? Where are the soldiers? How can they face down that brave old man?"

Floss was touched too, but would not admit it. "Bah! He's had dozens of warnings. He's too old to have any sense." But she bit her full lower lip and stirred against the huge wagoner who stood at her shoulder, unconsciously pitting his weight against her and Devon.

Devon pushed Floss with renewed determination. "Try again to move out. We can't stay in this horrible place and watch them bait him. What difference does it make if he is a Whig or Tory? If this is their precious liberty, I want none of it. We must get the soldiers."

Floss did not hear. She was struggling in vain, shoved from one person to another, only to end by cracking Devon sharply in the ribs with her elbow. Since both girls were short, they could see nothing now at a level with their own height, only broad, beefy male backs that enclosed them the more tightly as each new emotion swept the crowd.

"What's happening now?" Devon asked, to stifle her uneasiness.

Floss pushed and shrugged against the wagoner in front of her until she could see an oil-soaked club waved close at the base of the inn.

"They're lighting the torches!"

"They can't! They must get him out first. Why doesn't someone . . . ?"

A sound like thunder beat through the crowd and Floss and Devon felt its reverberations over the cobblestones, dodging the stampede that surged into them. In the wave of angry fear that swept through the mob, the grenadier guard burst out of hiding to drive off the rabble.

Trying to shield herself and Floss from the frantic crowd, Devon prayed there would be no shooting like the one in the same city five years ago, for this time there would be war. But no shots were fired. There was only the nasty crunch of club on skull and fist on leather jaw. Evidently, the authorities too were afraid of a musket hastily fired.

Devon and Floss were driven to the edge of the crowd, and Devon was trying to pull the soubrette out of the melee, but Floss, with a sharp intake of breath, held her back. Over the fighting, turbulent mob, the girls saw a shaft of flame shoot up the century-old wooden face of Gamaliel Mather's Green George Inn. In five seconds the whole building was a shroud against the wind-swept sky.

Devon's throat was tight, and no sound came out when she opened her mouth to scream. Floss pulled crazily at her shoulder, muttering something that sounded like a litany, over and over. Now, grenadiers and rebels had become aware of the danger to the old man and they broke from private fights to attempt an entry into the crackling inferno. Half a dozen disappeared inside. There were screams from the crowd, and Devon looked up tensely at the attic window. The old, wrinkled leaf was gone. Had they gotten to him in time?

Buckets of water were being handed up now and tossed upon the flames, useless gestures that served only to occupy minds haunted by unspoken fear. How had it happened? How had this good-natured lesson to an old Tory turned into tragedy? In the faces of those about her, Devon read the creeping horror, the knowledge that each of them was guilty.

The men staggered out of the building, one at a time, tattered jackets pulled up over noses, scarlet coats pulled down over faces seared and blackened and weary. But although one grenadier came dragging a half-dead rebel out into the air, and two of them bore out the struggling body of a Yankee sailor, none of them found the old man whose face and shaking hands were gone from the attic window.

A sharp, splintering noise, then a rumble of falling timbers. The interior of the building had collapsed. In an incredibly short time, the Green George was a charred skeleton standing uneasily in the wind. Coughing and sniffling, eyes enflamed by the heat and smoke, the mob separated, and each man went his way, and after them went Devon and Floss, leaving only a handful of British soldiers and Yankee sailors to clean up the remains of the fire before it spread to the buildings and nearby wharves.

Chapter Nine

THE TWO girls dragged their way down toward the theatre, saying little at first, but sharing a memory. Floss, in her confusion, tore her purse strings and went running after the purse's contents in the street.

Devon rescued Floss's mirror and could not help seeing, pasted on the obverse side of the round glass, an ink self-sketch of Denis Varney. She almost dropped the mirror in her surprise. Had he given Floss the miniature? She felt a jealous twinge and handed the mirror to Floss, who examined her pallid face in it and then suddenly slammed it into her purse and knotted the broken strings.

They walked on, but Devon kept seeing old Mather's faded gray eyes before her and shuddered. She felt a surprising thing then, Floss Roy's harsh voice, comforting and sympathetic. "I know. It's the same with me. Don't think of it. Think of nice things."

"Nice things! What nice things? People who go around inciting riots and then wishing they hadn't? Spineless, weak cowards . . ."

"No. You don't know anything about it, anyway. I meant things like—well—like bein' rich as a toff. I used to be poor, you know. Bloody poor, I can tell you," she confided in the tone of one who is rather proud of this distinction.

"Were you?"

"Gawd, yes. If it wasn't for de Guiche, I'd have gone to Newgate for throwing a chamberpot at the stinking master of the workhouse. I was in the workhouse, you know, after I was scullery maid at—" she hesitated, seemed to avoid some truth she had started to betray—" a rich toff's house in London. My old man died when I was this high, and there was no place else for me. When they didn't want me at the toff's house, Ma sold me into the workhouse. Anyway, de Guiche and Dantine happened onto my trial and paid the fine. If they hadn't I'd be in Newgate today."

So that was the link between Floss and the Dantine Troupe, a workhouse! Michael Dantine had understood the suffering and misery of a workhouse brat. But still, Floss carried Denis Varney's portrait in her purse. Mighty ungrateful of her.

Floss went on without malice. "But you wouldn't understand about people like me. Your kind sees just the pretty posies on top of the ground. You don't see the dirt and worms underneath."

Devon thought of the days when she had lived on a mug of ale, counting the hours until she could drink it, calculating the time of the feast to give herself the most energy. She said softly, with understanding, "Don't look back."

"That's right. Why look back?"

Then, at the same time, they both remembered the old man in the Green George and were silent.

They reached the doors of South Market just in time to run into Bob Traver and Kate who were engrossed in untangling one of her long braids from the frog of his blue travelling coat. Kate stopped laughing long enough to recognize the two bedraggled girls as they came up to join them.

"Well, my Pigeon," that to Bob. "Here is a pretty nosegay for the Company. And you haven't pulled each other's petals off yet. Or have you? What on earth have you two been up to? I'll wager you were caught in that crush over town. They were burning down the George. We got out fast. Everyone's been hours late on account of it. Lord! Bob and I were literally swallowed in humanity. Gad's my life, but you should have seen us!"

Bob Traver quietly took Devon's cloak from her, and Kate and Floss came into the theatre behind them, Kate still recounting her adventure to the stonily indifferent Floss.

The big room had been cleared of chairs and benches and was full of odd-sized bundles: painted backdrops and flats wrapped against dampness, furniture that could be made up like a good actor for a dozen roles, precious drapes of gold cloth, velvet and heavy satin hangings, the ever-present green curtain with which a stable could serve as a theatre, all rolled in thick carpets.

Kate went swaying down to the stage, her skirts sweeping floors and props free of dust. On the stage, the whole company was busy packing and crating, and the busiest were de Guiche and Michael Dantine. The only one missing was Denis Varney.

Devon was surprised that the Company was not yet ready to go, but before she could ask a question, de Guiche put the newcomers to work as they came up to the plank stage, Bob and Floss folding draperies, Kate and Devon packing the costumes. Devon cast a furtive eye at Michael Dantine, an earthy figure with his breeches tucked into his inevitable topboots and shirt sleeves shoved above his elbows. The black ribbon that gathered the ends of his unruly black hair had come untied and dangled over his shoulder. He was a picturesque fellow for some silly girl to break her heart over, but Devon reminded herself he must never add her to his company of Discarded Mistresses. He was working hard packing a backdrop for the Forest of Arden and even harder at pretending that he had not glanced her way, when she came up to the stage. She tried not to smile but the impulse was there, a tenderness she had to conceal. No doubt he was ashamed of his behavior last night. If he were sufficiently ashamed, he might mend his manners to her in public and act more like a gentleman to her in private.

In despite of all her efforts, her thoughts were full of him. But throughout the afternoon, she was also reminded of Denis Varney by the procession of imaginatively created flats passing in the hands of workmen, scenic properties to which his talent had given depth, perspective and a sense of imaginative reality.

After a while, she saw Dantine say something to de Guiche who nodded and a moment later came over to the corner of the stage where Devon and Kate were packing the bulky, modern wardrobe of *As You Like It*, with all its hoops, stays and panniers.

De Guiche spoke specifically to Devon. "What detained you so long today, Mademoiselle? We—the Company was concerned for you."

"I am very sorry. We blundered into that riot at The George. It was impossible to get away."

He considered this. "You looked very much dishevelled when you came in. We were afraid you and Varney had come to an accident."

De Guiche might speak, but the jealous idea was Dantine's. Devon suppressed a smile. "No, Sir. I was with Floss Roy."

"Indeed," said de Guiche. "We are relieved to hear that nothing untoward has befallen you." But as he turned away, she was aware that he did not believe her.

Nothing untoward. . . . She wondered if he would call the happenings at the burning inn *untoward*. . . . The old, old man staring at his own blood on his hand. The swiftness of the flames, fanned by the high salt wind. . . . But she had an idea that if she kept the picture to herself, the image would fade into an unreal nightmare and finally vanish.

Presently, Bob Traver came in after arranging about the carriages and wagons and went into a low-voiced conference with Dantine, who quickly lifted the conversation above a whisper. It was past four o'clock then, and there was still no sign of Denis Varney. Perhaps that was what concerned Bob and Dantine, and now de Guiche who had joined them. Devon watched the men with great interest.

After some heated argument, the heat coming from Dantine, he turned to address the already eavesdropping Company. "Listen to me, all of you. Because of the riot today, we can't go through the Boston Neck until I get a new permit from General Gage. That gives you until about seven o'clock to finish loading the wagons. Since the Green George is gone, you will either have to see to your own reckoning or eat off trays here at the theatre. And any of you who are not outside the theatre on the spot, at eight tonight, will be left to Boston hospitality. Bear that in mind."

He kicked aside the pile of footlight candles and hoods to reach the edge of the platform, and his boot hesitated over Devon's blue-ribboned bandbox that someone had set against the cold tin hoods. To the Company he added a postscript without looking at them. "Kate and some of you will need money. I know your proverbially flat purses. De Guiche will take care of you."

He cleared Devon's baggage with a long stride, leaped off the stage to the pit, and stalked up the jumbled, helter-skelter aisle between the shrouded stage props.

Chapter Ten

AT EIGHT o'clock that night there was a noisy concourse of players around the doors of the South Market Theatre. Presently, under Bob Traver's quiet, efficient handling, the principals and players were divided among the coaches and wagons, leaving the curtain man and a carpenter to drive the remaining wagons loaded with stage properties. The other wagon carried an assortment of workmen and the more valuable stage drapes—which these brawny passengers always adapted to sleeping quarters before the journey was over.

As Devon watched the others climb into the high coach, she let her shielded glance wander in search of Denis Varney. But he was not in sight, nor was his brother. When it came her own turn to step up on the carriage block, she ignored Bob's outstretched hand and pretended to have lost her little sewing case whose stout cord drawstrings were always securely pinned to the waist of her gown. She kept up this elaborate pretense of a search until every seat had been filled in the first coach and Kate was vowing to heaven as the coach pulled away that she washed her hands of Devon. The seamstress could walk to Roxbury, for all she cared.

"But I can't find my sewing case. I must have it," Devon explained in as plaintive a voice as she could muster.

Still, Denis had not arrived. Were they going to depart without their Company Master, or their leading man? She stifled her disappointment and glanced up to find Bob Traver's eyes on the sewing case that had come into view as she mounted the carriage block. They shared a look that had in it a silent understanding, before he beckoned those in the second coach to move over and make room for Devon and himself

As, one by one, the players shifted to the right, she saw their expressions freeze at the sight of something behind her. Her fingertips were just touching the open door when she felt powerful hands at either side of her waist and she was lifted down forcibly to the carriage block. The voice of Michael Dantine ordered Bob to mount in her place. The young man hesitated, looked at him for a long minute, then leaped nimbly into the coach, and almost before the door was closed, Dantine bade the coachman whip up and be off.

It was a high-handed procedure that annoyed while it startled her, but she knew he was anticipating protests; so she set herself to a stubborn silence, shrugged herself free of him, still without looking behind her, and crossed her arms in a manner that he could not mistake. One of her feet ominously tapped the ground. He did not know what to make of this. Signaling the driver of the waiting property wagon, he looked down at Devon's relentless form and said finally, "I have a mind to drive one of the wagons. Will you bear me company?"

The property wagon was pulling up toward them, the driver eager to relinquish his place and join his friends in the wagon following. Devon pulled forward her hood against the wind and readjusted her cape. Still, he hesitated, then, taking a chance of a rebuff, put one hand on her shoulder. His voice was very low; yet its power reverberated somewhere within her. "Don't *you* turn from me, Devon. Don't listen to their lies. No one could be all the things they say of me."

Her heart gave a lurch of pain at his voice, but she would not let him know she had forgiven him so easily for last night and for his base display of authority at the carriage block. Kate had prophesied he would try this weapon of pity.

She reminded him quietly, "You are exactly what you were born, Sir. And so you will always be."

His hand leaped from her shoulder as if his palm were scorched at the contact. He laughed harshly. "Since I was born a bastard and 'so I will always be,' I have a warm hope for the future; have I not?" And he began to fasten his greatcoat as he frowned up at the sky. She knew his thoughts were not on the chill, winter sky. She was aware of a sensitivity between them, as if his wounds would bring a drop of blood to the surface of her own flesh.

But the notion passed. She could smile at the unnatural fancy. Was this the way he had ensnared all those women whom he never loved? Suppose he did want to get her into his bed. If he ever got his way, what then? Having no further worth to him, she would be sent packing, a ruined woman with no hopes and no prospects. Better to take warning from those dark eyes of the Master-Player. It would be a disaster to yield to him, to be drawn into those swirling deeps where other creatures that had gone before stared at her with dead eyes.

The property wagon was before them, the coachman climbing down from his perch. A trembling invaded Devon's body. It must be the brisk, December air. Not the thought that she was riding into the stillness of a winter night with a man beside her whom she did not dare to like. No. It must be the beauty of the strange evening that made her suddenly glad she was not safe in the warm coach with Bob and the others.

Dantine swung her up to the high seat of the wagon and mounted after her. "You won't be cold, will you? I like the night. The days are hellish enough, but the night is clean. One doesn't see the filth, then."

She did not know what to say to such a philosophy and settled herself beside him to face the rising wind while he tucked a cloak about her feet for warmth. She was grateful for the small, thoughtful attention. Ahead of them, the coaches had long since pulled away from the South Market. Behind Dantine's wagon another, carrying its full complement of backstage workmen, stood ready, the driver muttering into the high collars of his heavy service coat, his team pawing at the cobblestones. Dantine took the reins and they moved off.

When they were under way, Devon, touching on a forbidden topic, asked, "Isn't Mr. Varney coming?"

He looked at her with hard humor. "What? And leave his wench before they've made a night of it? She's a pretty blonde. I saw them together at a corner gin shop this evening. Come now, Mistress, you know Denis better than that."

How glad he is about it, thought Devon. How he gloats over it! And she subsided, fearing to probe the matter further.

Devon looked back more than once, sentimentally, in the long drive past the ugly marshlands to the barricades. There was no love lost between her and the cold, great city of the North, but in travelling southward she was further separated from her mother and father who lay under the snow of Concord graves.

They passed the barricade of Boston Neck without trouble. Devon was touched and amused at the camaraderie between Dantine and the British soldiers. They scarcely glanced at his permit with the bold signature of the Military Governor's aide. Their trust in this master of a company of players was simple and pathetic, she thought. She liked them, those big, florid fellows with the smell of rum upon their breath and the hearty friendliness of men befriended far from home. This morning there had been dauntless old Gamaliel Mather. Tonight there were the soldiers stamping up and down on the icy ground, swinging their arms and slapping their own shoulders to keep warm, for they would never be permitted to thaw their chilled bones before the hearths of Boston Town. And opposed to these wicked Tories, what? The vague and idealistic mouthings of patriots like de Guiche and Floss Roy. And a mob of insensate murderers who burned old men alive. Fat, pompous little fellows like Sam Adams who had never been a success at honest labor, and dishonest smugglers like well-to-do John Hancock.

She waved to the soldiers as Dantine drove the wagon away, and every man at his post answered her. She had a glow of satisfaction. Surely, men like that would not take arms against decent citizens. They had no wish to persecute the suspicious Bostonians. They wanted only to be respected and to have the king's mandate respected. A simple matter, surely . . .

The wagon was soon rumbling into the sparsely wooded open country where low-lying hills rolled one into another under the distant black sky. Neither Devon nor Dantine spoke for a long stretch of time. She could see nothing of the road ahead except an immense loneliness. How did he see so well in the dark? A man should not have cat's eyes. Perhaps it was his long nights at sea that gave him those eyes. Finally, she glanced at him. He was studying the wagon ruts in the dirt and the patches of snow, pale against the earth. His face was free of the cruelty that seemed to her so much a part of his conscious mood. She was astonished to find how strikingly attractive he could be in repose. She must have stared at him longer and more closely than she had intended, for he looked at her suddenly, smiling. "Now, you see, I don't eat up little girls every night."

"No," she came back, flustered to have been caught admiring him. "Only every other night."

Waiting for his reply, she looked out over the snow-tipped rocks that dotted every dark field and hill slope. She felt a glow of warmth course through her as if she had been swallowing brandy. Her body was close against his and she did not move away. The feeling that coursed along her spine was too pleasant to throw off at once. She remained where she was and wondered if he shared this sensitive awareness.

He exploded violently at her words, but not without humor. "Blast me! Had I been your father—and the demons were kind to spare me that—I should have seen to it that you kept a respectful tongue to your elders, Mistress Devon."

She challenged him as she had longed to answer her equally masterful father. "And what would you have done to me, had I been your unfilial daughter?"

He looked down at her close beside him, and she waited, half expecting some sort of physical response and not averse to the idea. But he only looked at her for what seemed to Devon a very long moment, and then his hands twisted a little in the reins and he was looking ahead at the ice-crusted wagon ruts in the road. "Don't play at high games, Devon. Not unless you will put up stakes."

Her cheeks felt hot beneath her icy skin and she was humiliated. She decided not to speak to him again, but he waited so long before speaking to her that she was relieved when next she heard his voice. He was not looking at her and said carelessly, "Have you come around to forgiving me yet for last night?"

"Oh. That. Did you think you frightened me? I went back and laughed with Kate over you and your noisy performance."

"Why, you damned, heartless little bitch!"

"Thank you, Sir. Now we are back on normal terms again. Don't you feel more at ease when you are shouting at me?"

He laughed so loudly she was afraid the team would bolt, but she laughed too, because, for all his moodiness, he fascinated her. "It's good to be with you, Devon. I am never sure from one moment to the next what vulnerable spot you will find in my toughened hide. I seem to be one mass of bloody bruises since I have known you. And yet, a month ago, I should have said I had not an Achilles' heel to my name. Now, I will place myself in your pitiless hands again. Will you let me?"

She looked at him. She was prepared for any absurdity. He, too, was capable of saying the unexpected.

"Well then, long ago, more than twenty years before you were born, I found a kitten inside a heap of rotting garbage. It was very young and the bones stuck clear through its dingy coat. But in my hands it lay there, sweet and incredibly dear."

She stared at him, trying not to be moved, but unable to avoid his insidious influence.

He went on, softly. "I knew my small kitten loved me. But still, when I would rough it or play with it, the tiny teeth would snap down upon my fingers and give me a sharp, strangely thrilling pain. I could not get its love without that pain. And so I took what I could have. In sleep it lay next to my body for warmth, and one night they found it in the straw with me."

She moistened her dry lips. "No—please—no."

He shrugged. "There was a cauldron of foul, watery soup left over from supper, boiling on the coals for tomorrow's breakfast. The workmaster's sly one-eyed crimp held my kitten in midair, its little paws still clawing frantically, and my hands tearing at his sleeve. Then he dropped it into the cauldron...I don't know whether the kitten made a sound. But I shall hear until I am rotting in hell, the sound of that hot soup as it splashed upon the coals."

He was silent then, and Devon became aware of the horses' hooves upon the hard, frozen ground. Then Michael

Dantine's voice once more. "I never again experienced a feeling for another creature to equal the passion I knew alone for that kitten. I would trade all that I have known since to have my kitten again in my hands, frail and sharp-clawed, loving nothing in the world but me. . . . You see, Devon, it was *me* that pathetic heap of bones belonged to. Nothing else in my life has ever belonged to me as that kitten did."

After a little while he resumed coolly, "Now you have your cue. You may laugh." He looked down at her and his face softened. "There. It is no matter for tears. It happened before you were born. How could it possibly concern you?"

How young and how different the strange, burned man must have been in those days! Something more than a squirming, helpless kitten had died that night.

"Why did you tell me?" she asked finally as she turned away to hide the tears of which she was humiliatingly conscious.

"Can't you guess, Devon?"

Surreptitiously, she ran the side of her forefinger along her cheeks to destroy any trace of tears. She knew she was being swayed by his unhappiness, and this, too, despite Kate's warning.

"Well then," he said with a quiet that was almost gentleness, "in thirty-two years I had not again seen that kitten nor its like—until one night not yet a week gone. I saw it scurry across the gloomy stage of South Market, and I watched it for long moments before I dared to believe it had come home to me."

He looked at her once in an almost furtive way, as if uneasy over her reaction. She could not unravel her own emotions, and was aware that this was his most successful assault upon her carefully constructed defenses.

She said on an impulse, "I wish someone who loved you had known you then, when you were still—impressionable. Someone might have changed your view of life—made you see that there are precious things to be found in all the dark places of the world. She might have..." She caught herself in the middle of that dangerous thought.

He put one hand out and covered her hands where they lay twisting nervously in her lap. The sound of his voice lingered on the clear night with a haunting beauty. "Thank you for your lovely, foolish thought."

Suddenly, the slow-moving wagon swayed on Devon's side as if a weight had been put upon it and, startled, she released her fingers, shaking off with an effort the Master-Player's spell. A lean body had inserted itself onto the outer edge of the seat beside her, and, almost touching her as she turned, were the sardonic features of Denis Varney.

"Did I startle you? A thousand pardons. But I have a pressing engagement further down the road. Much further."

By now his brother had recovered from this infuriating interruption and demanded over Devon's head, "What in hell are you doing, leaping out of the darkness at midnight? Why weren't you with the others when we left town?"

Denis smiled blandly. "What? Ride in the carriages with a parcel of drowsy wenches and jawing patriot lads? Then I would have missed all the interesting endearments you and my little seamstress had for each other only a moment since."

Devon felt fury stiffen the body of Michael Dantine, while Denis on her right insinuated his body in under the covering of her cloak and snuggled up to her.

To forestall the fiery speech she knew Dantine was about to make, Devon said gravely, "Are you sure you have not caught an ague in your listening? The back of the wagon must be very chilly for a person so desperately unsure of himself that he has nothing better to do than eavesdrop."

She had scored a touch at an uncovered spot in that bundle of ego, and she was rewarded by Michael Dantine's hearty laugh, the second time in one evening. As for Denis, it took only an instant for him to recover his equilibrium and join the laugh at his own expense. Dantine broke off the merriment with a quick gesture which Denis obeyed on the instant.

"Listen. A rider. Are you pursued?"

Denis did not search for explanations. "Yes. A long-nosed Redcoat from the barricades."

"Alone?"

"So far as I can tell."

"I suppose you have been dabbling in treason again. What did I tell you about staying out of politics?"

Denis looked injured. "Sink me! Not a politic! Must be a wench I've won from the Redbellies. They've pursued me for hours, I'll take oath on't. I cut across the fields, let old Bess gallop on to what pastures she might find, and climbed on the wagon as you came along past the Providence cutoff."

There was a glib frankness about his story that made Devon uneasy. They could all be hanged if Denis were involved with the rebel patriots, and she had no mind to dangle from a stout tree for a reason so foolish as politics.

Hoofbeats on the crusted ground were now plainly audible. Devon sat stiffly, wondering just what Denis Varney had done to attract the Tory soldiers. She saw Dantine's hand tighten on the reins, and knew he expected violence. Of the three of them, only Denis sat indolently with his arms folded, surveying the undulating fields with their barren winter nakedness. The clatter of hooves announced the arrival of the Redcoat just behind the wagon, then around the side, and into the path of the slow-stepping team.

Dantine reined in sharply, almost throwing Devon from her seat, and bringing the horses to a nervous, shying halt inches short of the wooden-nerved soldier and his mount. Even in the half dark of a starless night, the three players could not miss the mouth of the carbine in his steady hand, leveled at a point just over Devon's head between the two brothers.

"Get a light there, Sirrah, and let me see your face."

Dantine did not move, so Denis went for the light, leaping off his side and obligingly scuffing down the road to the rear of the wagon. There he fumbled in the theatre properties for several minutes, calling out ridiculous things to his brother.

"Where could it be, Master? T'lantern's gone. Can't find it nowheres. Don't y'beat me, pray, Master. I be lookin' again."

Devon thought it a very bad performance from the elegant Varney, and wondered why the soldier did not guess the truth. Dantine was twisting the reins murderously in his hands, making a noose of them, as if, in his imagination, he pulled it tight around his brother's neck. The night was still except for the uneasy pawing of the horses. Then there was Denis Varney's voice again to enliven the scene.

"Master, ain't I looked enough? Happen the sojer'd like to look, too. Come back here, Mister Sojer."

To Devon's amazement this upset Dantine so that he threw the reins over her hands and leaped to the ground. "Never mind. I'll find it myself," and he went around to the back of the wagon. She guessed by the stillness of the British officer's form that he was similarly alert.

In another moment a terrific crack of hand on flesh was heard, the sound blunted by an indignant yelp from Denis. The scratch of tinder delayed the two men a little longer but when Dantine came around the wagon again he carried a lighted lantern which illuminated the angry set of his mouth but kept in darkness the young man trailing at his back and nursing a sore cheek.

"Now then," said the soldier, "I am informed contraband of war is being carried out of Massachusetts Colony on this road tonight. As you are doubtless aware, that is a hanging matter. Do you have arms in your possession?"

"You are misinformed, Redcoat. I am Michael Dantine. The barricades will vouch for me. My pass is in order. If you've done staring at me, I'll go upon my way with my servants."

The soldier dismounted, rubbed the fingers and thumb of his left hand together in a request for the light, and after a little pause, Dantine handed him the lantern. Still, the lieutenant's right hand was steady with the carbine. He waved the lantern aloft to cast its faint rays first over Denis who was now climbing onto the wagon, knees first, like a clumsy boy, and then over Devon's frightened white face. He flashed the light away, then back quickly. He was interested.

"Good evening, Ma'am. Are you a player too?"

She saw Dantine turn and look at her during this speech and knew he was wondering what was between her and the soldier, but she was busy with an answer that would satisfy him. "Ay, sir. That is, I am the seamstress and my— my brother here, is ostler and prompt boy and whatnot. We work for Mr. Dantine. This gentleman." She was so intent on keeping the lantern light off Denis that she went on brightly, "I am shocked you should think us carrying contraband, but please to search us, no matter what." Search anything, so long as you do not identify Denis . . .

She knew then, by the sudden tense attitude of Denis, that it was not himself, after all, that he was concerned about, but the contraband. Why should he be hiding contraband arms? Certainly not for patriotic reasons. But she knew almost instantly. There was good money in the smuggling of arms.

In her first glance at Denis by the edge of the lantern rays, she had seen that his garments bore him out in his preposterous acting of the stable-boy part. All the lace had been ripped off his shirt and the breeches were rent across both knees. He wore no stockings and the bright silver buckles were gone from his shoes. Under close scrutiny, the quality of his clothing might have given him away, but in his present state, he apparently held no interest for the soldier, while the wagon itself occupied his attention.

"Well, Mistress, and you, Sir"—to Michael Dantine—"if

you've no objection, I think I'll just be having myself a bit of a look at your properties. Do you care to come with me, Master Dantine?"

But after a cursory inspection, they returned and the soldier handed back the signed pass from the governor's secretary. Dantine had the lighted lantern which he hung on a peg at the side of the wagon. The lieutenant pocketed his carbine in the saddlepouch, saluted Devon and mounted his horse while Dantine got onto the wagon beside her and took the reins from her hands.

"Good luck on your chase," he called out to the lieutenant.

"Thanks. I've found only one other who went through the barricades at about the time you and your second wagon did. Incidentally, you will find them a little late in joining you. Two of my men are overhauling the wagon itself. I doubt if they expect to find anything, but there were some disputes and one or two black eyes before I left them. Well, this is what comes of doing business with female informers. The blond wench may have lied about the whole matter."

No one said anything in the wagon for a few minutes as it rattled away from the soldier; then Denis straightened up, becoming himself again. Devon was smiling, thinking of the blond wench who had betrayed Denis. That would teach him!

Denis looked over at his brother. "Rather well done on the whole, I thought. I liked it better than the time you smuggled the wounded rebel out of New York last month. That was a silly business where no profit was involved. But this! I'll go you shares on this."

"I'll forego my share," said Dantine acidly. "Do you think I didn't guess you'd a mind to stick a knife between his shoulder blades that time you invited the fool to the back of the wagon?"

"Oh, you noticed that, did you?" Denis grinned and then tried to look repentant. "I'll never do it again. And I certainly never will boast to a blonde again about my plans." He put his hand on Devon's head and roughed up her hair familiarly. "Next time, no more blondes, eh Devon?" He reached over her head and offered his hand to Dantine. "Here's my promise on it."

Dantine ignored the proffered hand, and after a little hesitation, Denis drew it back, examined it critically and smiled to himself. "I don't know why you're so angry. God knows you've better reason than I to cheat the Tories. And you've smuggled weapons yourself."

Dantine said, still staring at the road, "The difference is: I've never pretended to love the lobsterbacks—but you made deals with them in New York. You've served them and you've served the rebels. You'd serve anything, for a fistful of five-pound notes."

"Why be modest?" Denis asked blandly. "Make it ten-pound notes. And there is this to consider: I don't hate anyone. I am a kindly Christian. You have enemies. But what enemies have I? None."

Dantine looked at him for the first time in their conversation.

Denis smiled. A moment later he settled himself comfortably and went on. "I may as well tell you that our nice-mannered lieutenant was pursuing me and not the wagon; so, half an hour ago when I burst in upon your little romance, I had just dumped a dozen government contraband muskets into the back of the wagon. When the Redcoat came up, it seemed the ideal time for me to lash the muskets to the bottom of the floorboards while I made my running commentary and pretended to search for the lantern. If he had found me there, you know it would have been the Redcoat or me. . . . Now that I've explained so carefully, am I still in bad odor?"

Dantine did not answer.

There was a little silence. Denis turned to Devon.

"Are you really angry? I wouldn't have told about it only

I thought you'd be amused." He saw her difficulty in remaining angry. "You aren't really cross with me, Devon. Are you? Are you?"

"For God's sake, be silent!" Dantine shouted so loudly that the horses almost bolted.

Devon and Denis, who had both jumped, exchanged startled glances and when Denis, pretending fright, sought her hand under the cover of the robe, she did not pull away from him.

Chapter
Eleven

DEVON IMAGINED life would be less hectic once the Dantine Troupe left the political indigestion of Boston. But the Inns along the Middle Road, and later, the Upper Post Road, meant rehearsals at ungodly hours in musty lofts and foul cellars, unpalatable food, and strange bedfellows. At one time, Kate, Floss, Devon and a village girl, doubling as a temporary ingenue, shared the same bed. This required some last-minute arrangements; for Kate sprawled all over the big mattress and slept so soundly that when Devon and Floss shoved her off onto the floor under a couple of blankets, she knew nothing until morning. She awoke astonished at her night's peregrinations, apologizing to the girls for having so rudely left them.

Devon was busy with her own particular activities and too uninterested in the complex problem of finance to see just how the mathematical minds of Floss Roy and Gerard de Guiche handled all the reckonings of the troupe. She had not yet been paid her own quarterly salary, having earned only two weeks of it, and being in debt to Dantine for considerably more. The intricate method of paying actors by shares did not involve her or the backstage workmen, who were all paid flat salaries.

But of the stage Devon learned more than she had thought existed in the plain, outspoken language of Shakespeare and Company. There were times, and not infrequent, when the cast worked for seventeen hours with only minor interruptions of a utilitarian nature, the longest being a generous fifteen minutes in which to eat and digest a hearty supper. They worked as hard upon a twenty minute afterpiece by Molière as they did upon the beauties of *Othello*.

The big carriage wheels bounced over clumsy back-country roads into bordering Connecticut and back along the Upper Post Road, playing to shamefaced farmhands, gay young squires and daring burghers' daughters, and, not infrequently, to the town council itself. Every play was edited by Dantine and de Guiche so that it said what the men of influence at each wayside coach stop wanted to hear. Many a taproom was hung with blankets which, when they parted, revealed the awful penalty of avarice, infidelity and disloyalty or tyranny (depending on which side of the current political dispute held the reins in the town). The same play could serve either cause, depending on the inflection of a line.

More than once in the winter countryside all passengers were ordered out of the travelling carriages, the men to push, the women to climb up icy hills and down muddy slopes at dark midnight and winter dawn.

On the day before Christmas they arrived in a bustling little town at the foot of a steep incline, the lowest point in a deep-sunk basin of farmland. After some haggling conducted by the Frenchman with native thrift, the whitewashed ballroom of a posting house and inn was made to serve as a theatre. It was not a bad arrangement; for the east end of the room was raised, having served heretofore as the station for local fiddlers in the routs held there. A large clumsy harpsichord had to be moved to a point below the platform. The actors must exit into an ice-coated covered walk that connected with the carriage shed. A fireplace cut off a third of the stage. But it was still the most attractive theatre they had struck since leaving Boston.

Kate and Denis came in to look it over after the alterations were made and the tired trio, Dantine, de Guiche and Bob, retired to wash up. Devon and Floss, who had supervised the more artistic changes, were undecided over the harpsichord which Floss thought ought to be changed with the big hutch table. The doorkeeper would sit at the hutch table to collect eight shillings per head for the chairs, five shillings sixpence for the benches and anything from a tuppenny bit to a shilling from the standees.

"But we couldn't possibly put the harpsichord in front of the door. How would the audience get into the theatre?" Devon pointed out. "They would have to go clear around and come in the back way, through the inn."

"Make no mind of that," said Floss with pungent conviction. "It's the actors falling over the damned thing on their exit cues that I care about, and I say the lads should move it now."

There was prospect of a hasty exit on Denis Varney's part as he heard this, but Kate saved him, siding at once with Devon against her old enemy. "What the devil, Floss? If you can't get off the stage without tripping over a harpsichord, don't imagine everyone is so clumsy."

Denis backed this up. "My dear Kate, why blame poor Floss for her big feet and her unfortunate tendency to corpulence? Where her body carries her, she must follow."

She sprang at him with claws ready, but Kate and Devon got between them and soothed the ruffled Floss.

"Well then," Floss said, shrugging away the whole matter, "let it stand so. Let the stage exit be blocked and see who falls over the thing first. It won't be little old Floss; that I'll wager you!"

Devon wavered before this intense conviction. "Still, perhaps Floss is right. It's the Shrew tonight, and so many exits. What do you think, Kate? After all, it is your play."

"I say, let's all be on our way to the taproom. I'm as thirsty as a bawd in a church choir."

Denis made himself loudly heard. "Bravo! Come along ladies. My service to you. Yes, Floss, even you."

"Hoity-toity," said Floss, but she did not resist when Denis took her arm and they followed after.

Over a glass of Rhenish, Devon heard Denis Varney's plan for a walk up the hill to the ruins of Old Town. She was anxious to see the desolate place that had been destroyed eighty years before by a nomad Six Nations Tribe.

"It is haunted," Denis told the women. "They say that if you listen of a still morning, you can hear the wail of a woman as the scalping knife slashed across her skull."

"Don't!" Devon cried, spilling a drop of wine. "Good heavens, I don't believe a word of it."

Denis laughed. "Come with me, and I'll prove it."

She yielded to his wheedling and Kate's good-natured insistence as she had known she would, but she was a little surprised at his determination that Floss come along. She went to pick up Bob Traver, and upon his friendly but definite refusal the four started up to Old Town.

Snowdrifts were piled high on both sides of the steep coach road, and the churned mud of the roadbed had hardened under last night's cold, so it was easier to walk on.

Floss argued over yesterday's performance; Kate was talking volubly to anyone who would listen, and Devon was wondering how Michael Dantine intended to spend the day. She had paused a moment as the noisy group passed the inn, with half a mind to ask him to come along on the walking tour. His grim liking for solitude intrigued her, and while he was not nearly so charming a companion as his brother, she would like to have been able to break down that reserve of his. But it was a temporary notion. How would gloomy

Dantine, unfamiliar with the simplest pleasures of youth, know the conduct for a cheerful walking party?

Kate was frowning. "Now why did Bob refuse to come? Has he lost his silly affection for me? I daresay he has, fickle rogue."

Devon leaped quickly to the defense of her kindest friend. "I think he is too proud to bear the treatment you always give your admirers."

Kate took this to heart—for the moment. "Poor dog. Do I really treat him so badly? Damme—that's my silly way. I meant no harm. I must make it up to him."

Floss looked across Denis at the beauty. "You just can't see a fish slip off your hook, can you, Katie, dear?"

"Oh, they always bite again," Kate said airily. But Devon hoped kindhearted Bob would not bite. He deserved better than the role amoral Kate had in mind for him. After a few minutes, she forgot Bob. The top of the hill was a place of icy beauty. Even Kate lost her tongue staring beyond the low, broken stone walls which were all that remained of Old Town to the earth and snow of the valleys. It was not a very high hill; yet its steep ascent gave it a peculiarly grand aspect and made the sluggish ice-coated river in the valley below look an immense distance away, winding into a dead and barren country of mottled white.

Denis teased Floss who, though she protested and insulted him, seemed to like it. He stood on the stiff ground at the very edge of a sheer drop toward the stream below and grabbed her around the waist, under her cloak.

"Shall I drop you down? Wouldn't it be simple? And then, no more Floss. Here I go!"

She shrieked as if he actually intended to kill her, and the hysterical, high-pitched sound of her voice sent a shiver down Devon's spine. But after a few minutes, he turned his attention to Devon. "And what makes our little seamstress so silent? . . . Listen!"

Everyone jumped nervously at his command and, staring

at his upraised hand, listened in a sudden, unnatural stillness. Over the hillside, the wind moaned among the ruins, and there was no other sound. When the wind died for a moment, a cloud went over the sun and left the hilltop wrapped in noiseless white obscurity.

Devon, wondering what Denis had asked them to listen to, looked uneasily at Kate. Denis caught that look and said with soft persuasiveness, "Don't you hear it? A woman sobbing in the wind."

For a moment Devon was petrified. Surely, it did sound a little like . . . and then she saw Denis watching her slyly, grinning. She had been taken in. "Well," she defended herself with vigor, "I did hear something, and so did you all."

Floss relaxed too, and pushed him, half in anger. "What an actor! What a stinking fine rogue you are!"

With the best humor in the world, Denis waved his arm in a sweeping gesture as if to take a bow. The violence of his movement was stronger than anyone had suspected; for the back of his hand struck Floss at an angle across the upper half of her face. The blow was so hard it carried a sound both soft and resistant, as if it had struck through flesh to the bone. She reeled backward and was only just saved from a tumble down the snow-covered rocks by Denis's quick grasp of her wind-blown petticoats.

"Did I hurt you, Floss? There, now. It was damned clumsy of me. Are you all right?"

Floss recovered herself enough to shake off the alarmed Devon and Kate who had run to brush her off and exclaim over her.

"I'm all right. Small thanks to you." She skimmed her hand lightly over the left half of her face, near her eye, and winced.

Devon looked up at Denis. "She is hurt."

"Hurt? I am perfectly well, blast you! It's just that my cheek stings a little. I'll pay you out, and neatly, for this, m'lad. What was it you'd a mind for—a new soubrette?"

With gentle patience Denis explained to Devon. "Floss thinks I contrived this so that you might go before the candles in her place tonight. Isn't that absurd?"

Floss cracked outspread fingers across Denis's face, and as he lost his balance, she switched her skirts around and marched over to the road alone.

Kate rushed to console the stunned joker, while Devon was torn between the appeal of Denis and instinctive sympathy for Floss who was in pain and nursing her face with her handkerchief. Devon joined her, trying to offer a little assistance, feeling guiltily that she was the cause of it all. A sudden, needle-sharp wind swept across the hill, whistling among the ruins, billowing out the women's skirts and snapping their petticoats around their legs so that it was difficult to walk against the ruffled cloth.

"Damned little bastard!" Floss muttered finally. "Thinks I'm not onto him. The truest thing he ever said was that he wheedled me up here to get me off the stage tonight. He hoped I'd break a leg."

Devon protested vehemently, alarmed that Floss should share her suspicions. "That would be idiotic, Floss. There is no one to go on in your place. The ingenue we took on at the last performance certainly couldn't do the part."

"Don't play the innocent."

Devon stopped in the teeth of the wind and faced her. "I should be quite petrified, I promise you. I could never do it. Not without long practice. When I think about those odious creatures who sit across the candles and gape at you—Impossible!" The more she thought of it, the more she shuddered.

"Here, here, girls," Denis chided them, coming up with Kate at last. "No quarrels, I pray you. I dote on peace above all things."

Devon could find no words in which to answer such audacity.

On the journey down the hill, she listened with some

misgivings to the smooth working of Denis Varney's tongue. By the time they reached town, Floss was desperate over her fast-swelling face, and even Denis roused himself to the extent of loaning her his handkerchief which he soaked in a snow bank on the edge of the local Common for her use.

The first flakes of a new snowfall caught them as they crowded around Floss on the Common to examine what was going to be a colossal black eye. A moment later, with dusk upon them, they lost all interest in Floss Roy's face and hurried on their way.

As they crossed the inn yard, Michael Dantine stood waiting for them in shirt sleeves but otherwise with the look of one who had been in that position for hours. His black hair was powdered with snow; the fine flakes had blown upon his folded arms, and one of his boots crunched out a solemn tattoo upon the stones. Before Denis could open his mouth, his brother cut him short.

"So! You've finally recalled that we have a play to perform in two hours! Get in to supper and be quick about it . . . all of you!"

Devon did not look at him but hurried past with Floss between her and Kate, hoping that, in his anger, he would not see her face. Denis was not long behind them. It was as if each expected the sting of the bo'sun's cat upon the laggard.

When in ten minutes Michael Dantine ducked his head under the low-beamed roof of the dining room, Devon was eating rapidly and Kate was talking very fast to de Guiche. Even Denis bestirred himself to tell Bob and the Company a long and involved joke. Everyone was united in a conspiracy to keep the director's eyes from Floss Roy and her swollen, unnatural face.

Devon, furtively watching Michael Dantine, saw him reach for the salt pork and then help himself to the boiled turnips without looking up or speaking to anyone. She could not make up her mind whether he was being childishly cross or whether he was troubled by something more important than four tardy players. He ignored the table talk entirely and did not reply even when de Guiche addressed a remark to him. But when Devon trailed her sleeve in the salt trencher as she reached for her wine glass, Dantine handed her the glass across the table and her fleeting look crossed his own intent gaze. She murmured an inaudible "Thank you," and began to drink. Over the rim of the glass she saw he was still looking at her and wondered whether to risk a smile, or would he be suspicious if she were too pleasant? She was saved from a decision by the sudden drawing together of his dark eyebrows and the unmistakeable signs of rage that appeared on his face. He had seen Floss. She sat perfectly still and dared not look at the soubrette beside her.

One by one, the company stopped eating and waited for the explosion. Devon looked at the great walnut case clock in the corner beyond Bob Traver's chair. There were less than two hours until curtain time. Impossible to get another actress. Floss would have to go on. She felt a surge of relief. No question of a substitute now.

Michael said with the quiet, terrible voice of lightning before thunder, "Floss, my dear, where did you get that magnificent black eye?"

For a moment, Floss was stiff and frightened beside Devon. Then, Devon felt the soubrette's body relax. Floss was determined not to be cowed by the director. "Ask your loving brother."

"Well, damme," said Denis in great haste and virtuous resentment, "I flung my arm out and she was in the way. How was I to know she stood so close to me? Anyhow, I saved her from falling down the hill."

"And for that we must repay you, Denis. Remind me to set it down in my accounts."

Devon started. Her senses where Michael Dantine was concerned were remarkably acute. She could scent the breath of deadliness beneath the words. But the others at the table laughed faintly, imagining this to be a touch of his mordant humor.

De Guiche tried to smooth things over. "Can it not be concealed, the little black eye? A particle of wash, very white. A soupçon more carmine. Who will guess? One will say 'Ah, but ma'am'selle wears the kohl beneath the eyes.' What harm?"

Michael Dantine was frowning, with his hard white teeth set into a corner of his lower lip as he studied Floss across the table. He motioned to her. "Come over here into the light, by my chair. Now, turn your face. No, no. Toward the candles." He took one good look, swung her around to the Company and challenged them, "Now what do you say? Do you still think a bit of white and a dab of rouge will send her out tonight on a stage only two feet from the audience?"

The entire left side of Floss Roy's face was badly puffed and red. But Floss was by no means ready to give in. She wrenched herself free of his arm in a fury. "Just try and find someone else! You'll *have* to use me. If you don't, there won't be any show, and we can celebrate Christmas tomorrow with lean purses and hollow bellies. Besides, it's less than two hours till curtain. Just try it. Just try . . ."

"Be silent!" thundered the director while he looked over the Company, face by face.

Denis put in casually, "I don't know about the rest of you, but I've got to play tonight. I've a deuce of a reckoning with the taproom."

Dantine turned upon him a look of such menace that he subsided and began to toy with the stem of his glass. The rest of the Company sat unmoving. Whenever Michael Dantine looked Devon's way, she became busy over her cuffs, putting new pleats into the white lawn, looking innocent and hoping against hope that for once he would not notice her.

Suddenly, Bob Traver spoke in his quiet way, with that

unobtrusive authority that Devon had noticed before, and which even caught Dantine's attention. "The one person who can help us tonight is Miss Howard. She must play Bianca and the rest of us will pick up her cues."

Everyone looked at Michael Dantine, and when it was plain that he was not going to take off the bold juvenile's head, they burst into chattering agreement. Devon felt ice coursing through her body. Of the whole Company, she had not dreamed Bob Traver would betray her. She sat stiff and unsmiling, terrified, while Kate and Denis patted her back and lavishly encouraged her.

The director looked across the table at her. "How would you like that, Devon?"

She groped for arguments with which to resist the entire Company and especially Dantine, but found herself forestalled by Floss Roy.

"I knew it! I knew it! That Judas planned the whole thing. He did this to me deliberately to put her on in my role. By Jesus, I'll lay you out, my pretty lad!" She fell upon Denis Varney in a furious assault that took him by surprise and brought forth a yell as she fastened her talons into his queued hair. Kate and Devon pulled and hauled the two of them while the men rushed to the struggle. But the director reached Floss and her victim first and grabbed them by their collars, shaking them like two yapping puppies. He sent Denis crashing into the table to be pulled together by Devon.

Denis lost his temper for one of the few times in his life, yelling, "Keep that bitch away from me. I'll kill her, I warn you. I'll kill her!"

What the squirming, writhing Floss would have answered no one knew; for Dantine had one hand over her mouth and the other around her waist, forcing her back against his body. She was still waving a fist full of tawny hair at her enemy.

Michael Dantine's voice shook the Company and certain delighted eavesdroppers in the doorway as he addressed them all. "The next outburst of this kind will send both of you packing, and *by God, I mean it!*"

Denis, now fully recovered, laughed and opened his mouth to make some witty retort. Dantine reached over Devon's head to box his brother's ears as he might have chastised an unruly schoolboy. Denis subsided, his grin a little twisted. The master looked down at Devon coldly, appraising her possibilities.

His resolve was taken in such an unshakable tone that even Floss was hushed. "Well then, let it be as Bob suggests. Devon goes on as Bianca tonight."

Only Devon ventured in a shaking anger, "That is quite impossible, sir. As you must see, the hour is . . ."

"The devil with the hour. Bob, go and find a script for her. Kate, bring Floss's two costumes to the greenroom and be sharp about it. They will both have to be altered from head to toe. The rest of you finish your meal and we will all meet in the greenroom."

The plan was preposterous, Devon knew, and wondered when the Master-Player would realize it. But she went along indifferently beside him to the carriage house which was Dantine's greenroom, just as if everything would come about as he had said it would.

Chapter Twelve

THE FAMILIAR green curtains were hung across the east end of the ballroom, and already a queue had formed outside the public door. It was a large but oddly furtive group as if ashamed of this lure of the flesh. A good deal of whispering went on, and now and then an excited female giggle. The queue was buried in greatcoats and capes and calashes, using as cover against the steady snowfall everything from a month-old copy of the Boston *Gazette* to a square of sailcloth.

Devon saw her prospective audience from the windows of the ballroom on the way to the carriage house but was jolted out of rising panic by her companion, the Master. He hurried her between the rows of benches, past the stage, out under the covered way that connected the ballroom with the carriage house, quite unmindful of the snowflakes that sifted down her neck.

The carriage-house door stood ajar and there were candles set about the barny interior, which was divided into two dressing rooms by a single inadequate blanket. The big room had been used recently for the storing of two carriages, one belonging to a prominent citizen of the town and the other to the inn. Both carriages, bundled like fragile invalids, stood outside in the snow.

There was sawdust scattered at the entrance, and Michael Dantine's wet boots soon tracked it all over the floor. Devon stepped into a clammy mass more than once in the ensuing half hour, but this she scarcely noticed amid her greater trials. First, Dantine explained the scenes to her. She had known the play since her first childhood memory of her mother as the beautiful Shrew. But until tonight, Bianca had been just an insipid little ingenue, a sort of whipping boy for her beautiful sister.

As he paced up and down before her, Dantine explained just what would be expected of Bianca—when she must enter, and the various subjects of her dialogue. It was, for the most part, a utilitarian role, feeding other actors and situations, with only about a dozen sides in the entire play. She stopped him in the middle of one of his assurances. "But what if I forget to cue the other players?"

"That's of no account. You may rely on Kate or Denis to get you out of a hole. Or if they fail, Gerard will assist you. All that I ask of you is that you appear onstage and know what you are doing there. Not ten in the audience will have ever heard of Bianca, and they won't give a damn whether she talks or not, providing she looks pretty."

"I'll do my best," she volunteered, and added a quick warning, "But you may as well know I think I'm going to be stupefied with fear before an audience."

He dismissed this with a confident, "What is there to be afraid of?" and turned to hustle Kate into the room. She was loaded with the costumes and accouterments of both Bianca and Katherina.

"This is going to be fun," she told them gaily as she dumped the clothes on an old carriage shaft. "Poor Floss is locked in her room trying to tear the door down. Shall I dress and then get the neophyte into her costume, or what do you say?"

Dantine was already rummaging through laces and silks and stays, throwing his choices to Devon. "We will sew her into the costume and then rip her out of it for the change. While we are dressing her, she will be learning her lines. Bob! Where the devil is that fellow?"

Devon thought she might have had something to say about dressing in the presence of the whole Dantine Company, but she was uneasy over an explosion from the director. His good will might be needed before the evening was over. She and Kate together unfastened her gown and she stepped out of it while Kate unhooked her top three petticoats. The Renaissance costume required only one petticoat, and that to be without ruffles, for the costume would be—when she was sewed into it—a snug fit.

Bob arrived on the run, carrying the tattered pages of Bianca's script laced together with a corset string, and while Kate took in the side seams of the peach satin gown on its wearer, and Dantine laced it down her back, Bob cued her through her first two entrances. She had almost no dialogue in those scenes and it should have been simple, but her brain was a great empty funnel. Not a word of Bob's speeches made sense. Every time she was about to get her own action straight in her mind, Dantine pulled too tight on the stay laces or Kate screamed as she stuck the needle into her own thumb.

Just as it seemed that clarity must prevail at long last, the rest of the Company stumbled into the carriage house with ancient plaints about provincial tiring rooms, chilblains, bad liquor, and all ending on the theme that this was the most benighted village they had struck in the colonies.

It was only when Michael Dantine roared out, "A little silence, damn you!" that anyone remembered the delicate maneuver about to take place—the substitution of an inexperienced seamstress for the flamboyant, well-versed Floss Roy.

"Too tight?" asked Dantine, when Devon caught her breath sharply.

"No. No. It's all right." It wasn't all right and she had to breathe up and down instead of in and out, but she would never admit it to someone who had bragged that his fingers fitted around her waist. Kate, however, had no such vanity. She was biting off a thread and cried out, "Enough, enough!" between her teeth. "No tighter or I must take another pleat. There. Mighty handsome if I do say so. Turn around, sweet. What do you think, Dantine?"

Devon, observing herself with a hand mirror and a three-foot floor mirror propped against the rear wall, felt that there was some justification for Kate's praise. She really looked quite handsome and cut a far better figure than Floss ever had.

Dantine looked her over, nodded to Kate, and reached for the makeup, piece by piece. Under his long fingers Devon felt her face flush hot, and a pulse beat fast in her cheek. He larded her face for the paint to stick better, widened her lips with bright pomade, curved her eyebrows, exaggerating their natural high arch, gave her fascinating blue shadows on her eyelids and a hint of shadow under her lower lids. He completed his work with a heavy coat of yellow powder over her face and her throat and a dusting of powder over her shoulders and breasts, wherever her body was exposed by the deep cut of the gown. All through this exciting process members of the Company kept peering over at her to watch the transformation. She could not tell by their interested expressions whether they were overwhelmed by her vixenish good looks or astounded at Michael Dantine's art.

When she saw herself at last in the hand mirror, she could not believe the image was her own familiar face. An imperious coquette stared back at her rather cruelly, a face to rival Kate Merilee's, set off by the saucy tilt of the tall hennin that covered the crown of her head, leaving silk streamers to flutter behind her. It was as if Michael Dantine had taken a clean piece of foolscap and painted on it the face of a stunning beauty. It did not quite belong to her. It belonged to him. She smiled at her reflection, made a moue and winked at her director. He seemed a little startled, wiped his hands on the towel Bob handed him, and went off to help de Guiche into old Baptista's robes. He looked back once or twice though, as if unable to believe his eyes. Devon flirted with the men and found herself absorbing much of the attention ordinarily reserved for Kate. She was very happy and began to be a little proud of herself when she saw how Denis Varney and the others watched her.

He was in the midst of whispering a risqué story about de Guiche and a Venetian contessa into her ear when the prompt boy came in to shake off the snow and announce that the curtain was in ten minutes. Devon was startled into a renewal of her freezing stage fright.

What was Bianca's first action? Devon must enter with Kate and speak when spoken to. What did she say? Then what? Exit. Of course she could do it. It was childishly simple. She had only to follow directions. Only . . . what were her lines again?

When the Company began to file out of the carriage house and up the covered way, Devon felt her knees knocking beneath her skirts and doubted if she could actually go through with the performance. Even her stomach felt queasy. She hesitated in the open door and looked up at the fine snowfall out beyond the covered way. Her mother seemed so near, she fancied she could smell the faint perfume of her garments.

Michael Dantine was behind her. She had not noticed him and blamed him now for all her woes. "I'm going to have them hissing. I won't stand that. I won't!"

He closed his hands over her arms and held her back to him a moment, his voice pleading. The habit of command was lost for that fleeting time. "Sweetheart, don't disappoint me."

She said absently, to shake her mind off the terror of the waiting audience, "It is an odd night, luminous as if the moon were shining."

"It is always so on Christmas Eve."

As she turned her head a little to answer him, he kissed her hair below the hennin, where it was abundant and glossy. For that instant she was wildly happy, and amazed that this was so. She feared to move and tear out the chord which was taking root between them. There was not so much passion as warm tenderness in his caress, and she had an impulse to turn in his arms and kiss him passionately, more fiercely than any woman had ever kissed him, so that he would remember her a little longer than the others in his endless chain of females.

Then Kate called to her from the stage door. She freed herself with a deliberate, almost languid movement, and went rustling along ahead of him, up the covered way where the snow sifted gently down between worn and aged rafters. She was conscious of Dantine's eyes still upon her as the heady delight of his nearness wore off in the cold night. But in the ballroom, behind the green curtains, she began to wonder if he had used the caress merely as an earnest for her good behavior.

Beyond the thin curtain there was a rattle of chairs, a scraping of heavy benches over the smooth ballroom floor, and the drone of conversation—on the right, the high-pitched giggling voice of a girl, on the left, a jovial townsman. Somewhere very close to the curtain she could hear the nasal twang of an inland farmer's wife. Devon's ears seemed to catch acutely each individual voice of the seventy-six in the big room, and she felt that they must all be awaiting her, ready to sit in hostile judgement, perhaps to throw things if she missed cue.

"Kate, it's awful. Worse than I ever imagined. How do I look?"

"You look bewitching, my pet. All the lads are simply

perishing for you. I'll lay you ten guineas you could bed with any one of them tonight if you'd a mind to. I know. They told me so. It's only fear of Dantine holds them back."

"Thank you, no. I'm not like to survive the performance. Isn't it cold? Have you noticed? It seems to me that I'm freezing."

Before she was aware that anyone but Kate had heard, she felt a hand laid upon her forehead with all the solemn ritual as if Denis Varney were the King's Surgeon. "Devon, you have stage fright." He was grinning and looked very handsome in Petruchio's best Sunday hose and doublet. "This is absolutely nothing. Wait till the curtains part. You'll forget all your lines and feel like a country bumpkin out there in front of seventy-six heads, one hundred and fifty-two eyes. I've known girls, strong as oxen, to faint as they stepped on stage. But be calm. It happened to us all at one time." Devon snatched her fingers away indignantly, beginning to feel warmth generated through her anger.

"Hush, you fool," said Kate. "What are you trying to do, ruin the play?"

Before Devon could stop him, Denis captured her hand again and whispered, "Don't be frightened. You'll love it. . . . And they'll love you, and then we'll lose you to them forever."

"Quiet. Curtain!" cut in Michael Dantine's voice from somewhere behind them, and Devon, frozen again, stood stiffly beside Kate as the harpsichordist began a pretty little lament. The curtains parted, the footlight candles flickering in the sudden draft, and Bob Traver, as Bianca's suitor, Lucentio, passed quickly in front of Devon, to walk onstage.

Devon marveled for the first time at the ease with which the quiet, seemingly shy young actor worked before strange eyes. As Bob carried on his scene, quickly warming the audience to his troubles, she realized just what a task it was to open a scene, to grip the audience's attention and to hold it through the long introductory lines without any help from fellow players or pretty actresses. He might be a failure as Petruchio in Boston but he was the most useful actor in the Company—excepting possibly Gerard de Guiche who hobbled up behind Devon now as crotchety old Baptista.

Only seconds later came the cue for her entrance: Bob's voice announcing, "But stay awhile. What company is this?" and Kate was trying to keep her from rushing too fast into the scene. She dared not look outward across the candles, only ahead toward Bob.

From the audience she heard a strange sound like the summer sighing of aspen leaves. Were they laughing at her? Had they guessed her stupid inefficiency? Then she realized that the murmur was a tribute either to Kate Merilee's voluptuous beauty or her own looks in the peach gown, probably a little of both. When she had heard that sound previously, from the wings, it had been faint and far away. She had never before understood just how close an audience was to the players.

Suddenly, her stage name was spoken by de Guiche. "Bianca, get you in. And let it not displease thee, good Bianca. . . ." He continued his speech, but she paid him no heed and on the end of his lines hurried offstage like an obedient daughter, just missing the cumbersome harpsichord. It was only when she heard the dreadful little pause of astonishment which followed that she knew she had retired four sides too soon and neglected to give the one small speech assigned to her in that scene. She could have wept with rage; for now in the wings she recalled vividly every word in that four-line speech.

Bob Traver quickly picked up the scene with his line which followed Bianca's, and the scene went on its appointed way with only the wisest observers to guess that the Dantine Company worked tonight without its smooth perfection.

Kate came offstage soon after and stood with her arm around Devon's waist to watch the rest of the scene while Devon mumbled her second-act speeches under her breath. Presently, Bob came off, smiled at Devon, and went away to the tiring room. She was consoled by his smile as by Kate's presence but still shuddered to face Michael Dantine, the perfectionist. He was nowhere around and she had a creeping fear that he was waiting to pounce on her outside in the dark, covered way or down in the carriage house, and insult her before the Company for her failure. She remembered very well his furious bellowing, the pitiless cruelty of his sarcasm when another player faltered over a word. And to forget a whole speech, cut off two other actors and force a dead pause onstage—they were unforgivable crimes in his view.

Denis Varney was holding the scene now, a magnificent rogue, taking all attention as no other player had done so far. When the curtains closed over the scene, the enthusiasm in the applause was as great as for any play given in the colony. They could not guess that there was a nervous, fast-talking haste in the performance.

The second act came fast upon the first with only a momentary pause for a change of one backdrop and the shoving forward of a chair for Devon in her role. Devon had a vague recollection that her hands were to be bound for this scene and was just looking around for the prop man when Michael Dantine pushed his way among the waiting actors and ordered her to hold out her hands, wrists upward. As he bound them with blue silk ribbons, her eyes travelled stealthily up from his shirt to his grim mouth and still more slowly to his eyes. He was looking down at his work, frowning.

She said in a small voice, "I'm sorry. I'm terribly sorry. I told you it would be like this. I hate it out there." He pulled the ribbons tight and she winced. He began to loosen them. At one side, she heard de Guiche ask Kate in a whisper, "*Nom de Dieu*, she will carry it off, you think?"

Devon was panic-stricken for fear the director had heard this expressed lack of confidence. Then came Kate's throaty assurance. "If she doesn't, I will. Leave it to us, my lad. Devon and I are better than you think."

Dantine finished the loose knot in the ribbons and gave

her a little shove out onstage. She did not look back. Something in that shove was eloquent of his displeasure. When Kate took up her position standing over her, Devon murmured, "What does Dantine say? Is he very angry? He wouldn't talk to me."

"Devil a' doubt. Not that we care. You'll do nicely, my sweet. Sh! Here we are. Curtain."

The green curtains moved apart on their rollers with a little click-click-click that was the most nervewracking of all stage sounds. One of the hardest things in the theatre, Devon found that night, was to know just the propitious moment to begin a speech that opened a scene. Remembering Michael Dantine's constant drilling of "Tempo! Tempo!" "Keep it up . . . don't let it drop," and his tantrums every time there was an instant's lull, Devon began her speech before the curtains were completely opened. Her voice, which sounded quite attractive in her throat the second before it came hurrying out, was a whole octave above pitch, but she stumbled on, parroting line after line until Kate took up her cue. Devon looked out over the audience for the first time. How still and absorbed they were! Row after row of them clear to the standees in the dark rear of the ballroom, watched the stage with not a flicker of inattention. Along the window seats that lined the whitewashed walls, heads of late comers were craned a little forward in geometric precision the whole length of the room.

When Kate's voice paused, Devon made a reasonably good reply, though it was not quite Shakespeare in spite of the meter that her now rapidly running mind improvised. Her short scene ended with Kate's brisk pursuit of her into the wings. Devon had by this time gotten into the spirit of the part and could not stop herself quickly enough in the wings. She cracked her kneecap on the rear of the harpsichord—exactly as Floss Roy had predicted would happen. While she was still bent over with pain and anger at her clumsiness, the prop boy pulled on the tight satin sleeve of her gown.

"Master Dantine wants to dress ye for third act. Right now 'e says."

She rushed out the door and down the covered way in the thickly falling snow, groaning at the pain to her knee. By this time even the covered way offered no protection; for snow had blown through from the inn yard as well as down the cracks in the roof. The sloping white banks in odd corners sparkled with Christmas magic in the luminous night. Devon was suddenly struck by the memory of her last Christmas Eve in the dormer room of her father's house, when the Pelham girls who lived in town brought their plum cake and shared it with her, and they all exchanged Christmas stories. How different tonight was, with its nervous tension, its enmities: the bitter resentment of Floss Roy, now the disapproval of Michael Dantine.

She limped into the carriage house pressing her palm to her knee and grimacing. There were several of the Company hurrying around, changing for the third act and renewing makeup. It seemed to Devon's uneasy conscience that they were all waiting to see her scolded for her sins by the terrible director.

Dantine, however, was too busy for scoldings. He came over to her with a knife blade used for sharpening quills and told her to stand still while he ripped her out of her gown. He had meanwhile found another fifteenth-century costume which smelled of airless trunks and verbena sachet but which, miraculously, fitted her in almost every way. As she fingered the sheath skirt and the still unfaded folds of the overskirt, she wondered who in the long procession of Dantine Company women had last worn the lovely gown. It was too small for any of the present company. Some one of Dantine's forgotten mistresses, perhaps.

He inquired about her knee, which she felt was too high on her anatomy to discuss with him, and they had nothing more to say that did not have to do with the costume or her new headdress. This was a veil fastened by one corner to the center part in her hair that floated in a blue mist behind her. In the mirror which he held up, she saw and felt anew the miracle of the master's creation called Mistress Devon Howard, the actress. Over the mirror Dantine smiled down at her.

She was so relieved that she flashed him the most enchanting look she was capable of and took this chance of apologizing again. "I shall do better now, Sir. You are kind not to remind me of my past sins."

He said nothing, but the manner in which he said nothing made her wonder suddenly what it would be like to be kissed again by him.

Denis called out a witty, flattering compliment as he passed. She did not notice him. She was wondering if anyone had ever had such great dark eyes as the Master-Player.

Chapter
Thirteen

THAT NIGHT in her bed beside Kate, thinking over the evening's performance, she realized it was in her third-act scene with Bob Traver that she had first felt herself an actress. With Bob's smooth and always dependable aid, Devon managed a bit of amateurish but not unacceptable comedy which produced some laughs that heartened her, and she even got most of her lines right. After that, she began to be a little more composed, sure enough of herself to risk a bit of coquetry with the men who came to see the players after the last curtain. She found herself quickly back in the stride of her Concord girlhood, laughing off the silly compliments of male strangers who offered to unhook her from her form-fitting costume. She got rid of them and retired behind a screen, only to find Denis Varney impudently waiting to unhook her.

On Christmas morning, aside from a bruise on her left knee, there seemed to be no bad repercussions from her performance. She was aware when she awoke that there was a subtle change in her position with the Troupe. Although she scrubbed her face thoroughly there were still vestiges of last night's stage makeup, and she found that it gave her quite a bit of last night's stage aura. At breakfast, a country feast that made the food shortages of Boston seem far away, her voice was deferred to as if she were Kate or the still sulking Floss. When she ventured an opinion that the snowfall would shortly let up, several people spoke in agreement. Yesterday only Bob Traver would have been polite enough to answer.

After bolting down his pork steak and eggs, Denis Varney decided to stroll out in the town and pelt the tricorne hats of all the gentry going to church. No one except Devon was enthusiastic enough to accept his invitation to join him; she remembered all the snowy Christmases, rambling around Concord and the Middlesex countryside in past years, where she had won innumerable snow fights. Although her co-ordination was so bad she was never known to hit where she aimed, she was highly proficient at hitting where she did not aim.

Denis dashed up to get his new greatcoat, while Devon ate at her leisure and enjoyed her sudden importance.

Michael Dantine came in from a long walk in the snow, just as his brother passed him with a flip greeting on the way out of doors. Devon noticed this morning particularly how the director's big, imposing figure dominated the room and all of its occupants. He was in his usual morning mood, a very bad one, and his authority over the little world about him inspired the waiter to a frenzy of service. Devon smiled in secret while she shared the general excitement in all of his movements. Did he know how theatrical he was? Had he perhaps practiced these gestures many times alone before a mirror? It seemed unlikely. His vanity was on a different plane from that of his brother, and his theatricalism was perfectly natural to him.

The Master took his place at the head of the table and

asked someone in a harsh voice to pass the pork. Floss did so without speaking. She was waiting to be coaxed into forgiveness for their treatment of her Christmas Eve. He ignored her in a way that was all too noticeable to the players. Floss still looked battered and had a large red swelling on her cheek.

After a silence during which the Company waited in vain for some words of wisdom from the director, everyone rushed to cover the lull with animated conversation. Devon would like to have included Michael Dantine in her remarks but was still too much in awe of him to make any overtures. It was for this reason that she was the more startled when he addressed her pointedly over the noise of the table talk.

"By the by, Devon, I have been complimented twice this morning upon the beauty of last night's Bianca. It looks as though we may have another actress in the company. How would you like that?"

She did not know what to say in the presence of a dozen people who turned at once and looked at her, including one pair of especially hostile hazel eyes. She avoided looking at Floss Roy when she replied frankly, "If I could begin a scene in the middle of the role, I shouldn't mind. As it as, I think the theatre will be the better for my absence."

"Fiddle-faddle," said Kate. "Don't be modest."

"You don't understand. The first minutes on stage are too horrible to repeat every night as you actors must. In any other connection with the theatre I am yours to command."

While everyone in the Company looked a little shocked at her rebuff of his suggestion, Dantine gazed down the table at her and smiled. The Company relaxed immediately.

Devon seized the moment before she lost her nerve to say to him a little too loudly and rather too brightly, "Why don't you join us this morning? I am going to accompany Denis while he conducts the greatest battle since the Plains of Abraham with his snowballs against the top hats of the townsmen."

He seemed to be amused behind the hard mask of his face. "If Gerard and I joined this titanic battle of yours, there would be no play ready for the New Year's show."

"Small loss," Kate put in airily.

The window behind de Guiche's chair was suddenly jarred by a heavy ball of snow which spattered over the windowpane as it struck. Denis stood outside in the sloping field, sunk to the tops of his boots in soft snow and waving frantically at the faces in the window.

Michael Dantine was the only one who had not moved. He said impatiently, "For God's sake, someone go and humor the beggar and keep him out of my sight!"

Devon sprang up hastily to get her cloak and join Denis. It would take more than a casual caress to humanize the director, and she was cross and disappointed in him.

At the outer door of the inn a blast of slush struck her hair and half her cheek. By the time she had shaken off the mess, she was furious and in a spirit of revenge gathered up a handful of snow and ice and started in pursuit of the tawny-haired culprit. She called to him in the most seductive voice she could muster in the cold air, and as he turned, surprised, she threw two snowballs, one after another, missing him altogether the first time, but striking him square in the face with her second ice-crusted snowball. Laughing at his stunned surprise, she scrambled around in the trampled snow and began to run, counting on his vanity to keep him occupied with brushing himself off. But he was agile as a cat. He seized the flying folds of her cloak, winding her in it so that every struggle pinned her more securely. She was still mocking him when her face was within inches of his own: "Confess it. You were beaten."

He took her head between his gloved hands and kissed her suddenly on the mouth. She tasted ice upon his lips and her only reaction was amusement mingled with a kind of vengeful triumph. When he drew his hands away from her cheeks, she broke into open laughter. She was recalling all the little snubs he had given her throughout the past three weeks. "The irresistible Varney!" she taunted him.

After his first amazed shock, he began to grin and then, in a moment, to laugh. "Well, you've a damned plenty to learn about kisses, anyway. If you're a good girl, Devon, I'll kiss you properly some time. You'll not laugh then, I warrant you."

As he unwound her from the cloak, she caught a glimpse of the dining parlour window of the inn. Michael Dantine stood there alone, looking out at her and at his brother. And suddenly, she was not laughing. She said to Denis, "Let's go somewhere. Shall we walk past the church? We needn't go in if you had rather not."

He brushed himself off, twisted his long hair back into its confining brown ribbon and stepped lightly over the churned snow with her. As they passed the inn, she looked up. The window was deserted.

They walked over to the little green-steepled church across the Common and entered during the hymns. It surprised her that he could so easily pick up the hymn when she, who had sung it many times, was still unsure of the words. He had a fine voice and several of the congregation looked around to see what that excellent tenor looked like.

The sermon was a lengthy oration against the tyranny of the Crown, recited by an absent-minded old gentleman who did not quite know what he was talking about and who kept getting his notes hind-side before. Devon wondered what rebel parishioner had written the sermon for him, and then her attention wandered to the white walls where each window was garlanded with greenery from the not-too-distant woods. Around the altar were piles of fir boughs and pine cones brought in from the pathless forests of the frontier. The whole church had the heavy, spiced scent of the woods.

Suddenly, Denis reached in under the flap of his coat pocket and brought out a blunt bit of charcoal, not an inch long, and a little square of paper which he unfolded and spread against the back of the pew in front of him. He began to sketch, making thick rough lines that did not look like anything but a jumble of idiot impressions. She followed his eyes to see what the subject was. On a side bench down close to the pulpit sat a small boy, his mittened hands crossing each other and shoved into the wide sleeves of his coat for warmth. She could just see his profile, the high, slightly curving forehead, the button nose, the full mouth which was screwed into an odd, soundless whistle. He had the look of someone listening to sounds far away.

When she saw Denis Varney's sketch again, she was astonished. He had made the small boy clearly visible by a few lines; his button nose, his pursed-up mouth, the curl that stuck straight out of his knitted cap over his forehead, and something else had been sketched in, the object of the boy's searching gaze. In the upper corner of the paper was another childish face looking down at him, and around the face was a faint nimbus, a few charcoal lines that made of it the Boy Jesus. As she studied the sketch, she realized that the two faces were the same, the Boy Jesus and the small boy with the button nose. It was so lovely she could not believe that cynical Denis Varney had drawn it.

She raised her eyes from the sketch to his face. He was absorbed in drawing a jumble of fir boughs and pine cones, and his quiet features framed by his fair hair reminded her of some long-forgotten hero of her childhood. Young David, perhaps. Or the Angel Gabriel. He looked very young, sitting on the hard, church bench, very young with an indefinable purity of expression. He was a boy lost in a maze of cynicism and she felt torn by an earnest longing to protect and defend the strange and beautiful side of him that she had never glimpsed before.

She had not heard much of the sermon or of the closing service, and when she and Denis left the church with the congregation, she was still thinking of Denis and his sketch. On the way back to the inn she mentioned it to him.

He grinned at her and she saw his eyebrows go upward in derision. "They call me St. Denis. Didn't you know?"

"No. Don't joke. I mean it. Give it to me. I promise you I will take care of it."

But he did not take the sketch from his pocket again. When she looked disappointed and a little affronted, he said coolly, "I never give away anything of myself. I am not like my whining brother who gets his women by sniveling of his sad past. My past has been a good one, a merry one. I like it. But I share it with no one. I am being honest with you, you see. Count it to my credit. One day I may need it."

The Angel Gabriel of the church bench had vanished in the rising winter wind. She shook her head over him, but his bad manners no longer disturbed her. Although she was considerably younger, she felt old enough to have been his mother. He talked such nonsense. One never knew when to take him seriously.

On the way back to the inn they passed Floss Roy scuffing dejectedly along, and Denis made his peace with her by the friendly observation, "Damned neat bonnet there, Floss. How the devil do you keep it on in this wind?" Just as Floss was preening herself under the praise, he stuck in his little dagger. "Too bad your face is swollen. Have you tried ice? They hauled in a wagonload this morning from the river. I wonder how long you'll be out of the Company."

Devon, hiding the gesture by the fullness of her skirts, kicked him on the shinbone just above his shoe top and talked very fast to Floss, trying to mollify her once more. Belatedly, Denis drew attention back to himself by leaning against a stone border and nursing his leg.

When Devon inquired sweetly into his state of health, he groaned a little. "Nothing. It is not worth mentioning. I had a sudden spasm across the bone here."

Chapter

Fourteen

KATE'S VAGARIES amused Devon. During Christmas dinner, she noticed Kate's efforts to spin her web of enchantment over Bob Traver and wondered at his quiet, tactful resistance. Kate was evidently ready for another romp with the man for whom she frequently showed such contempt, and was intrigued by his refusal to come when she whistled. She offered him a tender, browned turkey wing, a slice of roast goose, a refilling of his wine glass, but he politely refused all these temptations. Occasionally, when Kate was talking with great animation to de Guiche, Devon caught Bob studying her, and in his unguarded eyes was an anguish that would have startled Kate Merilee.

Once, Devon's glance crossed Michael Dantine's and she flushed at having been caught prying into Bob Traver's life. Dantine looked away after a long, and to Devon, embarrassing pause, and she finished her now-cold slice of turkey without glancing at anyone again.

Devon was very happy during those days around the New

Year. Despite her pronouncement of "no more plays," she found herself on the stage twice in the week after Christmas, playing a demure and shaky Phebe in *"As You Like It"* and achieving something of a minor triumph New Year's Eve as the saucy maid Maria in *"Twelfth Night."* She did Maria with a cockney accent which Denis taught her. It was not until the last act that she was aware of any offense. Somehow, by following Denis's instructions, she had made a credible burlesque of Floss Roy's normal voice. When Floss stamped offstage glaring at her, she pretended uneasily not to understand, but it was simple to see Denis Varney's sleepless little brain in back of the insult.

New Year's morning Kate brought her the Worcester *Gazette,* a local folded sheet devoted chiefly to Whiggish politics and diverse news of the southern Massachusetts counties. On the back page, squeezed between an ad for a restorative to manhood and a column of crop advice, was a three-inch review of the New Year's Eve play. Devon had been sewing the last ruffles on a new petticoat which was her New Year's present to Kate, and she hurriedly stuffed the white cambric behind her as Kate swished across the room.

"Wait till you see, my sweet. You won't believe it!" She thrust the little newspaper into Devon's hands, and stood smug and satisfied while the seamstress skimmed over the lines. The writer congratulated Worcester for its good judgment in packing the Meetinghouse where the great Michael Dantine had presented "that interesting and uplifting dialogue *Twelfth Night* by the English moralist, Shakespeare."

"No, no. Further along," Kate interrupted impatiently.

Denis Varney's Malvolio was highly praised, along with a compliment for Bob Traver as the young Duke. But none of the women was mentioned except Devon, and she was not referred to by name.

"Perhaps the most promising luminary of this celebrated troupe is the actress who played Maria. Here is a vivacious little beauty whose mature voice and innate sweetness will carry her far in the European theatre when combined with a trifle more experience."

Devon looked up at Kate who was swaying her skirts excitedly in her hands. "What does he mean—more experience? I rehearsed and rehearsed that. I couldn't have had more experience."

Kate stared surprised, with her mouth open.

Then Devon laughed and said, "It's the most ridiculous thing I ever read, of course. Everyone knows you were the best. But would you mind if I kept it?"

Kate brightened at this and said that the Company principals all had a copy, though Floss had stuffed hers into her chamber pot. Kate tried to peek at the pile of white cambric behind Devon and was pushed away indignantly.

"No spying. We are not having a London Christmas but a Colonial New Year and you'll see it tonight and not before."

A little later, when Bob Traver came in to congratulate Devon on the article, he stayed to compare notes on their New Year's presents. She realized after a few moments that he had actually come to get her advice on something and now hesitated. She set about to woo his trust. During the past weeks, and especially after the *Gazette's* praise half an hour ago, she began to develop more fully all her girlhood tricks of charm that brought gratifying results. She smiled very often, teased prettily, looked sweetly wicked and pretended to find all men fascinating, dangerous rogues. Denis and de Guiche loved this. Bob was the same kind Bob as ever. Only with Michael Dantine had this saucy, impudent Devon failed. Since Christmas Day he had not smiled at her. She was amused at his childishness and kept on flirting with him as with the other males of the Troupe. But in Michael Dantine's case, she had a notion that she was playing with gunpowder.

Bob intently studied the petticoat she was finishing for

Kate's present, while Devon smiled at his absorption. "Do you think Kate will like it?" she asked, holding it against her waist and laughing at his embarrassment. "Don't be so modest, Bob. One would think you didn't know women wore petticoats."

He recovered gallantly. "She will like it especially because it comes from you."

She said, "Thank you, Bob dear" without being at first aware of the endearment.

He looked pleased, the color suddenly high in his cheeks. He reached into his breeches pocket and took out a small ring case which he placed in her hand. "I thought perhaps, since we are friends, that you would advise me about this."

She stared at the ring with its lacy gold band and the graceful arrangement of pearls in the figure "K." He explained in a low voice, "A betrothal ring. What do you think of my chances?"

She did not know what to say, feeling herself a traitor to her dearest friend, but she did not want Bob to be rebuffed. "Then you are confident she will accept you?"

"She has been so attentive this week, so . . ." He exchanged glances with her and then looked at the ring for a long time. When he raised his head she was startled at his short, sharp laugh. The other Bob Traver was looking at her, the man she had barely seen once or twice, a harsh, bitter person so unlike himself she was startled and uneasy at the change.

"Good God! Am I confident? Who can be confident of that harlot?" Suddenly, he grabbed the case from her, shoved it into his pocket again and hurried out of the room. She was struck with amazement at this act from calm and gentle Bob, and jumped up so quickly to run after him that she strewed her sewing across the floor.

In the open doorway she stopped and considered what purpose it would serve to encourage him in his dream. Marrying Kate would be like chaining the wind. Could she tell him that? Better let him go. But she was puzzled by him. For one fantastic moment, he had shown her a man capable of any excess behind those calm, brown eyes.

Hours later in Michael Dantine's study she arranged her carefully wrapped presents on the closed top of the spinet before the eyes of the entire company. It was impossible to resist peeking at the other mysterious boxes, especially one bulky little packet which had her own name scrawled across the wrapper. As she reached over to squeeze it, Denis cried out noisily, "Forfeit! Forfeit! You touched that package."

"I didn't. I only . . ."

Denis reached over and pulled her to him by the sleeve of her velveteen gown. She fell onto his lap and struggled to get up while the Company laughed at her discomfiture. She could feel Varney's fingers prowling over her breasts as if to pinch her and struggled to free herself. It was all very well for him to flirt with her but that he should appear to be so familiar with her body in the presence of Michael Dantine was the outside of enough. After an emphatic slap across his face, Denis let her go, though his good humor was in no way impaired.

Dantine passed out the gifts. While the players restricted their presents to themselves, he had not forgotten a single member of the family troupe. Every carpenter, ticket-taker, prompt boy and actor received something from the director. Sitting on the arm of Kate's big milord chair, Devon was very excited, as if she had drunk too much wine. The smallest present from Kate Merilee or Denis came with a smile and a good-natured joke. She felt a little annoyed with the director. He who was such a great director somewhat overplayed the romantic villain. A small gift and a smile were infinitely more acceptable than a fine gift and a sour look.

The first present Dantine handed her was from Kate, and proved to be a bedgown of the most shocking cut, made of costly pink camlet with almost nothing above the waist, a fashion that was all the rage since its introduction from the new French court. Devon was stunned by its magnificence and its nakedness while everyone insisted that she try it on and let them judge it a perfect fit. Kate explained that she had ordered it made according to guesswork and had even hemmed the sleeves and twelve yards of skirt herself. This from indolent Kate aroused many disbelieving "Ohs" and "Ah-ahs" from the Company, and Devon could not help hugging her. Warmhearted Kate returned the hug with a kiss.

Everyone was demonstrative and it was a noisy room for a little while. Devon soon became too busy opening presents to care what anyone else received. Bob Traver had given her a leather-bound journal with gold leaves and with her first name written in gold upon the cover. It was a beautiful thing. She skimmed through the glossy pages wondering what would be written on this page in the middle of the book or that one toward the end. It would take years to fill it up. What would she be doing on New Year's Day next year? 1776 seemed a long way off, but it would be something good, surely. Her luck was rising.

On the frontispiece was written in Bob's neat, readable hand, "To Devon, with the deepest regard of her obedient servant, B. Traver. Written at Worcester, in Massachusetts Colony, One January, Seventeen Hundred and Seventy-five." She smiled at the formality.

Kate was exclaiming over an exquisite little medallion watch from Bob and then Devon glanced over at the giver. He replied to her unspoken query with a faint shake of the head. So he was not going to give Kate the ring! She did not know whether to be glad for his sake or sorry for Kate, and felt as if she had betrayed her two best friends in somehow discouraging him.

The odd packet Devon had wanted to squeeze turned out to be from Michael Dantine and was a dainty pair of black kid slippers which laced over her ankles in the manner of the shoes she wore. She turned them over quickly, hoping to see high heels. But they were flat sandals to make her as short as ever. Evidently he had these made in strictest imitation of hers, which she now wore padded with paper over the hole in the sole. The old shoes had been chosen by her father who believed in beauty only when it was utilitarian. When she took out Dantine's card from the toe of the right slipper, it gave her a cool shock. Across his own imprinted name he had scrawled two words: *Kind Wishes.* The heelless shoes did not matter now—they merely bore out the indifference of those two words. How foolish she had been to think he had ever borne any but the most professional interest in her!

She received other presents; a bottle of very nice scent from Floss—by one of those quirks of fate, the same as Devon had bought for her. Floss's note said, *A Happy New Year to a good seamstress.* Devon hoped there was nothing personal in the emphasis on her former position. De Guiche gave her a little ivory brooch which aroused everyone's envy. There was a verbena sachet from the prompt boy whose name puzzled her for a moment. She thought him very sweet to favor her, and told him so. He turned scarlet and shuffled his feet as usual.

The last present must surely be from Denis, and she opened it with quick fingers. It was a man's handkerchief, lovingly stitched by some mother or other loved one, but in its folds was a soiled piece of paper with Devon's name on it. The handkerchief came from the old carpenter she had often seen hammering around on sets and carelessly talked to while she waited in the wings for the players. She took his hands and thanked him with considerably more pleasure than she had offered the director; for the gift from the old carpenter must mean a great deal more. She was deeply touched by the sentimental tears in his eyes at her thanks.

She looked over her gifts, feeling rich, yet missing one. Denis Varney. She had given him a handmade claret satin cravat similar, except in color, to the black one she had made for Dantine and the blue and green ones for Bob and de Guiche. Without wanting to, she looked at Denis. He was sprawled in his chair, resting on the middle of his spine, with his stockinged legs thrown over the arm. Propped on his knees and held in place by one hand was a brandy goblet, whose convex side was the drawing board for a little sketch made with his tiny segment of charcoal stick. After a moment or two, he glanced over at her but made no motion that he had seen her. She wondered what subject was engrossing him.

Michael Dantine was fingering his black satin cravat with slow, stroking motions. Devon wished she had not been so informal on the little square of thick blue notepaper that had gone to him with the present; for she had said "To Dantine, with the admiration and affection of Devon Howard." Affection, indeed! And in return he politely sent his kind wishes. She wondered what he had done with her square of notepaper. Had he tossed it on the floor with all the other assorted cards and papers that came with his presents? Men had no sentiment.

She and Kate were busy measuring Kate's new petticoat when Denis unwound himself from his chair, finished his brandy, and sauntered toward them.

"A trifling gift in honor of the New Year." He bowed and presented Devon with the sketch he had just made. It was a profile of herself, with her own familiar features, none of them flattered, and yet the whole had a kind of wanton appeal that she was sure could be found only in Denis Varney's imagination. Where had he got that twist to her mouth, that full, upward curve of her lip, and the derisive arch of the eyebrow? Even the cheek had a shadow that added to the general wanton effect. She was swept by a sudden wave of uneasiness. She could not be what Denis Varney thought her. What made him do these things?

Everyone crowded around to see the sketch and no two of the company saw it in the same light. The nose was wrong, the untidy tendril of dark hair over her broad temple wasn't quite correct, the lips were certainly not Devon's. But they all agreed that it was a very good likeness.

Floss Roy said, seeing Devon frown, "It isn't like you was handsome, old girl. It does favor you quite remarkable."

Devon had to agree to this, though it still seemed to her that Denis had sketched all the worst facets of her personality. No one else in her life had ever found her a wanton. She was both repulsed and fascinated with the idea, with the traits she must possess that he could think of her like that. Before the evening was over she had forgiven him for the drawing and was beginning to treasure it, to see that perhaps she was like it, underneath. Only he, of all who knew her, was clever enough to see it. Could he help it if he drew what he saw? And it was such a personal gift, too. In the corner was written in a spidery, flourishing hand: "To the Enchanting Miss D. from the enchanted D."

By the time Devon went to her small back bedchamber she was loaded with presents and a lighted candle and yawning after her last glass of hot negus. She was in the midst of a wide yawn when she collided in the midpassage with Michael Dantine who was deep in rum and dour thoughts. She begged his pardon. He grunted and picked up her packages, presenting them to her all helter-skelter, not answering when she remarked how fortunate that Floss Roy's vial of rose scent was not spilled on Denis's sketch. While he was busy restoring her property she noticed a familiar, neatly folded blue sheet of her own notepaper in his waistcoat pocket and studied it in surprise.

With the rescue of the last package, he remarked ironically, "You have quite an assortment of tokens from your various lovers, haven't you?"

She transferred the candlestick to the forefinger of her right hand and slapped him across the face. For a moment she thought she saw a pinpoint of light in the dark pupils of his eyes. She backed away a step or two, half afraid he would strike her in return.

He saw her movement and stood aside, with the frigid reminder, "You were never quite so forceful when you slapped my brother." He bowed stiffly and went on down the hall.

She turned into her bedchamber puzzling over his contradictory behavior. In spite of his bad manners lately, and his cool holiday greeting, he carried her own New Year's message in his waistcoat pocket like a sentimental schoolboy. Then she smiled as Denis Varney's sketch rolled open on the bed—very roguish, very sly, with mouth half virgin—half wanton in his peculiar conception of her.

Chapter
Fifteen

MICHAEL DANTINE was gone before
dawn the next day, to search the countryside for new book-
ings and to arrange advance handbills. The performance of
All For Love that night was flat and uninspired, the audience
meager; Kate and Floss quarreled over a silver cloth tunic
and tore it in two; Devon somehow caught a chill and had a
red nose and a cough and was cross with everyone.

The performances in the next month were not much better. As they neared Boston again the political unrest had
eccentric effects upon the cash box. One night a hall would
be packed to the rafters with noisy, drunken partisans who
saw in the play a thousand shades of political meaning. The
next night would bring hardly a score of paid admissions. On
three occasions there were more men upon the stage than below the candles. Twice the play was abandoned and no shares
paid because de Guiche and Floss were attending a rally for
patriots united against the Boston Port Blockade. The Frenchman and the Cockney girl were as violent in their politics as

they were in their unreason. To Devon and Kate, it was much ado about nothing. Bob Traver and Denis seldom opened their mouths about the recent actions of Lord North and the Tory party, although Bob often came in at strange hours and met strange people who proved to be Sons of Liberty or Members of the treasonable Committee of Correspondence. Just as Devon decided he was a clever patriot masquerading as a rather stupid young actor, he would turn into the stupid actor again, before her eyes, and she did not know what to think.

At Floss Roy's insistence, Devon accompanied her and de Guiche to a meeting of the Middlesex County patriots who were organizing what seemed to her rather dangerous Committees of Correspondence. All these organizations fell into a mold of threatened violence—hints of night raids and tar-and-feathering parties. Floss assured her that this was unusual, that such talk was merely oratory. Devon did not like it.

There was considerable heat on the part of Denis and the stage workers about the light cash box at the recent performances. Denis summed up the general dissatisfaction one night after the profits had been split, when he announced that if this was the glorious New Year, he was damned if he wouldn't rather wear out the old one all over again.

Devon wondered sometimes what Michael Dantine could be doing. Did he spend all his time arranging play dates, and if not, how did he spend his nights? When she asked Denis, he laughed. Bob Traver said casually that he supposed Dantine had some amusements—perhaps he read the new plays or talked at the taverns with other travelling men over a mug of rum.

But Kate looked at her oddly. "Dantine?" she said. "He has his women, of course . . . No particular women. Just someone to entertain him tonight, and another tomorrow night, as he chooses. Why not? Michael Dantine has no ties. He's free to do as he likes, isn't he?"

Devon, looking independent, was forced to agree that

Michael Dantine did indeed have no ties. She wondered what Kate would have said if he still loved her. Would she take the matter of his women so calmly then?

Devon was not on the stage again as long as de Guiche controlled the company and Floss Roy controlled de Guiche. Never having conquered her old "entrance" stage fright, Devon was—or should have been—grateful to them both, but sometimes, perversely enough, she imagined that she might have given a different reading to the lines, or that they could have made a happier choice than the young village girls they broke in to play minor roles. They had three new girls in two weeks. One was dragged home by her irate father, one eloped with a prop man, and the third was as bad as Devon had been in her first stage appearance. Devon dressed them and mended for them and went about her way, noticing with resentment that when she was just Devon Howard, seamstress, few of the public wasted a second glance on her. Or if they did, they were promptly called away by the actresses, by their loud cries for help in getting into and out of their costumes, a dressing privilege usually reserved for the eligible young males who swarmed backstage between scenes. Though flirting amused Devon, she could not bring herself to allow strange men to dress her.

Sometimes Denis paid her attentions. More often than not, he was carrying on silly, obvious little amours with the new actresses, and the smiles he tossed her way were but a sop to assure that he kept his popularity with her. She despised him for that, but no one could make her laugh as he did. No one could amuse and lighten the moments as he did when he chose.

"What you need is a red-blooded lover," Kate said one night before their performance on the outskirts of Cambridge.

"Oh, hush," said Devon sharply. She said everything sharply these days. After having known Dantine and having had a taste of fame as well, it was hard to let them both slip away again. She had been in an amusing tête-à-tête ten minutes ago, only to have Floss call the gentleman away to fasten up her corset.

In a barn on the road to Menotomy they were doing *Hamlet* on de Guiche's assumption that the authorities of Harvard College would approve its classic flavor. It was also de Guiche's idea to double as King Claudius and his ghostly brother, and his skill in characterization was not quite up to it.

Floss was fatally miscast as Ophelia, and talented Denis Varney proved worst of all in the title role. Among the entire cast of de Guiche's production, the only genuinely moving performances were those of Kate, a surprisingly good Queen Gertrude, and Bob as staunch young Laertes.

During Denis Varney's first soliloquy, there was a disconcerting echo from the back of the crowded barn, and after the first act curtain he spoke about it as Devon hooked up his tunic. "God knows Hamlet isn't my role. It's an idiot character any way you play it, but what the devil was going on in the back among the standees? I swear, all my lines had an echo or someone was mocking me. Did anyone else notice?"

"Probably the structure of this damned cow barn," Kate suggested, putting her head over the blanket partition, continuing to make her change as she spoke, and de Guiche agreed with this theory. Devon was not so confident. It seemed to her that mischief was brewing among the standing college students, and with misgivings she watched Denis, recklessly sure of himself, go to the wings for his next scene.

There was a low drone of comment on the second act. The tragic, virginal Ophelia achieved a number of laughter-provoking whistles. It was not until the final soliloquy of the act, however, that the damage was done. Denis, looking romantically evil and clearly not the melancholy prince, began his lines: *O, what a rogue and peasant slave am I!*

To the horror of Devon who stood listening in the wings, an intelligent but alcoholic response came from the rear of the standee section, among the Harvard students gathered there.

"Oh, Hamlet, speak no more."

The entire audience burst into roars of delight and for a few minutes Denis could not go on. He made no sign that he was thrown off his stride and during the first lull, resumed. On the lines: *Am I a coward? Who calls me villain?* the crowd went wild again at the response of another student voice in the darkness: "Then yield thee, coward, and live to be the show and gaze o' the time."

Denis stood up and slowly circled the stage. Devon could see his clenched fingers and his tense, set expression of disdain. He began to speak again quickly, almost incoherently. He had lost all sense of timing. . . . *O, vengeance! Why, what an ass am I?*

And from the back of the crowd: "My ears have not yet drunk a hundred words of thy tongue's uttering, yet I know the ass's sound."

With a cry of choked fury, Denis rushed off the stage, shoved his arm full force against Devon who stood in his way in the wings, and slammed the outer door so hard behind him it shook the building. The green curtains came quickly together. The Dantine Company was through for the night. Devon and the ticket taker refunded the night's proceeds while Bob Traver talked with dozens of still hilarious students, agreeing that the episode was the damndest joke in years, that tonight's Hamlet was a scene chewer, and that Harvard's students had proved their superiority in Shakespearean repartee.

As soon as she could escape, Devon ran around to the outside kitchen which was tonight's tiring room, to find out what had happened to the victim. She could not remember having seen Denis Varney really humiliated before. He had been angry when Floss leaped onto him with sharp claws but nothing to equal the white rage on his face as he passed Devon in the wings tonight.

There was great excitement in the smoke-blackened kitchen where Denis was enacting a performance far superior to his showing on the stage this evening. His long, black hose were in ribbons on the greasy floor, hacked up by a large carving knife he had snatched from the mantel over the fireplace. Overturned on the floor was a knife box, one of whose dull-edged dinner knives had evidently been used without results upon the flimsy material. By the time Devon saw him he had changed to his own street clothes but was still slashing away at the limp black velvet of his tunic with the carving knife while the other players eyed him, fascinated. Kate was pulling her dress over her head and making muffled comments; Floss was nervously watching from her corner and de Guiche expostulating to deaf ears, but nothing fazed Denis Varney. He was trembling in a kind of nervous seizure, his face ashen.

He's gone mad, Devon thought with concern, *and why was nobody helping him?* After an instant's pause in the doorway, she walked to the center of the floor—he had it pretty well to himself—and said more coolly than she felt, "Is there something I can do?"

He looked from the tattered tunic to her face, the heavy knife blade turning, its point just denting the breast of her gown. She could feel the sharp steel tip through the lace of her bodice.

"What do you mean by that?" The tawny iris of his eyes had dissolved into the black pupils. For that instant he looked like his brother in a killing rage.

She pretended to be surprised. "I mean, may I take care of your costume?"

There was a period of breathless silence. No one in the big, smoke-stained kitchen moved or spoke while Denis Varney's reaction was in doubt. He looked down at the glistening blade in a puzzled way, as if he had not seen it before, and then he looked at her.

She smiled, hoping that her face revealed more confidence than there was in her heart, and strove very hard to keep an easy, bantering note in her voice. "I daresay you have an engagement tonight. You don't want to be late, do you?"

He went on staring at her, his eyes almost imperceptibly reverting to their normal focus while she gently took the knife from his fingers and stooped to pick up Hamlet's hopelessly ruined black hose. She was rising with the carving knife in one hand and the hose in the other when the outer door opened, sending a cold draft and a bar of moonlight across the corner of the room, and she looked up, expecting to see Bob Traver.

Michael Dantine stood in the doorway, stamping the mud of the road off his boots while he surveyed the scene before him.

With one impetus, the company recovered its wits and everyone rushed noisily around to make a pretense that the evening's excitement was the normal state of things. De Guiche came over to the director and greeted him, but his fingers shook as he nervously rearranged his neckcloth. Devon, watching as she laid the knife and hose on the carving table, felt that the night's debacle was the Frenchman's doing and judged by de Guiche's uneasy behavior that he feared discovery.

While Devon hid the torn hose behind her back, Michael Dantine advanced to the center of the room, acknowledging the many greetings by the careless wave of a gloved hand. His manner was indifferent, even contemptuous. He began to pull off his riding gloves while Denis was getting himself together and brushing ravlins off his breeches. He had dropped the tunic on the instant of his brother's appearance.

"Well, sirrah, haven't you a tongue to greet me?" the director inquired directly of his brother.

Devon resented him bitterly. Did he know what Denis Varney had been through? Surely, he must have heard of it. How could he treat the agitated actor like that, just after she had spent so much nerve-wracking effort calming him?

Denis turned on him, striving hard to be his old, arrogant

self. "Good God! I forgot to salute! It's the Commander in Chief." He began combing his hair, keeping a wary eye for treachery.

But Dantine was done with these courteous little insults. They were too constraining. His weapon was the mace. "You should *kneel*—to the Cambridge public. By God, that you should! In my entire life I never saw such a monstrously foul performance. All the slime of Newgate never stank like that Hamlet of yours."

Devon noticed that Denis's fingers tightened around his comb, but he was now able to smile, more emboldened as he answered. "At our next little mud hole I shall out-act you every foot of the way . . . once we are clear of these Harvard toffs. Perhaps then too, your lordship will see fit to step onto the stage. As I recall, you haven't done anything very stirring yourself in eight weeks. What is the matter? Are you fearful of the competition?"

Michael Dantine smiled grimly. "That's as may be. To-morrow night we do *Beaux' Stratagem* . . . you and I, and the others, and we play it here before these Harvard toffs."

Denis swung around to face him. There was panic in his voice. "I'll not play before them again. That I swear!"

"You'll play before them tomorrow night. *That I swear!*"

There was a death watch between them. Over Denis Varney's face came a slow understanding. All his panic was gone; in the iris of his eyes the pupils were tawny and dangerous as a yellow panther's. His voice was low, hardly over a whisper. "But of course! *You* did it. You put them up to those tricks tonight. I might have guessed. It wasn't my performance. I wasn't a failure. It was you out there in the back of the theatre—you and your little hirelings."

Michael only half heard him, as one hears a troublesome child. "What madness will seize you next? Gerard, find me the scene plans. We will go over them tonight in your chamber. I want to adapt them to that miserable barn."

As Michael Dantine left with the Frenchman, Denis called

to them, every word weighted with care and horrible clarity: "How I shall enjoy paying you for tonight! How I shall savor it and chew it and swallow it and digest it! Listen to me!" He ran after the two men and shouted to them from the open doorway, his voice carrying far into the clear night. "Dantine! . . . All right then. Run away. But that's my promise to you."

He stood in the path of moonlight smiling, his hair and features and figure silvered. Steel bright.

There was a hush inside the kitchen, then everyone went about his business. There were no jokes, no laughter and camaraderie tonight.

Devon was already in bed and Kate just climbing out of her last petticoat when a heavy knock on the door startled them both. Kate hoisted the ruffled straps of her petticoat over her shoulders and hurried to the door. "Now what the devil's this?" And her rich voice changed ludicrously to pleasure. "Oh. It's you."

Devon stuck her head around the musty brown curtains of the bed but could not see the visitor. The voice, however, was undoubtedly Michael Dantine's. "Kate, run across the corridor to Gerard for a few minutes like a good girl. I want to talk to the seamstress. Here. Cover yourself with my coat."

"But what . . ."

"Gerard will explain. It's about tomorrow night's performance."

"Yes, but . . ." She was hustled across the corridor before the rest of her objections were voiced, and Devon jumped out of bed and ran for her dress by the fire, shrilly ordering the director to stay outside for a moment. Without time for petticoats, she scrambled the worsted dress on over her body and kicked off her bedgown. Michael Dantine rattled the latch and opened the door briskly.

"I'm coming in, whether or not the requirements of your precious modesty are met. Ah! I see you are comfortable."

He came across the room and stood there before her, propping one boot on the fender and holding his hands out to the blaze. She wondered what on earth he wanted of her. There was a draft across the floor that chilled her back even as her face burned in the firelight.

He said finally in a tender tone, "Did you miss me, Devon?"

She assured him that everyone had missed him, "Because the players need your direction."

"Oh, business. That isn't what I had in mind." He sighed as if the subject bored him, or saddened him. "Well then, to get on with tomorrow's play. Do you know *Beaux' Stratagem* very well?"

"Tolerably."

"Would you undertake Dorinda?"

She was startled. Dorinda, the heroine's role, while not so exciting a part as the soubrette, Cherry, was still a woman of spirit.

"You need not if you don't choose," he added quickly.

"I should like to, if you think I can." She could not let stage fright interfere with that. How wonderful to play a part again and also to wear all of Dorinda's beautiful changes of costume, all her hoops and stays and panniers and all her paint and powder! During the past weeks Devon had missed the adulation of those three performances, the compliments and the smiles. But much more, she had missed the wonder of losing her identity in an exciting life that was not properly hers.

"Good. Then it's settled. Come here." He took her by the elbow and put a soiled manuscript into her hand. She glanced through the yellowed, dog-eared pages expecting him to leave, but he did not and she thought of Kate shivering in de Guiche's room, wanting to return to her own bed. "Poor Kate. You had better go and tell her she may come back now."

He did not release her elbow but drew her closer to him. He had not found her words amusing, nor appeared to notice them. "Devon, be human. Let me see whether your body is as cold as your heart."

Irritated that he always took her at a disadvantage, she tried firmly to free herself. He would not be denied. He pulled her up against him until she was standing on her toes and bent his head far over her. She closed her eyes, angry at his impudence, but keenly aware of the slow approach of his face to hers and his rough mouth upon her lips which responded with a passionate eagerness that astonished her. But there was pain in his embrace. Through the folds of the single garment she had hastily pulled on, she felt his body, toughened by the workhouse and the slave deck, against which she was crushed like one of his African blacks, in a death grip that left her weakened, without breath. Weakness washed over her gradually as if his lips were draining her body of its blood, and she fought for breath, moving in his tight embrace with a growing panic.

The night was torn by loud voices in the corridor, and rising above the confusion of sounds came Floss Roy's raucous shriek of displeasure. Devon dragged herself away from Michael Dantine and breathing fast, pulled her gown into position, smoothing out the wrinkles as Kate Merilee burst into the room almost as dishevelled as Devon.

"Tell her, Dantine. For God's sake! She's raving!"

The director stamped out into the corridor, cracked someone loudly across the padded portion of the anatomy, while Kate slammed and bolted the door behind him.

"It's Floss. The bitch caught me in de Guiche's room in my petticoats. Whew!" She fanned herself with the lowest flounce on her petticoat. "What a day it's been!"

Feeling very warm, Devon looked innocently at the ceiling and began to unlace her gown.

"Yes. It's been quite a day, all considered."

Chapter

Sixteen

By THREE o'clock the next afternoon the Company had been rehearsing for ten hours and fifteen minutes, and Devon could scarcely believe that the terrible director with his incessant shout of "No, no, no!" and his bad-mannered shake of the head in the middle of an actor's speech, was the man who had asked so tenderly, *Did you miss me, Devon?*

Nothing she did during the rehearsal satisfied him. Her posture was a horrible example to the Company. She had a shocking habit of clutching the furniture during moments of stress, and worst of all, he set up Floss Roy as an example to follow in the correct memorizing, if not the reading, of lines. Floss was always annoying in that respect. She did not spend hours crouched before the dying fire learning her role, yet she was letter perfect, or improvising when she did forget.

It was just as well that Devon ate no dinner. Despite all her resolution to take the performance calmly, her stomach seemed to turn over on the instant that the callboy gave the half hour signal. She tried to take her mind off it by attending to her looks. Before leaving the kitchen tiring room she took a glimpse of herself in the cracked mirror.

Christmas Eve's glamorous stranger stared back at her. While Michael Dantine was busy making himself into Gibbet, the Highwayman, she had managed the painting of her face, the luscious exaggeration of her lip line and powdering of her shoulders, but her headdress was the work of Floss, Kate and Denis Varney (who had proved to be the most artistic of the three collaborators). Her hair was thickened and given added body by a quantity of false hair, the whole built up almost a foot above her head and heavily powdered. It seemed to her as gorgeous as the much-emulated hair style of the queen of France.

As the play opened, physical nausea drowned all other sensations until her first scene was behind her. Then, with perfect timing, she was at ease and began to play Dorinda with verve and insouciance. It astonished her that she who had received so many reproofs at rehearsal could suddenly understand the role while facing a hostile audience. They did not seem hostile tonight, and yet she was sure that the same students were there in the back of the drafty barn, standing in wait for the propitious moment to strike. She no longer cared. If they answered her, she would ad-lib back to them.

She realized toward the end of the act that they liked her, that an occasional whisper in the audience was in her favor. Armed with this confidence, she developed the character, playing it for all the romance she could extract and occasionally directing her lines away from Kate or Bob with whom she had most of her speeches, aiming them at the audience.

They loved it, and in the fashion of most actors, she began to love them. Could they help it if Denis had been bad last night? They had paid several shillings and gotten a tuppenny

performance. The Harvard students and Cambridge townsmen were discerning. Tonight, with Denis magnificently in
his element as the gentleman rascal, Archer, he aroused from
his old enemies no more than a few hoots at his first entrance.
He waved in the direction of the derisive spectator and
went on with his characterization. They liked that.

But it was Michael Dantine, after all, who stole the show.
Devon had never been present when the director gave a
public performance and was curious to see how his florid
personality would register before the students. An indica-
tion of his popularity came when, upon his exit, a trickle
of applause broke into a torrent that stopped the show for
almost two minutes. Devon shared no scenes with him and
could observe from the wings the power and confidence
with which he endowed Gibbet, the Highwayman. His
comedy technique verged on overemphasis, though his timing
and magnificent voice captured the lion's share of interest
in a production studded with excellent acting. Devon thought
it unfair to Denis who was equally clever, but the natural
gifts of stature and voice were undeniably Michael Dantine's;
and when to these were added his night-black hair coiled in
greasy ringlets over the tattered white shirt collar, and the
cuffs of his breeches were shoved into piratical-looking boots,
he was everything a highwayman ought to be. The audience
thought it would be a shame to see such a capital rogue hanging at Execution Dock.

That night at the last curtain Devon shared the applause
with Michael Dantine and Floss Roy, who had acquitted
herself brilliantly in insolent Cherry's role. As Devon curt-
seyed low, it occurred to her suddenly that this was the first
time she and not Kate Merilee had been called for a curtain
call.

She hurried up to the inn, bundled in the greatcoat of a
young Harvard admirer who had asked her to meet him
when she completed her change. She had also promised to
let Denis escort her to a students' party which Kate was

attending, but she was too excited over her evening's triumph to hear half that was said to her. Passing the taproom she saw Michael Dantine with de Guiche and Bob Traver grouped around the tapster. The director waved to her with a half empty glass of arrack and she went in for a moment.

"I must hurry. I have an engagement."

"No matter. Gentlemen, I give you the Dantine Company's new leading woman: Devon Howard! Drink up!"

She saw during the toast that he was still the highwayman. His hair was dripping wet, and he had not queued it up since the grease of his role had been washed out. After changing to his top boots, he was still "Gibbet." When Bob and de Guiche lowered their Flip mugs, Bob excused himself and left, with a smile for Devon. As if in tacit conspiracy, de Guiche went about his business soon after. Without consulting her Dantine sent the tapster off to make her a Hot Rum Fustian and then took her and ushered her to the high-backed settle before the fire where they were out of view of the tapster and the rest of his custom.

"I must go in a moment," she reminded him, but he paid no attention to this, and when she had sat down on the settle in a gingerly, temporizing way, he took the place beside her, stretching out his long legs and crossing them at the ankles, his feet resting on the fender of the fireplace. His action pinned her into her corner. He might at least have smiled at her when correcting all her acting faults this morning, or later between the acts. Why did he always make it so difficult for anyone to be nice to him? If only he would treat her as Denis did—Denis who always came back with a quick smile and flip remark to top hers!

She managed to say casually, "The play went well; didn't it? I remarked some in the first rows who seemed very engrossed."

"Yes, on the whole we redeemed ourselves for last night."
And then, before she could follow the tangled undergrowth

of his thoughts, "What is this so-called engagement you have tonight?"

She explained briefly about the student, omitting Denis, and craned her neck to look around the settle for the tapster. It was time she tasted her drink politely and went on to her room. He put out his arm in a jesting way and when she tried to push it aside she discovered that however jesting it seemed, his arm was inflexible.

To her haughty frown, he replied in the tone she always hated, "I don't wish you to go with your precious college students."

"And why not, pray?"

"Because you are going to stay with me."

"Indeed!" She began to be really angry. It was not that she would rather have been with Kate and Denis and the students but that she was resolved for once to win a bout with him. "And what is so attractive about your offer? Why can't I do exactly what Kate is doing and accept the invitation of a very nice young student who wants to talk to me about going on the stage."

"My dear little perversity, I know what Kate is going to do, which is not talk about going on the stage. Kate is a delightful wench. I don't deny it. But I will not have you following in her footsteps. If she persists in involving you in her pleasures I will see that you share someone else's chamber and company."

"Who else's?" she inquired brightly to hide her rage at his audacity. "Bob's perhaps, or maybe de Guiche's? But Floss wouldn't like that. Oh, I know—let it be your brother."

His eyes were like coals burning in a high flame as he slapped her face. The blow was so sudden she had not time to move and took the sting of his palm over her left cheek. The quick little pain did not matter. Her father's knotty hand had been nearly as hard. But no one else had ever touched her in anger.

She drew back as if to avoid another blow, and saw him

wince at her gesture. Good! That had hurt him too, and she despised herself for the passionate tears that made her vision of him suddenly dim. She cried out in a voice ragged with shock and the moment's hatred, "What a cheap liar you were last night!"

For an instant they remained at stalemate before Devon stood up slowly and made an attempt to move past him.

His fingers fastened like teeth upon her wrist, and instinct warned her not to challenge his strength and his desperation. "Devon, I have the right to make you listen. Shall I tell you why?"

Giggling voices came very close, a pair of lovers looking for a warm place before the fire. They paused, embarrassed at sight of them, and Dantine's hold on her wrist relaxed, as if he recognized his failure. He swung out of the seat and took long strides toward the tapster while she stood before the settle looking furious and perplexed at the same time. Let him go off and get drunk if he chose, the cowardly way to forget he had struck a woman.

When she reached her room she found Kate smoothing on a pair of rare silk stockings, the color of her own flesh. "Hurry, sweet, hurry. We shall be late."

Now that Devon had quarreled and been unforgivably insulted by Dantine over her evening's engagement, she realized how much she regretted it. It was depressing, and new to her, to know that she would like to have lived the past hour very differently. She was so used to his preference for her that she often forgot Kate's warning. There had been other women before her. She could not play fast and loose with him.

With a sigh, she changed her clothes and began to search for her violet sachets to tuck into the many folds of her costume. Then she remembered having dropped one of the sachets on the kitchen floor in the excitement of changing into her last-act costume. Well, no matter. She would attend to that when she returned from the students' rout tonight. Meanwhile, Kate was again urging her to hurry.

A few minutes later she and Kate met the students, fully a dozen of them, and she could not help reflecting how dull and stupid they would be after the Varney brothers. The boys from Cambridge were neither dull nor stupid but she had scarcely said ten words to them before Denis appeared with a horse and carriage, offering his driver and himself at her service while they drove to the Ordinary in town on the Post Road. He seemed to take her acceptance for granted, so she got in beside him amid the good natured hoots and envying sighs of the students who then rushed to add themselves to Kate's entourage.

Denis sat quite still in the carriage while she rubbed her cold-nipped hands briskly in the folds of her cloak, wondering what was the matter with him. It was the first time they had been together since his wild spell last night. Surely he was not still remembering that.

"You know, Devon," he said at last. "You are going to give Kate a run for her place very shortly or I miss my bet."

"What nonsense! She is the most beautiful woman in the colonies."

"Good Gad, my girl! La Merilee may have been that, once —but I saw the hold you had over the crowd tonight. It's witchery, as I told you long ago. But you are a liar. You're innocent—that's how you've twisted that great behemoth, my brother, around one of those fingers of yours. Even I feel it, and I'm immune to all of the ordinary charms."

"Do you know—you prattle!" But she was smiling. He reached for one of her hands and brought it to his lips but said nothing more despite several efforts on her part.

The carriage came to a halt before the red-brick Ordinary and still he kept looking at her and frowning a little. She said, "Ha'penny bit for your thoughts. Or are they worth more?"

"I was thinking about you."

"Then they certainly are not."

Denis considered her. "Although you are painfully moral and have all the gaucherie of a child about to lose her maidenhead, I will admit you look better to me than anyone I've known recently."

She pinched him on the arm he extended to help her down and he withdrew his support at once, allowing her to step squarely into a snowdrift. As she stamped out scuffing her wet shoe on the dirty road, Denis took her hand politely to escort her up the steps. "I think I shall marry you one day. I promised myself the best, and if I can't get it, I shall take you."

"And if *I* won't take *you?*"

He looked at her. He had stopped laughing and was suddenly cross. "Don't joke. I mean it. You always turn aside everything I say to you. Once in an age or so I mean what I say."

She was still smiling and he backed her against the brick wall of the Ordinary while she struggled in good humor. "Denis, I know you so well."

"That's it," he cried eagerly, shaking her. "You know me because I need you so much. I needed you so much last night it damned near killed me. I'll—I'll marry you. I swear I will. Tonight, if you say so."

"Of course not. I don't love you."

He said with blithe confidence, "I'll make you love me. I'll work at it. You'll see." Then he was quiet again, while she stared at him. He started to move away, but instead leaned forward, his cheek against her own, his lips softly upon her neck where the warmth of her hair protected it. She suffered the caress as she would a child's, wanting to cry, not understanding her own emotions. Wasn't she glad for his proposal?

She said good night to Denis at what he claimed to be "the obscenely young hour of one-thirty in the morning," and was about to go into her bedchamber when he stooped over her doorsill and came up with a folded note. "A love message from one of my rivals, I'll wager. Shall I open it?"

She snatched it out of his fingers, suspecting it might be a joke, or perhaps a note from some student, but in any case she had no intention of letting Denis Varney know all of her affairs.

When he had gone, Devon read the note by candlelight and did not know what to make of it. The writing had the broad black force of Michael Dantine's hand.

COME AT ONCE TO MY ROOM. TRUST ME. IT IS OF VITAL IMPORTANCE THAT I SPEAK TO YOU.

A likely thing. Did he imagine she could be so easily co-erced into his bedchamber in the early hours of the morning? She tapped the paper against her teeth, considering. Down the corridor she saw Bob Traver opening the door of his small, rear bedchamber and resolved to entrust him with her problem. As she went toward him she noticed that he was in travelling coat and carried a riding crop. Where had he been riding at this hour? Unless he was indeed one of those rebel Sons of Liberty.

At sight of her, he hastily threw the riding crop into his room, closed the door behind it, and faced her. Without ex-plaining, she showed him the note. He frowned over it while she prompted him, "It is in his writing. I would know it any-where."

"Would you?" His gravely pleasant voice made of the question something significant and she hastened to explain.

"Certainly. I saw it on my New Year's present and on many of the plays."

"What do you propose to do?"

She had her mouth open and a firm answer ready but his question troubled her. "Don't you think—hadn't I better—" She swallowed. "I think I should answer it."

"If you wish. Shall I wait in the corridor in case of diffi-culties?"

"If you would."

As she started down the corridor, he put his hand on her arm momentarily. "Devon, there is something odd about this note. He is either drunk or mad to write such a thing. It is not like the man I know."

She looked down at the paper crumpled in her hand and thought she knew the answer. "We—I have reason to think he may want to apologize for . . . you see, we quarreled to night "

"Then go, by all means. But I shall wait close by."

"Thank you, Bob. It is nice to be sure of one friend."

He smiled. "Perhaps I am just curious to see how this little episode turns out. Go now." He gave her a little shove and she knocked on the door of Michael Dantine's room while Bob retired to the alcove by the second floor staircase.

The director's voice answered her knock, harsh and thick with drink. "Come in, damn you! You're late."

Affronted at this address, a curious preface to an apology, she went in nevertheless, and closed the door quietly behind her. The room was saturated with the sick-sweet smell of rum and the odor of gin that was still strange to her. For an instant, in the dim rushlight, she could not see, and blinked her eyes.

Without looking up, Michael Dantine said, "Set the bottle down and get out."

So, he thought her the tapster. That would explain his peremptory tone. Moving from her place against the door, she stared across the room at him. He was sitting on the side of his bed, leaning forward, a wooden mug in his fingers. She could feel the stiffening of every muscle in her body, the nausea rising within her at the overpowering stench of spirits, at the sight of him.

And of his companion; for he was not alone.

In the flickering rushlight his shirt and the tumbled white sheets of his bed were the only pure brightness in the room. Devon finally looked at his companion, a slight wench with a terribly young, starved face. She hovered over him on the bed, putting her weight on one of her knees which was bare of her gray, stuff gown. The girl was winding a strand of his black hair over her forefinger but the result never satisfied her and she kept winding the same resilient strand over and over for an endless time while Devon stood paralyzed.

Michael Dantine shook the rum mug again and threw his head back to drain the warm dregs, disturbing the girl at her play. He saw Devon at the same time that the girl saw her. His eyes were enormously black. No other expression crossed his features for a long pause.

Devon heard her own voice, like a thunderclap in the still room. "I had a note from you. I came as you asked. What is it?"

He came very slowly out of his stupor and she saw that his hand shook as it closed over the rum mug. But something other than drunkenness had him in its grasp. A moment ago his hand had not shook, his eyes had not held in them so much horror. And at last, she understood what she had been too sickened to understand at first. He had not sent her the note. He had never in his nightmare life expected to have her come upon this sordid scene.

She began to move, feeling her way behind her until the bolt of the door was under her hand, and faltered, "I beg your pardon. I thought . . ."

But still he could not speak and the girl who had sat taking in this strange meeting, spoke up finally. Her voice was an old hag's drunken rasp out of her young, pale mouth. "What be ye waitin' for? Go 'wye. Nobody wants ye here. Begone."

Devon's foot crushed something soft upon the floor. She looked down. Her own lost violet sachet lay on the floor of Michael Dantine's bedchamber. Had he found it and brought it here? It was soiled where her slipper had trod upon it. She kicked it aside and went out into the corridor, closing the door behind her.

Bob Traver came to her in a few steps. "Devon, what is it? Are you all right?"

She shook off his hand. "He didn't write the note. There

was a woman with him. It was all a joke. A stupid, humiliating joke someone played against me."

He said quietly, "A humiliating joke, Devon, but not against *you*."

At her door she turned with sudden violence. "It's no use, Bob. I can't be like Kate and the others. I could never forgive a man who—who took such a creature into his bed."

"Devon, be generous."

"I despise him!"

"He loves you."

"He showed me so tonight, didn't he?"

He opened the door for her and she hesitated an instant, looking up at him. "Bob, dear, thank you. You are much too good for this rascally troupe."

He kissed her lightly on the cheek and went on down the corridor to his room. It was only then as she touched her cheek that she realized his kiss had grazed the soreness made early in the evening by Dantine's angry hand. Strange that it did not hurt so much as the thing she had seen a moment ago, in his room.

She stood still. *How can I hurt him? How can I return the pain I am suffering?*

She was never to know for a certainty who had sent her blundering into that room. Who had hated Dantine so much? Or who had such a wicked humor? It was clear from Dantine's freezing treatment of his brother that he suspected Denis. Once, when Denis complained at not being given a leading role all month, Devon overheard Dantine say, "If I could prove, as I suspect, that you wrote that note—"

"What note?"

"We won't argue the matter. But if I ever find the truth, I'll kill you!"

Chapter

Seventeen

DEVON'S CAREER went forward to the sound of growing applause and then lusty shouts and whistles at her first appearance each night. As her career and rising popularity took her further from Denis, his complaints grew louder. In desperation, he played at falling in love with Floss Roy, to the discomfiture of Gerard de Guiche. Devon watched with amusement, knowing that Denis despised Floss. She had been a little surprised at Floss's swiftness in succumbing but reflected that those who protested so loudly of their hatred often were the first to yield. She could hardly blame her for finding Denis attractive.

They played in Charles Town late in April, and Devon, fearing riots after the political upheavals in Middlesex County, was delighted to be given an ovation in midscene. She did not know why, for her performance in *L'Ecole des Femmes* opposite de Guiche and Denis had not been a whit better than Kate's wildly passionate work in the previous evening's *Venice Preserved*.

Sitting hunched over the firelight after Kate retired, she had been learning several serious roles. In spite of an omnipresent stage fright on her first-act entrances, she felt that her future lay in acting. A stronger motive kept her fascinated by the stage. She could do all the daring and romantic things tragediennes were always doing, and still be Devon Howard— secure in her independence, her growing reputation as the most exciting actress in the colonies.

At last Denis discovered that Devon was too busy with her own attentive lovers of the drama to notice his byplay with Floss. Early one morning in July, when Devon had been up late the previous night at a rout, she was aroused by an impatient rapping on the door. She was not in too good a mood. Last night's young Philadelphian had spent most of the evening haranguing her about the injustices of the Home Rule, boring her for interminable hours. He had discussed the Concord shootings, called the soldiers "wild beasts" and condemned all Englishborn as children of the devil.

The sounds at the door eventually made Kate curse and roll over in bed; she hadn't come in until five and needed her sleep. For some reason Devon thought the early visitor must be Dantine, since his brother never arose before it was absolutely necessary. She and the director had not spoken in private since the night at Cambridge, and she still awaited some kind of explanation from him. On several occasions he had seemed about to speak, but he never did. She hurried on the dressing robe he had bought her before Christmas and went to the door.

Denis Varney whistled at sight of her. He was tremendously impressed. The fact that he was up at this hour surprised her so much she looked beyond him into the hall, just in case someone else might have driven him to this desperate measure. He was alone, dressed to put a London dandy to shame.

He said brightly, "I kept my word. I've searched for seven weeks and haven't found the best woman ever created; so

I must take the best I can find. And here I am, suitably garbed for the occasion." He flipped out of his cuff a handkerchief with a yard of Valenciennes lace, and patted his nose gently. She laughed at his foppish airs, but did not know what he was talking about.

"Devon, I am chagrined. Don't you recall our little conversation some weeks ago about solemnizing my penchant for you?"

She could hardly believe it. "Are you still proposing marriage to me? I thought you had long ago found better arrangements."

There was a shriek in the bedchamber behind her. Kate stumbled across the room entangled in bedclothes.

"A proposal? Wonderful. Wonderful! Come in and make your declaration in style. Devon! Bring the dear scoundrel in and close the door."

Devon obeyed, a little puzzled at Kate's enthusiasm, and watched Denis cross the room, flip his handkerchief back into his cuff, and explain his motives for this unheard-of action. "It's drastic, but damme, what else is left? Do you know, Kate, that for five nights in a row I have tried to wedge in a pleasant evening with our little belle here and not succeeded yet? Well, Devon, don't just stand there. Give me the prescribed reply and we will consider the matter settled."

Devon sat down quite suddenly on an arm of the slat-back chair. His cool assumption of her answer was too much to accept standing up.

Kate was wild with excitement. "Devon, we're on pins and needles. Say 'yes' and have done with it. Denis, my lad, I'm proud of you. An honest man, and at your age, too."

Denis grinned. "Nothing at all, Kate. I'd have done as much for you . . . if I had to."

"But," said Devon in a carefully perplexed manner. "If I married Denis, I should have to give up all my . . . my friends across the candles. My gentleman last night, for instance. He was an utterly charming young man, very engaging and romantic. And yesterday I went riding to the up-country with Major Colton. The night before, let me see . . . that was my devastating lieutenant from New York. And on Tuesday it was that awfully nice little Quaker. Remember him, Kate? He was so sweet and naive. Oh no, I couldn't possibly trade them all for just one Denis Varney."

Kate and Denis looked at each other. Kate said in an incredulous tone, "Are you sure you know what you are saying?"

"Oh, yes. I know exactly what I am saying."

Kate sat down on the bed and sighed. "I never thought I'd see the day. Denis, you may as well face the fact. You have been refused."

"Twice," said Devon.

Denis did not smile. "Kate, will you favor us with your absence for a few minutes?"

Kate wrapped herself in a robe and, protesting all the way, went to the door. "These Varneys. First, it's Michael Dantine, now it's Denis. Must I spend my life in the corridors so that you two may have a 'few minutes' with the little flirt?"

"Not at all, Kate. I have nothing to say to Denis that you may not hear." As Devon started to rise, Denis reached forward and stopped her. "I mean it, Kate."

By this time, the door into the corridor had slammed and Devon made her position quite clear. "Denis, I know this will seem incredible to you, but I don't regard it in any way remarkable that you want to marry me. Two nights ago, I received a flattering declaration from Lieutenant Wickerly. Last night the lad you laughed at, the one from Yale College, also made me an offer. Both of them were fully as eligible as you."

Denis said with the first white gleam of his anger, "What you are saying, of course, is that you find me ridiculous. You don't love me."

"I haven't said I find you ridiculous. And I do like you

very much, in any case. But as to your being ridiculous, I remember very vividly a time you made me ridiculous . . . the night at Cambridge when you forged your brother's note and let me blunder into his room." It was an accusation made at hazard, for there had never been positive proof.

He looked at her startled. "But I didn't—what makes you think I sent you the note?"

"Why did you do it?"

"Now, Devon . . ."

"Why?"

"If I had done it, you might credit me with doing it for love of you—not that I did do it!"

She was enormously relieved. She didn't want to believe him capable of such a vile trick. But she said, "You couldn't love anyone but yourself."

He smiled. "But next to myself, I love you." He leaned over her and kissed her lightly on the bridge of the nose. She turned away, trying to be haughty and imperious but could not hide her amusement, and he was sure he had won. He straightened, brushed imaginary grains of dust off his suit and shook out the lace at his cuffs. "Suppose we made it a tentative 'no,' subject to revision."

She laughed and agreed to think it over. He took her hand, examined it inside and out, then sighed and gave it back to her.

By breakfast time everyone in the company had heard of Denis's proposal and did not doubt for a minute that Devon would marry him posthaste. After all, one didn't get a genuine declaration from Denis Varney every day in the week. To all pleas for a direct answer, Devon replied with a shrug and a cool smile. She had Denis where she had always wanted him—or would have, except that he took her eventual acceptance for granted. Only Floss Roy was upset; and who paid any attention to her problems?

Looking at Dantine and remembering the moments when they had been so close, she was surprised at his almost insulting lack of concern. Wasn't he going to stop her? Or forbid the betrothal? His only reply to Kate's loud remark about it was one indifferent glance upward from his plate, and the pertinent comment, "I knew some little fool would finally relieve you of him, Kate. I congratulate you upon your freedom."

The whole room was tongue-tied, and Devon reddened, but although she could think of a dozen razor-sharp replies, any one of them might cost her job. As she sat angrily mulling over an imaginary dialogue between them—she had given herself some brilliant, unanswerable lines—Dantine glanced at her. She thought she detected some malice in his expression before he shifted his attention to Kate. "What had you planned in the way of entertainment for tonight, Kate?"

For the first time since Devon had known her, Kate was flustered as an ingenue. "Nothing—nothing at all. Why?"

What a liar, thought Devon, who had heard her boasting for a week that on Thursday night she was spoken for by the richest, handsomest devil in Philadelphia.

Dantine said heartily. "Good. We may renew an old friendship."

The disgusting creature! It was just like him to be coarse, and at breakfast, too. Somehow, that made it twice as bad. And he hadn't made a single effort to stop her engagement! Did he actually want her to marry Denis, in heaven's name? As for Kate, it was plain why she had been anxious to marry Devon off—despite her warnings against Dantine, she still wanted him for herself. During the rest of the meal, Devon was distractingly charming to Bob and de Guiche and any other males who appeared within her range.

For the first time in weeks they had a real theatre in which to present the night's play. Philadelphia law prohibited any such goings-on inside the township, but just outside was a convenient building which had housed certain temporary theatricals in the past and was now the headquarters of the Dantine Troupe for as many nights as the most brilliant city in the colonies would support them.

Rehearsal that morning astonished everyone. Instead of pushing the sleepy players onstage and forcing them through their places like colts to be trained, Dantine called them to order and spoke about the new play he had been working on during the past weeks. It was an adaptation of Mr. Richardson's novel, *Pamela*.

Someone whistled, and Kate said in a tone of acute boredom, "What's the plot? Can you give it to us in a sentence?" She yawned and patted her mouth.

"My dear Kate," said Dantine pleasantly. "You may as well save your yawns for the night of the play. You will not be appearing in more than three scenes. However our lovebirds, Mistress Devon and Mr. Varney, will be more vitally concerned, since they represent the focal points of tender virtue pursued by rampant lust."

Now, what is he stirring up in that vulgar head of his? Devon wondered.

He had taken the most melodramatic scenes from the famous novel and woven them into a tale guaranteed to act as an aphrodisiac upon any town gallant. All of Richardson's careful morality was blown away like barley chaff, leaving the straight, lurid story of a beautiful servant girl and her handsome master determined on seducing her. It carried through the complicated details of his kidnapping of the fair Pamela, her attempts at escape, and the climactic moment in which Mr. B, perhaps in desperation, offers to marry her, whereupon she falls happily into his arms.

Pamela was a delightful role. Devon found during first rehearsals that it was easy to extract high comedy from the heroine's evasions of her employer. Denis, on the other hand, was not quite her mental conception of Mr. B, with his domineering ways and his force. Denis was too civilized. Still, she was not averse to playing light love scenes with him. Not at all. They made a very pretty couple, as she had heard him say many times. They went over the love scene at the end of act three at least half a dozen times during that Thurs day rehearsal. The first reading had been highly successful until that moment. Then everything went wrong.

Dantine was deadly. "I implore you, Pamela, put a little conviction into it. Surely, your partner is sufficient inspiration. Mr. B, I am sorry to awaken you at this unseemly hour. May I trouble you to take your betrothed in your arms?

". . . My dear Denis—since you are obviously not Mr. B— that is not a sack of meal you are trying to seduce.

". . . Mistress Devon, I am sure your partner is not going to rape you here on the stage, so will you please furnish a little more warmth?"

His voice went on inexorably, "Mr. B, have you eaten something indigestible?"

Devon no longer needed her script for her lines and was sure that if she lived to be a hundred she would still remember this miserable scene which she knew backward and forward and upside down, including the slap which she had administered to Denis's now reddening face for countless times in the rehearsal already.

Denis was entering again. She felt him creeping up behind her and was chilled. Why didn't he stomp in like any other mortal? Why must he have that catlike tread that made her think of prowling things? They began their dialogue. It could not be wrong this time. It sounded exactly right in her ears. And then the attempted embrace, for the seventh time.

"Damn it! Relax!" whispered Denis into her ear. How dared he make such an accusation, as if she were the cold one? She whirled around, ready for the slap the script called for, and knocked him over into the chair behind him.

Kate and the others roared at his plight. Floss Roy did not laugh, although she, of them all, might have been the most amused to see her old enemy ridiculed. Devon looked at her curiously. As Denis picked himself up with Kate's help, trying valiantly to control his temper, Devon glanced at the director. He was not laughing. He was perfectly serious—

almost too serious, like a man who is laughing inside himself. For a brief moment she hated him.

Dantine now said with unbearably sweet patience, "Denis, try not to be so clumsy. Bear in mind the anxiety of the rest of us to get on with the play. Now—once more."

"Be damned to you, you hell-kite!" cried Denis as he dashed off the stage and disappeared into parts unknown.

With the director giving Mr. B's lines from his place in the pit, the play progressed rapidly and satisfactorily to its final scene, although Devon and Kate, who played Mr. B's sister, found it a little difficult to act with an invisible man.

Chapter
Eighteen

DENIS DID not come in that night for the opening performance of *King Henry IV*, in which Bob Traver made a personal triumph as the noble traitor, "Hotspur" Harry Percy. When Devon asked Kate about Denis next day, she passed the matter off as a triviality. "Nothing to be alarmed about, my pet. He probably wants you to pine and sigh for him. When you've demonstrated enough affection to warrant his return, he'll pop up and marry you before you can change your mind. What worries me infinitely more is old Floss's empty seat at breakfast. Did she leave last night after the performance, or this morning before we were up? I've an idea she followed Denis, but if I know the dear rascal, he will send her packing."

Intending to ask about Kate's night with Michael Dantine, Devon lost her nerve and instead gave instructions to the seamstress who was fitting her new street suit with velvet panniers.

Kate helped her out unwittingly. "Why do you frown?

The suit looks enchanting. You should be all smiles. Heaven knows *you* got some sleep last night."

Devon stepped out of her gown and made arrangements for the next fitting. When the woman was gone, she turned to Kate, saying as casually as she could, "And did you enjoy yourself last night?"

"Prodigiously."

Devon began to pick up snips of gold brocade off the floor of her bedchamber. She did not look Kate's way. "His disposition was so bad yesterday, and after that scurvy trick he played on Denis at rehearsals . . ."

Kate laughed. "You're talking about Dantine. He never came near me last night. No. I kept my engagement with my Philadelphia beau. Gad's life, my dear, he's fabulously rich He's promised me a necklace of emeralds as big as robin's eggs. Old family heirloom. Trust little Kate to fetch the heirlooms out of their musty vaults."

Devon tried to conceal her pleasure over this information.

Nothing was seen of Denis until the first performance of *Pamela* eight days after the brilliant opening night of *King Henry IV*. During that time, rehearsals continued with no leading man. Devon mentioned the matter to the director. It was after rehearsal on Sunday evening and the players were arguing over their wardrobes for *Pamela*, which was laid in the present time and required elaborate hooped new fashions for everyone.

"Dantine, I find it difficult to talk to an invisible figure. I never know where Mr. B is going to stand or what he will do."

The director was busy supervising the placing of props for tomorrow morning's rehearsal and asked indifferently, "Have you no imagination?"

"Yes. I have an imagination and it tells me that there will be no leading man for *Pamela* next Friday."

"Run along and see to your costume, Pamela. You are squarely in my way."

So there was no satisfaction from him. Devon went over to the hired seamstress from Philadelphia's most fashionable mercer's shop and made known exactly what she wanted in the pert chambermaid's costume. The other players made way for the play's star and she felt that difference in her position. Even Floss was civil, not jealous at all. She had come back yesterday and been treated very politely by Dantine instead of being given the door for her desertion. It was a little odd about Floss Roy's sudden access of grand lady manners, but Devon was too busy to think twice about her.

Thursday evening there was no performance, and the company held a last dress rehearsal for this most daring play in the Dantine repertory. The theatre felt damp and depressing in the unseasonal downpour of rain, and Devon was not the only player who coughed her way through a dreary failure of a dress rehearsal. At the end of the fifth act Dantine addressed the company as they stood in a tired semicircle around him. His manner was quiet, almost kind as he covered last minute points.

"I know you are exhausted, but bear several points in mind: you know your lines. That is a beginning. But the entire performance is still white. It lacks red warmth. It lacks flow and continuity. It needs blood."

"It damned near has mine," whispered Kate in Devon's ear. Devon pinched her to silence. The director went on, oblivious to the by-play.

"More important, the tempo is far too slow. I know it is difficult for you when there has been no leading man except such of you who have walked through the role for our convenience. But I give you my word, tomorrow night you will have Mr. B."

He looked them over and added in the good-humored tone he reserved for special occasions, "One last suggestion: Be of good cheer, all you with your hangdog countenances. I am a firm believer that a bad dress rehearsal makes for a good performance." He paused. "And God knows the dress rehearsal could not have been worse."

Several of the players smiled feebly. Devon was too tired to smile—she was so disappointed at the evening's debacle that, for the first time in months, she wished herself back in Concord, Massachusetts with her father.

Michael dismissed them on the final remark, "You'll bring the whole town to its feet with cheers tomorrow night; so be off to your beds now. A carriage is at the tiring room door. For God's sake, take care not to carouse too late. And don't stay out in the rain. Good night."

Devon was changing slowly and dispiritedly into her street gown when he stopped before her. "Devon, you look tired. Sleep late tomorrow. Have your breakfast in your chamber if you like."

She smiled at him but was too tired to reply. How could she possibly rest when Denis was still gone and they might lack a leading man for the great occasion tomorrow night? If only Mr. B could have been played by someone in whom she had confidence, her own lengthy role would not trouble her so much. Even Bob Traver, physically unsuited as he was to the role of the scoundrel–hero, might have reassured her by his own competence.

She crawled into the high, cold featherbed that night aching in every bone.

A terrific upheaval awakened her a long time later. Kate was rattling and pulling the blankets off her. "What the devil, my pet? We've let you sleep all day, but you have less than three hours until curtain time. Come on. Sit up. Dantine has sent in your dinner on a tray. Wasn't that sweet of him?"

Devon could scarcely open her eyes. Lead weights were suspended from her lashes, and she groaned. "My back!"

Kate looked startled. "Are you sick? Oh, you can't be! Not today. Where does your back hurt?"

Devon could not pull herself together enough to tell her.

Besides, she wasn't quite sure it was her back. "No. It seems to be my head."

Kate put a cold hand on her brow and Devon screamed. "Warm your hands!"

Kate sighed and got off the bed. "You aren't dying if you can scream like that."

Devon turned over painfully, caught a glimpse of the steaming food on the big tray and sat up with more groans. Perhaps a hot cup of foaming chocolate would coat over the rough cobblestones of her throat. She drank a long swallow and the heat seemed to lift her headache a little. She took a spoonful of porridge. But something was wrong. Her body still ached and she was too tired to do more than play with the spoon in the porridge. And tomorrow night, she must do *Pamela*. No! Not tomorrow—tonight!

Impossible. She knew she could never walk across the stage. "Kate, I feel horrid. It's no use. I feel horrid."

"Where? Just tell me where."

"All over."

"You must have a rheum. Your head is hot and you do look feverish. But we're going to get you over it by tonight if we have to stuff you and prop you up on the stage. That's one thing a good actress has got to do. She must play unless she is dead."

"Suppose Denis isn't here." She thought a minute. "And suppose he doesn't know his lines—how could he know them?"

"Darling, finish your porridge. Try to spoon up the cream if nothing else. I'm going to get a few things. We are about to start our treatment right now."

With the symptoms of every disease she had ever heard of, Devon dawdled over her food, drank a little more chocolate which burned her throat, and coughed until her stomach muscles were sore, meanwhile trying to sort out one particular symptom for closer study. Of all times in the year, why must she be sick today, her first performance in a role that might have made her famous throughout the colonies? Kate came hurrying back into the room with one arm full of bottles and decanters and swinging a red-hot poker in the other hand. Devon sat up in amazement, forgetting to cough.

"Now, we shall see just what Kate the Surgeon can prescribe. First of all, I won't bleed you. I don't believe that ever helped a soul, and besides, leeches make me sick to my stomach. Mmmm, almost wish I was sick. What heavenly rum! Smell."

Devon loathed the sweet small of rum which reminded her of that night in Dantine's room in Cambridge, and wrinkled up her nose at the proffered decanter. Kate snatched it away and set all her bottles on the tier table before playing tapster. What she concocted was so formidable that Devon ducked under the covers and pretended to be asleep, while Kate, humming a tune, went on mixing odd things—pouring in a dose of brandy, a seasoning of salt, pepper and two chopped nutmegs, three spoonfuls of last night's meat sauce, several thimblefuls of raw whisky, a number of other liquid ingredients which she sneaked in with guilty haste—and she capped the pewter mug by filling it to the brim with rum. All of this she stirred vigorously with the poker, and the resulting noisy puff of steam frightened Devon out of any ideas of feigning sleep. It was an effort to sit up in bed again but she did so, offering to take the mug and drink its contents after Kate had gone.

"Nothing like that, my pet. What do you take me for? Drink it down." She gave the bottom of the mug a quick nudge so that its hot contents flowed more swiftly into Devon's throat. The empty pewter mug fell onto the floor while Devon fanned her mouth and broke into a spasm of coughing at the same time. Then she pressed tightly on the top of her head to keep it from flying off.

Kate laughed. "You'll be yourself in time for the performance. It never fails. In an hour there'll be no more rheum to bother you. Of course, I guarantee nothing for tomorrow."

"Never mind tomorrow," gasped Devon. "After tonight nothing matters."

Kate was right. The curtain was at five-thirty, and by four forty-five, when the company began to dress for the performance, Devon's world was bathed in a lovely pink fog and she knew that even if there was no Mr. B, the evening would be delightful. Stage fright, what was that? Fever? Completely gone. Kate was a wonder. She repeated that any number of times while she was dressing and Kate patted her on the back saying, "Yes, yes. I'm a wonder. I know. . . . Here, sweet, you have your dress on backwards. . . . Now, you've got your neck in the sleeve. There. That's better."

Word had been unofficially passed among the players that Bob would do Mr. B in his own personal wardrobe, since it was plain to everyone that Denis would not be in the company tonight, and his clothes would not fit the taller Bob. Devon thought the change a comforting notion. If she suddenly forgot every line or even dropped dead, Bob could be depended upon to cover up for the audience. The prompt boy stuck his head in to call "half-the-hour" as he tossed a folded, sealed letter to Devon and then whistled at the picture she made in her costume.

Through the fog of Kate's potion, Devon stared at the spidery writing and tried to read it.

Floss came up behind her, dressed in the fierce, black habit of wicked Mrs. Jewkes. "Is it from him?"

Devon ripped the wax and read the single sheet. At first, it danced in luminous, unsteady characters across the page but she was finally able to focus her eyes upon its message.

Devon, pet, I am asking you to come to me and I expect you will think it another trick. I need you. I am flat on my back and all I can think of as the damnable moments tick away, is you. Devon, pity a poor devil! I need you so. I'm lonely as hell, and not feeling quite my charming self. I'm lodged at the Sign of the Busk in Deacon Alley east and north of Dock Street. Come and let me know those ripe lips of yours. Nothing will get me to my feet more quickly than your sweet smile. Come the minute you receive this. I am desperate. I mean that. Desperate.

Floss said, "What are you going to do?"

Devon had a nagging sense of responsibility, as if she dealt with an unruly child. She muttered distractedly. "I don't know. I don't know. Half an hour till curtain. Time enough if I take a carriage and bring him back. Maybe they can delay the curtain for me. Floss, he's ill, and he's desperate. I've got to get to him immediately—he might do himself harm."

"Are you mad? And what of the play? Dantine won't hold the curtain. You know that."

Devon began to search for her coat, and finding it, thrust her arms haphazardly into the sleeves over Floss's loud protests. Kate saw her and heard the story of Devon's intended treachery. As Devon hurried across the room, Kate called very calmly, "My sweet, at least put on your shoes."

In her stockinged feet, Devon ran back, stepped into her lavender-heeled stage shoes and shoving Varney's letter into her tight bodice was on her way again. Everyone stood aside, spellbound, as she passed. No one could believe that she really intended to desert them all. Her wooden heels clapped noisily down the little passage to the stage door, but just as she had her fingers on it, a hand reached around her and slammed it shut.

"*What the devil are you up to?*" asked Michael Dantine in the most deadly voice she had ever heard him use to her.

"Nothing. Let me go."

He shoved her away from the door and into the wings before him. The curtain man passed, raised his eyebrows at the angry tableau and went about his business. Devon wrestled with the director in a fury.

"You little bitch! Running away from me on the most important night in our history, weren't you? Running to

Denis. Pretty little Denis who got stabbed in a drunken brawl over a street harlot. Yes. I know all about it. But Denis can do no wrong. Denis is forgiven. He is not like his vile brother whose touch pollutes your dainty flesh. Get into those wings for your opening cue, and if you try this again, I'll kill you." He shook her, and between the chattering of her teeth and Kate's earlier rum potion, she scarcely knew what was happening to her. "Do you understand what I am saying? Look at me. I'll kill you! Now, get over there in the wings and don't think you can escape during the performance. *I* am playing Mr. B tonight."

She let him push her into a corner where she stood obediently, while he went back to the tiring room to put on his cravat. She wondered how Denis was feeling and who was taking care of him. Poor Denis. If anything happened to him, if he took his life in a fit of despondency, she would never forgive Michael Dantine as long as she lived.

The first notes of the spinet startled her as the orchestra struck up an English country tune. The green curtains moved across on their squeaky rollers and she peeked onto the stage. Kate, as Lady Davers, sister of Mr. B, was receiving one of her brother's abandoned mistresses. The house, beyond the footlight candles, was the most impressive she had seen since joining the company. Everywhere possible in the big theatre, benches, chairs, cushions and boxes were crowded with quiet, expectant patrons. The aisles and walls were likewise blotted out by the standing crowds.

Belatedly, Devon recognized her cue and rushed to her entrance. Just as she put one foot before the audience, she remembered her coat and shook herself free of it as she stepped onto the stage. She prayed under her breath that the coat had not been dragged onstage behind her like the tail of a kite.

She could never afterward understand how her lines in the first two acts flowed so smoothly when she was too tipsy to know what she said or did. But she recalled very well that

Michael Dantine, in his first entrance, looked breathtaking in his black suit, fine new top boots, and his hair queued to just the right air of careless respectability. His shirt had starched frills and a black cravat—the cravat she had made him for the New Year's. She did not soon forget the gasp that went up from women in the audience during the few seconds after his entrance.

Bitterly angry with him, she thought it would be easy to outwit him in stage angles with her key role and capture the play. But as he stood silently in the flicker of the candles while she spoke her lines to him, he dominated the entire stage and beyond the stage, the vast, silent breathing pit of the theatre. It was no use trying to outdo him. She knew how Denis must have felt, battering his own tricks against the monumental poise of Michael Dantine. She found her scenes with him stimulating, and if she had not seen his eyes in the play's moments of intimacy, would have believed his fury forgotten.

By the time act three was upon her, Devon had shaken off the rum potion and was rapidly overtaken by all her morning's symptoms of chills, fever and aching that made it more difficult to concentrate on being sweet and romantic.

She was waiting in the wings for her cue, wondering a little about Denis, but more concerned that she herself should get through the next two acts, when Bob Traver came up and surprised her by his light touch upon her face. She had been too tired to renew her rouge and he was doing it for her.

"Never mind, Devon. It will soon be over. It moves fast. Then you must go to bed. You aren't at all well."

She looked up at his comforting face. "How have I been so far?"

"Haven't you heard the applause?"

"I suppose so. But they don't shout and whistle and tear things as they did in some of the other places."

"Nevertheless, I'll wager they understand better what you are trying to convey as an actress. It is an audience such as we have tonight that puts an actor on his mettle. They appre ciate subtleties. They will talk about the Dantine Company's first performance of *Pamela* for a long time."

"That may be," was her skeptical comment.

With the opening of the act that had sent Denis into a rage a week ago, her nervousness increased, but it put her on her best behavior to play up to Michael Dantine's brilliance, and she got through the scene to the last dialogue more successfully than she had expected. Then she met the full weight of Dantine's revenge.

Pamela faced Mr. B, separated by a small tea table in the rose arbor, virtuously warding him off with noble senti ments.

For heaven's sake, sir, pity a poor creature who knows nothing of her duty, but how to cherish her virtue and good name.

Mr. B began to move around the table with Dantine's purposeful stride, his dark eyes alight with what the rapt audience called lust and which Devon could see was hatred.

Here's ado with your virtue, foolish girl. Pretty fool, how will you forfeit your innocence if you are obliged to yield to a force you cannot withstand?

He reached for her and she had a wild inclination to elude him as if the whole staged scene and Mr. Richardson's dialogue were real and ominous, but she allowed herself to be trapped in his arms according to plan. Close to the candles she heard a young woman's audible sigh and felt better. It was pleasant to be envied, even if she and her hero did hate each other. His heavy voice had a depth of meaning that was real enough to make her heart jump. What an actor, she thought . . . in spite of his hatred of me, I could almost believe he loves me still. She was conscious of his daring dialogue then.

What a foolish hussy you are! Let the worst happen that can, you will have the merit and I the blame.

A gasp from the audience followed. She struggled in his embrace more than her role required, resenting the cruel force of his fingers on her upper arms, but his voice went irresistibly on, to the accompaniment of a concerted tension in the audience. Philadelphia had never seen such a shocking demonstration.

Whoever blamed Lucretia? All the shame lay on the ravisher only. And I am content to take all the blame on me, as I have already borne too great a share for what I have gained by it.

She came back nobly, very much the actress.

May I, like Lucretia, justify myself with my death if I am used barbarously.

Ah, my good girl, he taunted her. *Ere we are done, we shall make a pretty story in romance, I warrant you.* Before she could slap him, according to her role, he added what was not in Samuel Richardson: *But first, we will destroy these little vestiges of a forgotten love.*

To her speechless horror, Dantine put his hand deep into her bodice, snatched out her letter from Denis and tore it into a dozen pieces, scattering them on the stage.

She heard the scream that went up from some startled matrons in the audience, crumpled forward into his arms as required by the plot, and thought she would actually faint dead away of shame and mortification as the curtains closed on act three.

Chapter
Nineteen

DEVON'S RECOVERY was aided im
measurably by the Pennsylvania *Ledger*'s review which Dantine sent up Sunday morning.

> Mr. Michael Dantine's excellent company of players
> presented last night for the first time, a dramatization of
> Mr. Richardson's famous novel, *Pamela*, in which the
> director himself assumed the leading male role. Of the
> daring and immodesty involved in this undertaking, let
> us say little. It is sufficient to note that two ladies in the
> capacity audience swooned and one lady had to be
> borne out of the theatre by her escort during certain
> intimate and shocking scenes between Mr. Dantine and
> Mistress Howard, the enchanting Pamela.

Devon skipped down a paragraph.

> Mistress Howard approached her first three acts with
> an exquisitely light manner, which, at the end of the
> third act, turned to the desperation and near tragedy

suitable in the changing mood. In view of this, one feels it mere quibbling to note that she wears lavender and green instead of the gown of grey russet which Mr. Richardson explicitly mentioned. . . . Philadelphia and the Colonies are fortunate indeed to witness the birth of so bewitching a challenge to the throne of the great Siddons. The Mother Country may have her Sarah. We have our Mistress Howard.

Devon laughed. The critic could thank Kate's rum potion for the "exquisitely light" manner. And how had the old fellow ever recalled that Pamela wore grey russet?

Devon sneezed around the inn all day Sunday, unable to go out in the rain for one of the long summer walks she would have liked toward Deacon Alley and Denis. But after another and less alcoholic dosing by Kate Merilee, she was almost her energetic self on Monday and before seven in the morning hurried out to see the invalid.

The red brick town was splendid in the light of sunrise, with the mist rising from the river bank and the busy workmanlike efficiency everywhere, unlike the riots and pandemonium of Massachusetts Colony.

There was great political activity in the city but she noticed at once the difference between the judicial enthusiasm here, the constant knots of men thoughtfully discussing ways and means of achieving reforms and unity in the recent congress of colonies, and the rabid mob spirit of Boston. If she had not seen the tense closing of the fist of one Philadelphia dandy, and the set jaw of a lawyer, she would have dismissed the Philadelphians as talking dreamers.

As she walked down broad High Street, so different from the tortuous, strangely memorable little streets of Boston, she was aware of other differences. Where were the Redcoats who added color and menace to the streets of the northern city? For all its calm talk of teaching the motherland a lesson, Philadelphia was singularly unaware of any danger. It was easy to be a patriot in this neat, red-brick town, easier than to face down a Redcoat with his long service sword dangling against his thigh.

She had crossed beyond the State House and headed toward Dock Street when a huge placard on a brick wall beside her proclaimed the first performance of *Pamela*. In spite of her concern for Denis, she had to give the placard a reading.

"THEATRE GEORGE REX"
IN CLAPHAM ROAD
JULY 30, 1775
at Six O'Clock

The Famous Moral Study
P A M E L A
by
Mr. Samuel Richardson

presented by
THE DANTINE COMPANY

The Persons:

Mr. B. ....Mr. Dantine
Lord Davers .... Mr. Traver
Jewkes .... Mr. de Guiche
Lady Davers ....Mistress Merilee
Mrs. Jewkes ....Mistress Roy
Pamela, a serving maid ....Mistress Howard

Pamela, a serving maid . . . Mistress Howard. What a professional sound that had! She knew at last why her mother had so loved the stage, even when it treated her shabbily. She loved it for moments like this. Devon looked around self-consciously, wondering if any of the passersby recognized her. They did not seem to. She smiled wryly at her own conceit and hurried on.

The place Denis had chosen for lodgings, or perhaps they had chosen him, appeared disreputable on the outside and dank and dirty on the inside. She asked a scullery maid scuffing through the lower hall which was Mr. Varney's room and was waved up the rickety little staircase. As she was ascending, being careful lest her skirts swept against the stained and seamy walls, the scullery maid leaned her chin on the stair rail. "Ye be 'is lydy, ma'am?" Devon looked over her shoulder. "Perhaps."

The girl sighed. "So be they all. A body ain't got no chance agin' fine feathers. They was a blonde here a week gone, come Monday, an' yestiday an' day afore."

"Yes. I know. Which room is his?" The maid leaned further over the stair rail. "Front un. 'E couldn't find 'is purse but 'e 'ad sech a way wi' im."

"He has that," agreed Devon as she went around the upper hall rail. At the closed door she hesitated, remembering another time when she had come at a summons and broken into a man's bedchamber. But it could never be like that again. Seeing Denis like that would not be so terrible a shock, nor would she care as much. Denis was simply—Denis.

In answer to her rap came his voice, a little excited, unusual in him. "Just a moment, darling. Count to one hundred like an angel. I saw you from the street in your sweet summer things. You've a beauty of a hat."

Smiling to herself, she began to count. No. This was not the greeting she had received that night from Michael Dantine. While she waited, she rearranged the tilt of her new Leghorn straw—all her share from last week's productions of *She Stoops to Conquer* and *Twelfth Night* had gone for that hat. Then she examined her fashionable new gloves before rattling the door latch again.

In his most endearing voice he asked her to enter and she saw him across the room in his bed beside the sunny window. Even in this hovel, his room was neat and white and very clean. He looked delicate and helpless in bed, and she hurried across the floor, forgetting to make a stately entrance and a beautiful picture in her new outfit. He took her to task for the omission.

"Stand perfectly still, my pet. Devon, I dreamed the other night that you stood where you are standing now, and in my dream you were the most enchanting wench I had ever seen. But I was wrong."

"I'm not surprised." She awaited the insult, and from him it was sure to be one, while she thought up some witty retort. But when he spoke, the words vanished from her lips.

"Because I see you now, and you are lovelier and sweeter than in my dreams."

She laughed in relief and in embarrassment, so surprised she could not think of anything to say. He patted the side of his bed and motioned her to sit there. She came over, sat down beside him and spread her skirts out carefully to be sure her ankles were covered. He reached out a hand to pull her to him and she brushed the hand aside while looking softly concerned.

"Poor Denis! Tell me about your wound. Is it very painful? How did you happen to challenge the drunken beast?"

He looked perplexed. "What drunken . . . Oh, *that* one. Why, devil take it, he came at a young maiden on Dock Street and I stepped to her rescue. I was unarmed and the blackguard stabbed me in the back."

"In the back?"

"Well, almost in the back. Between the ribs."

"Between the ribs?"

"Yes. Toward my heart."

She turned away and he tried to catch her expression. She sobered instantly. "Yes. Yes, go on. It's very exciting."

"Damme, I'd have sworn you were giggling then. Look here, ma'am, how much do you know about my wound?"

"Nothing at all. I was shivering over your narrow escape. That was all." She purred over him sweetly. "It frightens me to think of you, the defender of virginity, in such deadly peril. . . . So you nobly defended the little maiden, and the Redcoat, without provocation, stabbed you. Almost as if you had stolen the maiden from him; wasn't it? But go on."

He was offended and turned his cheek to the pillow. Studying him for a moment or two, she softened. He did look
rather worn. Perhaps he was suffering. She did not enjoy his
suffering but rather the power it gave her to comfort him.
He felt her change of mood and his slender artist's fingers
moved slowly over the coverlet to her hands.

"Come and kiss me, my dear . . . my very dear."

She hesitated. Then, because he did look so irresistibly
young, young enough to be her own child, she leaned forward
and kissed him warmly on the mouth. When she would have
moved away from him, he raised his head a little and kissed
her flippantly on the cheek and clutched at her bare arm like
a small, roguish boy. "Devon, we could have fun if we were
married. Don't you see? We could play all the stages of
Europe. And you'd have your independence and I'd have
mine, but we'd always have each other, too. We could organize a troupe of our own. The Varney Troupe. We could
play all the good roles ourselves. We'd have a capital time of
it. Only . . . it must be you. I couldn't do it with anyone else.
I'd lack the courage, the drive. You give me that drive. You
lift me up. It wouldn't be like marrying—the others. Do say
yes, Devon."

"What others?" she demanded, pitching onto the essen-
tials.

"The others I've loved, of course. The others I've promised
shall share the Varney Troupe with me. Who did you think
I meant? My other wives?"

"But your brother would—"

"Are you afraid of Dantine? What the devil! Sometimes
I have a feeling you love that fellow."

She sat up stiffly. "Don't be ridiculous! I'll marry you."
Love Dantine, indeed! Well, she thought wryly . . . my
promise may be quite useless. Dantine will never let me do
this—never! Dantine will see that I break this promise . . .
Aloud, she said briskly, "Now, to get you on your feet.
You look very thin. Have you eaten regularly?"

"Not likely I have! Where would I get any money when I haven't worked for damned near a fortnight?"

"Oh dear, it isn't right. You look so—so transparent." How like a child he was! Truly, he needed her. Even if it actually came to marriage, it might not be too bad. He needed her and from need must come love. Besides, he was so very un-like her father!

She began again, "Let's get you some breakfast now. What would you like?"

He looked pathetically eager. "Anything. I haven't eaten since Saturday night. That was when my last ha' penny went over the counter."

"Outrageous. You poor thing. I'll supervise your breakfast myself. Before I am done with you, my dear, you'll be as big as Dantine." She slipped off the bed and her foot touched something on the floor that tinkled like glass. She looked under the bed.

Denis Varney's tray of breakfast sat there with the food and coffee still where he had hastily deposited it when she rapped on his door. She looked at him, trying to be severe. He peered over the side of the bed in astonishment.

"Good Lord! Now, how long has that been there?"

Chapter

Twenty

EVERYTHING BEGAN to happen too quickly, urging Devon toward the marriage from which there seemed now no escape. Not that she wanted to escape. But curiously enough, she dreamed that she wished to escape. It was very weird, inexplicable.

If only Dantine had needed me as Denis does! If only Dantine—"

She often fancied these days that she hated Dantine. It was maddening that she could never get him out of her thoughts, and yet, it seemed clear that whatever feeling he had once known for her was gone.

And suddenly she began to hear the date of her wedding spoken of as a definite thing. It seemed that one evening, between acts, and in a fit of momentary depression, she had agreed to Denis's persistent coaxing.

During the month before the wedding, while they played the Maryland countryside, Michael Dantine watched with the indifference of a bored audience, offering no comment to her romance, and but one decision. This, however, was implacable. Michael Dantine would play Mr. B. in all future performances of *Pamela*, even when, as Denis was careful to explain before the entire company, it was more proper for Denis himself to play this romantic role opposite his future wife. He elaborated on the fact that the love scenes between Pamela and Mr. B. were being almost as thoroughly discussed in Fredricksburg as the doings of the Continental Congress in Philadelphia, or the Committee of Correspondence. And, Denis carefully added, "Moreover, if you will forgive me, it may be regarded in some quarters as distasteful that you should make love to a young, beautiful woman. You are, you must admit, rather—"

"Ugly," inserted Dantine.

"Oh, let's not be crude. Call it—miscast—as a maiden's romantic dream. This," he added, "is no reflection upon your notorious success off the stage."

Devon and many another member of the company looked uneasily at Dantine but he took it with the ironic comment, "This is your unalterable opinion?"

"Now, Michael—dear brother—don't misunderstand me."

Michael Dantine looked across the garden props of *Pamela* and smiled grimly at him. "It is impossible to misunderstand you, dear brother."

"Seems to me," Floss put in acidly, "there's a deal of pother about that blasted play. Wasn't it Varney who was meant to do Mr. B in the beginning?"

For the first time in the argument Michael Dantine was at a loss for an answer, and Devon, watching him, knew that Varney had never been meant for Mr. B. and that Floss was either crafty or simple not to have guessed it before speaking.

"How true," Denis began but was cut short by Dantine's voice, as irrevocable as always. "I have made my decision. To your places. No more nonsense."

They moved to obey, though Floss, very daring lately, continued to mutter among the players. "Lord and Master says so. Fine nob he's grown these days! All to make love to his brother's sweetheart."

Michael Dantine's long arm reached for her through the press of players and pulled her into the front rank. "Now, here's impudence. Understand me, you slut. One more disrespectful word against any of my players and out you go!"

Bob and de Guiche tried to draw the excited soubrette out of the director's clutches, but she was determined not to be outdone in ferocity by the Master-Player. "Damned loud, ain't you, black galleybird? But I know what I know. You'd best go gently with me and maybe I could do you a bit of a turn."

Denis had gotten back into the arena again. "Damn it! Must your tongue wag at both ends?"

Floss swung on him. "You too. She's spun her little web over you, too. You fool! She is playing off each of you two ninnies against the other." De Guiche called to her but she made a furious gesture of hatred at the players and fled from the stage.

"What the devil's the matter with her? Well, let's get on with the rehearsal," said Denis matter-of-factly.

No one else had a better suggestion and all of them except Dantine went back to their positions. Less angry than puzzled at this insurgent in his docile ranks, he went after Floss. When Gerard de Guiche could no longer stand the suspense, he excused himself hastily and followed him.

"What a happy little gathering that must be!" Kate remarked as the rest went back to rehearsal. Devon took her place upstage, breathing hard and furiously, and the play went on.

The Company reached the thick, shadowed woods and golden rivers of Virginia in September, where, at Alexandria, they presented *Pamela* as their opening play. What had proved shocking and daring in Philadelphia was welcomed

205

with huzzahs and thunderous applause by the Southern planters and their wives, who had journeyed over long stretches
of abominable roads in order to see an entertainment dear
to Southern hearts. In less than two weeks the players were
a fixed object in the Crown Colony. The same audiences
came back night after night for the changes of program,
since, according to custom, no play was repeated in less than
a fortnight, and usually not repeated at all. But *Pamela* was
given three times in twenty-two days, and at each performance, many of the same faces were seen in the audience, particularly young dandies in the pit and young ladies of social
position, from barmaids to planters' daughters and burgesses'
wives.

It was obvious to the Dantine Company that positions in
the troupe had subtly changed in the past months. Dissen-
sion had been reduced to a minimum, and sometimes Devon
missed the peppery honesty of Floss, who was minding her
manners. But there had been other changes. Denis Varney
and Kate Merilee were no longer the chief targets of backstage gallants and fluttering ladies.

One night, after the third performance of *Pamela*, Devon
found a dozen dandies offering to unhook her gown, while
Kate was left to several excited girls who wanted to know all
about the Master-Player himself. Michael Dantine never had
time to dress or change in the hubbub of the tiring rooms
and long before five-o'clock was usually equipped to go
onstage. After the last curtain, he went off to the nearest
taproom and was not seen again until the next morning's
rehearsal. The growing evidence that strange young ladies
found him romantic in the greenroom bored and disgusted
him.

Devon was very polite to the director during performances. In their love scenes it seemed to her that no woman in
her right mind could resist him, but when, with the green
curtains closed, they went their way, Devon convinced herself that his spell was broken.

They began rehearsals early that fall for *Othello,* with Devon as Desdemona and Kate as Emilia, while Dantine and Denis played the Moor and his evil young ancient, Iago. Kate had never liked Desdemona and was physically much more suited to robust Emilia, but Devon liked the lovely victim of Othello's jealousy and thought there was rather more in the character than usually shown. She had to admit, also, that it was stimulating to play opposite Michael Dantine.

But it was haunting as well. If he truly loved her, Dantine would never be permitting her to marry Denis. He would have shown some gentleness, some . . . real love for her.

It was easy for Devon to forget the world's troubles when her own life was changing so rapidly. After stories drifted into Virginia of the bloody stand made by rebels on a little hill in Charles Town where she had lived, and so near where her parents were buried, Devon no longer cried her own uneasy consolation: "Impossible! Countrymen do not fight soldiers. City lawyers and townsmen do not pick up muskets against their own army!" For it had happened up North, above the very ground where, a few months ago, the Dantine Troupe had played *L'Ecole des Femmes* and *Venice Preserved,* and one battle's shadow fell upon the house where her father was born.

She believed now, at last, that countrymen did fight soldiers, but she could not understand it, the insanity of her own people, when to her myopic gaze, they had been so well off under the rule of the Crown. She vowed to the furious patriot, de Guiche, that she would never understand what was accomplished by rebellion, beyond the substitution of one form of tyranny for another. De Guiche did not care what she thought. He had turned more vehemently than ever to his Whig activities, and was waited upon at all hours by firebrand Sons of Liberty and by the quieter but no less dangerous members of the Virginia Committees of Correspondence. Bob was even more mysterious, and she was sure he was engaged in treason.

The Southern Colony was governed by that staunch loyalist, William Murray, Lord Dunmore, whose banquets at the palace in Williamsburg were the Mecca of Denis Varney's dreams. Devon shared her future husband's admiration for the spacious palace grounds, and preferred the jolly loyalists to de Guiche's glum set of rebels, but she liked to keep in friendly relations with both sides. This was easily managed; as the whole colony had suddenly fallen in love with the captivating Pamela she found herself as well liked in one camp as in the other. When necessary, she equipped herself with jokes that could be pointed in either direction and would take criticism from no one except Bob Traver, who several times suggested that she curb Denis's current dallying with the Tory cause. In response to these hints, she did what she could but had little influence.

If only her dreams—nightmares rather!—were not so persistently filled with the odious Michael Dantine. One other thing disturbed her: his remark one night after she had played both rebel and loyalist camps against each other: "The wench will end by turning into a female version of my estimable brother." She was sure that this was no compliment, but uncertain why she should think so. Surely it was wise to keep the peace, to see both sides in a dispute, especially when there had been no bloodshed in Virginia. It wasn't as if the rebellion would reach this civilized colony. When the populace did not like its governor in Virginia, they forced him to abdicate to his sloop in the Chesapeake, as happened in the middle of that summer, and there was an end of the political trouble.

Then, Governor Dunmore began to act from his exile in the Chesapeake, his long hand reaching out to his capital city, his agents still in control of the Virginia courts, and she realized that the difference between Northern and Southern revolt lay in manner rather than degree—for here, too, there was violence.

In four days, several men among de Guiche's agents had been quietly hustled aboard ships, bound for London and the traitors' dock, and Denis reminded Devon how well it was to have friends in both parties, for he, of course, had been untouched.

Chapter
Twenty-one

THE DAY seemed to be arriving long before Devon was ready for it. The whole thing still appeared dreamlike, but there was a new and chastened Denis to remind her almost hourly how much he needed her and that she was the only real love he had ever known. If Floss Roy showed her jealousy and cynicism in various ways, that was not too great a matter. More important was how little Michael Dantine seemed to care.

After a sultry October day all the windows in Devon's bed-sitting room remained open until eight o'clock at night. Miriam, the housekeeper at the inn where the players stayed, was just closing the windows as Devon tried on her wedding gown before going with the rest of the company to a rout at Yorktown. Intent on her examination of the ivory figured taffeta gown, Devon did not notice the housekeeper until she knocked against her as she left the room. Devon looked after her. It was the first time she had seen the woman drunk.

Everything was a little mad today. In the morning, Denis

had dragged her out of bed to ride upriver and look at the lovely Christopher Wren house he had suddenly thought of buying for her. It seemed amazing that Denis should be up at dawn, and even more amazing that he should have so much wealth with which to purchase the house on the James. But after all, it turned out to be mere speculation —he was hourly expecting to have money from a Yorktown shipping venture, which Devon suspected was smuggling. They would go to New York and organize a Varney Troupe, but Virginia would be their home. He had so often repeated how delighted she would be, that she occasionally believed him. It was when Denis removed his persuasive self from her vicinity that she was troubled. Troubled by him, and by her long quarrel with Dantine which would never be patched up.

Bob next came into Devon's room, closing the door behind him with a decisive slam that made Devon jump.

"How do you think I will look tomorrow before the pastor?" she asked him, twisting and turning before the long oval mirror. She swung around and, curtseying, gave him a nervous smile.

"You are the most beautiful bride I have seen in quite some time," Bob said seriously, as if he had weighed the matter.

She was surprised by his tone. "What is it, Bob? Why so sober?"

"Where is Denis?"

She stared at him in the mirror's reflection. "He's about, somewhere. Why?"

"A letter came to Gerard from an old friend, and he thought Denis might be interested." He leaned back against the bedpost of her dimity-canopied bed. "But perhaps it is just as well. It is a little surprise for him. I think we may not show it to him after all."

She did not know what he has talking about and cared less, for his manner suggested that there were graver matters to discuss. He appeared watchful, as if he did not trust her, and she was astonished at these manners from kind, ever-loyal Bob Traver. Or was this the other Bob, that one who had several times made her suspect a hidden strength, even a danger about him?

"Devon, I am going to ask you a question and I believe you will answer me honestly. I assure you that a great deal depends on my trust in you. It may even mean the lives of men you know. Do you understand?"

It was as if he read a speech from one of the Company plays. Only Bob's quiet announcement gave the words any reality.

"I—I think so."

"How long was Denis with you this morning?"

She twisted the betrothal ring Denis had given her and began to worry because it was tight. It was very tight. What had Denis done? Had he robbed someone? "I've nothing to conceal. We were together from a little after dawn until well onto two o'clock this afternoon. We went to choose the home we may have one day. Denis has made a privateer-ing venture and we shall be rich. He had an investment in a sloop, all rigged for speed and action. He's turned serious since I agreed to marry him. Perhaps I am a good influence on him. Do you think so?" She leaned toward Bob from her perch on the little stool in front of the mirror, knowing he would recoil a little, as if such flirtations offended him because he knew they were insincere. But he did not recoil. He took both her hands at the wrists and stared at her, study-ing her expression, the slightest blink of her lashes, the curve of her mouth.

"That is the truth?"

"Of course it is. What is this catechism, Bob? Has Denis done something?"

"It is important that Denis was with you between dawn and noon. Sometime between those hours a courier carrying dispatches for the Committee of Correspondence was tortured and murdered on the Yorktown Road hard by the old swamp."

"Why not report it to the authorities, to Lord Dunmore's men? Aren't they the proper persons to investigate?" Thank God, Denis had been with her during most of those hours!

"Devon, you are singularly blind. The governor is back of this attack on the courier. Whoever committed the murder did so in the interests of the Tory cause."

"Not Lord Dunmore! He couldn't murder anyone. He is a gentleman. Besides, I know him."

Bob smiled grimly. "Less than a year ago, he left an entire command to the mercy of the Shawnee Indian Confederacy on the Ohio frontier."

She sat down suddenly, unable to digest all of this indirect evidence against Denis, who was, after all, a friend of Lord Dunmore's.

"I am sorry, Devon, that this should put a shadow upon your wedding tomorrow, but rejoice as I do that Denis is not involved."

She grumbled, "One would think we were at war. . . ."

He said quietly, "Some of us were at war before the firing on Lexington Common. Perhaps you did not perceive that. There are many things you do not perceive, Devon."

"That is obvious. I thought you were my friend. I did not know you were a spy for that idiotic Sons of Liberty thing." She broke away from sarcasm. "Oh, how stupid! Why can't you rebels leave things as they were? They won't improve in your hands. It will only mean killing, like that poor fool this morning. And he was a traitor, after all."

"Don't talk like that. His body was hacked to pieces. He had been tortured to betray his colleagues and to get the dispatches he carried."

She was unnerved and uncertain enough without these horrors. And precisely what was the time Denis spent with her? Could it be that he had sought her out only to provide himself with false evidence of his innocence? Shaking a little, she shouted at Bob: "Name of God! Must you keep talking about it? How could you even think Denis capable of such a crime? Anyone in Williamsburg might have done it. Or in Yorktown. It is probably the work of some—some wandering Redskin."

"A Redskin who stole the dead man's papers?"

She turned her back on him and he left with a perfunctory bow. She hoped he would stay away. For the first time in her life she hated Bob Traver.

Why did he have to come around planting such doubts in her mind? Not that she believed Denis capable of torturing a man, for any reason. But possibly Denis had robbed the courier and someone else had tortured him. It *was* odd that Denis had come to see her so early this morning, as if he had been up for some time previous. What did she really know about him beyond the fact that he was pleasant-humored, and spoiled, and loved her? He did love her and he was as far removed as possible from the kind of man who had ruined her mother's life. He needed her more than ever now that he was in danger. . . . But had he really tortured that courier? Preposterous!

If only Dantine had been different! If only he could love one woman completely. But there was his past, Kate's warnings, her own sight of him with one of his harlots. Oh, Dantine! Dantine!

When, at nine o'clock, Kate and the crowd came by to take her along to the Yorktown rout, she refused them, knowing that tomorrow would be a strenuous day, with her wedding at noon and a performance of *Othello* at six that evening. She had a ghastly moment's doubt: *Must I go through with the marriage?*

Denis Varney lingered, asking in vain to see her wedding gown which she had covered with a cloak. But she refused him. She wanted no bad luck before the wedding. Her dreams, her queer prickling doubts—they were bad enough. But strange little things had upset her today, as if a malignant influence were at work.

One thing about Denis. He would never enslave her, never crush her as her mother had been crushed. And he needed her.

Denis pulled a small blue rosette of satin from the breast of his shirt and put it in the palm of her hand.

"For good luck, sweetheart. Wear it on your gown to-morrow."

With the others gone down the corridor, Denis smiled at her, one of the few tender smiles he ever bestowed on anyone. "Darling, I said a long time ago that I wouldn't give away anything of mine. I didn't know about you then. I was afraid of you and what you were beginning to mean to me. But from this moment, the Varneys, husband and wife, will share." He laughed. "Sounds impressive, doesn't it? The Varneys!"

She did not know why the idea gave her such a troubled conscience, but Denis caught the feel of her doubts and kissed her lips. He was tender and warm and his caress banished for a moment her sudden, sharp fear of the morrow. Her arms went around his shoulders and the back of his head, almost in a gesture of protection. She was not aware of it for a few seconds. Then she drew away from him, pushed him out of her room, kissed and sent him on his way to the rout. She looked down at the blue rosette and cradled it in her hand.

For a long time the inn was quiet. Michael Dantine had taken for the troupe the entire second story of a pretty white tavern on Nassau Road, only a couple of squares from the little dusty brick theatre skirting the Palace Green, and the windows in Devon's chamber faced on the lovely October foliage of the garden.

She reopened one of the windows and was leaning her arms on the sill, careful not to soil the tight sheath of her sleeves, when she was startled by a rapid knocking on the door. She had imagined herself pleasantly alone, free from invaders, and was astonished to hear Michael Dantine's booted step upon the floor behind her. She looked over her shoulder, trying to control a sudden ridiculous bad conscience and spoke quickly. "I thought you had gone to the rout."

He stood there in the middle of the room, staring at the picture she made at the window, all in white except the shining black mane of her hair. "I? When have I danced a jig like an idiot, to a lot of sawing fiddles? No. I came to talk to you. Have you a few minutes?"

"For my employer?" she asked. "Surely, that is your right." She came over from the window and stepped back up on the stool in front of the big oval mirror. "Please begin your little talk. I promise you I shall say all the polite things."

He walked around in a circle for a moment, kicking at the logs in the fireplace, rubbing dust off the bedposts, and finally taking his stand like a block of onyx in back of her, so that he could address her mirrored reflection.

"Devon, I swore to myself that I would let you destroy yourself if you chose, but I cannot. By God, I cannot!"

"You cannot what?" Her voice showed the beginnings of irritation that he should read her thoughts.

"He is not what you think him, Devon. He is not amusing and charming and gallant. You've seen the silver web, but the spider is inside."

"Oh, my sweet saints! What now?"

"He is evil. He is wholly evil. Can't you see that?"

She said frigidly, "From you, that is amusing. What has he done that you have not bettered?"

"A man was murdered on Yorktown Road outside the swamp today."

She turned on him in a defensive fury. "With scarcely any interruptions he was with me from dawn until two this afternoon. Where were you during those hours?"

Michael Dantine took a long breath and looked at the

high white ceiling for a moment, gathering ammunition while she turned back to the mirror and pretended to examine her pale skin for blemishes. She got tired of waiting for him to speak and said after a little pause, "If you have used your last argument, there seems to be no more to say." To her intense annoyance her voice cracked. "I would very much appreciate it if you would go."

She gave her skirts a brief flick with her fingers and studied her reflection with determined interest. But she hated what she saw, hated herself. Hated Dantine for being what he was. She could feel him move a little so that, as she stood on the small stool, her back brushed his shoulder. She stifled her nervousness, wondering who would hear her if she screamed, remembering how conveniently he had seen the whole company off to the rout. Were any of the servants around? She recalled Miriam, the housekeeper, with that whisky on her breath, and the mischievious twinkle in her eyes when she switched her heavy bulk out of the room.

Devon said with all the conviction she possessed, "Understand me plainly. There is nothing between us nor ever has been."

His answer lashed harshly upon the end of her shaky voice. "How do you know what there is between us? You cold-blooded little bitch!"

"That may be, but I'm no scrap of meat that a tiger will fight over to prevent another's having it."

She ran her shaking fingers over the lace ruffles across the breast of her wedding gown and picked off a loose thread from the low-cut bodice. In the glass she watched him as he turned away, took a few steps, and then came slowly back into the mirror's range again. His coolness matched her own.

"Well, then, Devon, the tiger is safe under lock and key, and the scrap of meat may go about her business in peace if she will give the tiger a small sisterly kiss."

She smiled at his reflection and was answered by his own

smile, slower, infinitely moving. The sight of that smile twisted her heart, touched her in a way she had never before experienced. She tried to treat the moment lightly.

"In that case, I see no reason why you should not have a properly conducted kiss. Come closer. I've no mind to move from this stool."

He accepted the offer coolly enough, taking a step or two behind her until she could touch him by an easy movement. She smiled to herself. She would give him a kiss he would remember. None of this "inhuman" talk would ever be cast at her again.

But something happened, something that was not in her calculations. As she was turning to him, she caught sight of his eyes, no longer indifferent but intensely, shockingly vital. Before she could move out of his reach, one of his hands clasped her left arm tightly below the shoulder, and he lifted her toward him. His other hand tore away Denis Varney's blue satin rosette from the low point on the breast of her gown. As she strained away from him in sudden understanding, he dragged her body close, and his lips were upon the hollow of her flesh bared by the torn rosette. She scratched at his left hand and kicked him with all her strength. He dragged her off the stool, caught her free hand between their bodies, and as she twisted her head away, kissed her on the throat. She screamed. The sound tore from her and was strangled by his fingers as they closed over her throat, tightening their pressure until her last panicked resistance was gone.

"That's for these past months you've had me on the rack. I knew long ago I would conquer those pastures where, I venture to say, not even sweet Denis has been allowed to prowl. I wanted you that first morning after we met, when I saw you sitting up in my bed at the Green George, very much the shy maiden, but not concealing all of your charms."

As she pulled herself together, he offered his hand to help her, but she moved to avoid his touch and stood before him, her face cold and white in the candlelight, her trembling fingers concealed behind crumpled skirts, so that he might not guess the extent of her inner conflict.

"And now that you have asserted your masculinity, what satisfaction have you? Do you imagine I would ever surrender Denis for such animal tactics as these?"

She could see that the shaft struck home and was infinitely satisfied. He stared at her an instant while she braced herself to withstand violence. But none came.

He said slowly and distinctly, "I could kill you for that tongue of yours."

She laughed, with a note of hysteria that she hoped he would not guess. Her brain warned her to make no resistance, to lull him into a false security, for he was watching her, judging what her next move would be, like an animal, stalking its game. She tried to remember the distance across the room, planning every step to the door.

He looked down at her, brushed a wisp of hair from her face, following the vagrant tendril with his hand. She shuddered to the light motion, torn between fear and a strange, brandy heat that filled her veins at his feather touch.

His voice, infinitely tender, exercised its old hypnosis. "What perverted animal has told you that the relations of a man and the woman who belongs to him are evil? I was resolved on having you the moment I saw you that first night, with the candle flame trembling in your fingers. Do you think I was not aware of the warmth of your frightened little body as you struggled with me for the candle? Just as you did a moment since. And the night Floss struck you—when I saw you faint and picked you up and carried you home to the Green George—I will admit it, I wanted you then, that night.

". . . But as I knew you better, it was more than that I wanted. It was the other part of you as well. I wanted that smile of yours that you were always wasting on Bob Traver and the prompt boys and the curtain men. I wanted the warm vitality of you beside me in the evenings when I worked on the plays, and your laughter when you were with another man—any other but me. You were never like that with me. Yet, tonight you are as you were that first night—for then, you were not a part of their lives, but of mine. Sometimes you make me want to hurt you. You drive me to it. I want you that way, all ways."

She looked at him, feeling the old dread, that if she yielded to the base, betraying passion he aroused in her, she would be destroyed as her mother had been destroyed.

He went on quietly. "I used to wish that you suffered, and then I would be indispensable to you. Sometimes, when you drove me to it with your flippancies, I wanted to break your little neck. I could, you know, so easily. . . ."

He had not moved; yet he seemed very close above her, oppressively close. She felt as if by some curious mental suggestion he was willing her to faint, and she steeled her tired body against the impulse and against the effect of his gaze. She knew now how the other women had felt, the others Kate had warned her about. Kate herself.

"Devon?"

How quiet his voice was, hardly above a whisper. She could feel the trap closing upon her, the pincers tightening. She could not look at him and saw his breeches and boots instead.

Then his voice shattered her. "Devon!" and she raised her head. "This is our last chance for happiness. Don't throw it away. You love me. I knew it tonight when I kissed you. Your body responded to me as it always has, though you are blind to it. You know that, don't you?" He took her by the shoulders and shook her. "Don't you?"

She saw the door beyond him, far across the room. She would have to circle the big Chippendale table and her canopied bed that lay just beyond the range of firelight. Then, there was the heavy milord chair, beside the door. She noticed everything as she remained submissive in his hands. In the moment when he relaxed his grip on her shoulders she took a hasty breath and, torn and dishevelled as she was, made a sudden dash across the room. The table's edge jagged into her left side and she paid no heed to the numbing pain. She heard his quick footstep after her, and in horror felt his booted foot come down upon the hem of her heavy skirt. There was a tearing sound. Her skirts were in long, ragged strips. She scrambled away, throwing the footstool over her shoulder at him. It struck the table and the candelabrum crashed under its weight, throwing the room into a darkness illuminated only by the flickering glow of the fireplace.

Behind her, he caught both her wrists, pinned them back until she thought her shoulderblades would crack under the strain, and dragged her toward the bed.

His voice was close to her ear, his mouth in her hair. "You said I had used my last argument. But I have not. There is still another. Do you understand?"

She gathered her strength in a final, desperate effort to free herself. He tried to scuff off her slippers beneath the torn skirts; one shoe was tight, and he tore it off, throwing it across the room. When her questing foot touched the floor again she looked up at him, her face drawn and livid. She used her last defense, the cruel, cutting lie.

She laughed, the brittle sound crackling through the room. "Do you think I would give you satisfaction? *I who loathe you*? What woman could want you, having known him?"

He freed one of her hands and twisted her hair between his fingers, forcing her head back into the hollow of his arm. Her cry of pain was foreign to her, a gasping, breathless sound stifled by his arm and the breast of his shirt as her body was lifted to the cold sheets of the bed.

She was frantic with fear of this island of sensations where the mind and body met. The fright was drowned in pain, waves of white-hot iron that scarred forever upon her the possessiveness of Michael Dantine. Her body screamed at the violence done to it; yet even in pain, there was a concord between them. His will absorbed her spirit so completely that no separate being existed. *She was Michael Dantine*, and there were no worlds she could not conquer.

Under the assault flowed a throbbing, inexplicable delight that ebbed with the gradual reassertion of her own will. And she thought at last that this concord had happened before, to the woman who loved her father and was destroyed by him.

Chapter

Twenty-two

SHE COULD see a part of the fireplace,
and she could see Dantine standing there, his features high-
lighted by the red embers. His hands were interlaced against
the mantel and he was staring at the grate below, as he had
been for long moments. She observed him curiously. Except
for a rent in one of his full white sleeves and the torn ruffle
of his shirt, he might have come from a quiet evening of
piquet with de Guiche.

He felt, though he did not see her move. His contempla-
tion of the coals had not changed and she was startled by the
deep music of his voice in the night stillness.

"It is two o'clock. You still have ten hours in which to
make your plans."

"My plans?" She realized that she had only whispered
the words, yet he heard them.

"We will go over to Norfolk and get a preacher if you
like, or up to Fredericksburg. You liked the town."

"Did I?"

"Yes. I heard you tell Bob one night that it was a perfect town for a wedding. It was after we had done *Pamela* and you were more receptive to romance than usual—though not more receptive to me, it seems."

Had he never stopped watching her in all those past months that she had hated him? It gave her a hunted feeling.

"You mean," she said with irony, "you are willing to make an honest woman of me? That was what you meant when you said you could force me to surrender—you thought you could force a disgraced woman to marry you. I would rather go into the streets than yield to you. But why marry me? Am I so different from your other victims?"

He was cool, only faintly curious. "What others?"

"Why, there were . . ." She stumbled for names to fling at him. "Kate and—and Floss and all the women who shared the honor of your bed."

"Floss never shared my bed," he corrected her indifferently.

Devon said fiercely, "If she did not, she was the only one who did not. I know what you are. If I had not known before, I should have been informed the night I saw you in that room with that—that horrible creature."

"That horrible creature, as you call her, was a pathetic caricature of you. It was I who found that violet sachet of yours and gave it to her. I tried to get drunk enough to imagine that she was you, that her body was yours and her mouth was yours, and her pliant flesh was yours. I failed. But it was a tribute to you, no matter what you may think you saw."

The shock of the night's events was beginning to displace her lethargy, and she found the courage to deny his spell passionately, because it hurt to deny it. "You lie! Long ago I knew. Before I ever saw you, I was warned. You never loved any living thing, any more than a storm loves the . . ."

He wheeled about from the fireplace. "You can say that to me? You, who never saw anything you could not have for the asking? You, who are wrapped safely in the swaddling clothes of Bob's love and Kate's love, and my love? Yes. *My* love! Call it lust. Call it anything you like, but you know I would crush the life out of anything that harmed you. Without me, you would have been lost a dozen times. I have been your father and your mother and your husband. I have been all the things you deny. You never in your stupid, ignorant little life have known what it is to want something so much you would sear your eyes out to get it."

She had always supposed the perfect love was gentle and giving. Dantine's passion disturbed her as much by his revelation of her own shocking response, as by his violence. "I know what your protecting love is. It is pain and torture. You can only bring hurt to the things you love—as you have tonight."

"You loved me tonight. There is always pain with love. You loved me an hour ago in that bed."

She screamed at him. "If you were on the rack—if I saw you burnt at the stake, I would love you. But nothing can ever happen to you. Only to those you love. I know what you made of Kate. And the others. I *will* marry Denis. He can be hurt. I am as strong as he. I would marry Denis if God himself forbade it! I would marry him in hell, but marry him I will!"

As she stared at him, he passed her, slammed the door and she was alone.

She got out of the bed and found her way to the window. She looked down at herself. Ten hours would not mend that wedding gown.

After a while, she sat down at the window seat, drowsy in the dying firelight, trying to understand what had happened to her and why she could not tear Michael Dantine out of her body as her quick tongue tore him out of her life. His lightest touch drove her to a trembling, childish frenzy that was not all terror; yet she did not hate him for tonight. She feared him because of that influence upon her.

Even now, she looked hastily over her shoulder to see if the dark phantom was still near. She took a long deep breath, knowing that her feeling for Denis and her ambition to be her own master was as nothing to the bond of pain and terror and voluptuous delight that held her to the man who had used her so brutally. What a lover he might have been, she thought, if it were not for that inhuman, masterful streak of his.

She knew that there would be angry black-and-blue marks on her throat and body in the morning, and dark, unhealthy smudges under her eyes. "A fine looking bride, I'll be bound. I'll pay you out, my fine master. I'll pay you out. I'll go through the wedding in spite of you."

But could she? Could she bear to do so?

Over in a dark corner she could see one of her shoes. She worried over finding one shoe and not the other. And then her fingers found a soft bit of satin, and cupping it to the firelight, she saw that it was the blue rosette she had worn at the breast of her wedding gown. It was crumpled and unstitched and fell apart in her fingers. Suddenly it was wet with her tears, and she buried her face in the tattered seams of the stained white gown and could not stifle the wild sound of her own sobbing.

When the first sounds of dawn reached her, she roused from her aching half sleep and began to consider what must be done. She thought of asking Kate's advice but Kate would have thought last night an adventure. There was no one else she could talk to. Long ago in Boston, Denis had believed her capable of an affair with his brother, and Denis, with his easy morals, would be the last to believe that Dantine had been her first lover. But desperately as she had fought the idea and as she fought it now, the real crime of Michael Dantine had been his success. He wanted to fetter her to him and had succeeded.

But if she yielded to that compulsion through which, for a little time last night, she had found an almost unbearable joy in his nearness, it would mean subjection to him and his whims and sudden lusts forever. She would never again be free to be herself, but always a mirror of her stronger husband. One day, her mercurial affections would drive him mad and he would kill her. But she would not be destroyed. She was of stronger stuff than her mother.

She was scarcely aware of the passage of time, and when her eyes began to ache, and she looked up, frowning, at a sudden piercing light, she saw that it was the sun. She started up, went toward the windows and pushed open the shutters. One of them was badly cracked. The sunrise had speared its way through those cracks. A hot, red sunrise.

She looked out, grateful for the cool air rising out of the garden. The garden itself was caught in that brief moment before the onset of winter when autumn colors were at their richest. The entire garden, precisely and geometrically laid out, still managed to shed enough leaves along its gravel paths to make it appear that the world was awash with scarlet and gold and all the endless shades between rust and earth brown.

She pressed her flushed cheek against the window frame and closed her eyes. She was aroused from disturbing daydreams by Denis Varney's voice as he came striding through the gate at the far end of the garden.

"Ahoy, Mistress Devon. You look like the Rosy-Fingered Dawn herself."

Shaken, Devon backed away from the window.

"Denis, no! It is bad luck for us to see each other before the ceremony."

But he was already below her window, laughing, in excellent humor, the sun sparkling on his coppery hair and his slight, stripling figure. He was a perfect creation out of romance.

She thought, *I must be mad to have these doubts.* She said sternly, "Go away. Do not look." But while she took a dressing sacque from the wardrobe and hurriedly put it on, she knew a remarkable fact. She had absolutely no feeling of embarrassment or shyness at being seen in a state of undress by Denis. And she should feel *something*.

Or had Dantine robbed her of that too? No! Because all her feelings were still present, bundled together into a fierce and violent passion against him.

Denis leaned one elbow against the windowsill. As if reading her mind in all its turmoil, he called to her, "Sweetheart, the housekeeper tells me she heard my esteemed brother shouting at you last night."

A pulse beat strongly in her throat. She put her hand up to hide this sign of her agitation. "Yes, he was here. He—he told me I should not marry you."

Denis laughed, but the laugh did not reach the tawny iris of his eyes. "Come here. Let me show you what a liar he is!"

She went to him, slowly and with a numbness that frightened her. When he put his hands on her shoulders and drew her to him, she let him kiss her but it was beyond her power to return that kiss. He did not let her go but shook her impatiently.

"You are cold. What has happened to you? Is it Dantine? Something he said?"

She tried to draw back, terrified lest he guess the truth and bring to a bloody climax his long feud with his brother.

"You are talking a great deal of nonsense. What could he possibly say that would influence me?"

"Very true, sweetheart. And how well he knows he had better not! Because then I must ruin him forever in your eyes."

"You are being very silly. You know I detest this kind of talk. Why will you go on?"

He raised one hand to her face, held her chin between thumb and forefinger. She tried to avoid his careful gaze, but his eyes were hard, inescapable. "Devon, he is a monster, this creature who craves you. He is not human. Do you understand me?" As she turned angrily, his thumb pinched hard into her chin. "You are not listening. You cannot believe anything that Dantine tells you. Not anything."

"Really, Denis, you are being very strange. Why should he tell me anything? What is there to tell about you?" She tried to laugh, to relieve the somber moment. "Surely I know all your faults."

"At least I did not murder my father."

She huddled deeper into the dressing sacque, feeling only that her flesh was tipped with ice. Very slowly, she absorbed what he had said. The most ghastly thing about his oblique accusation was that she knew instantly it applied to Dantine. This, then, must be the event that held the two brothers together: Denis Varney's knowledge of his brother's crime.

She said with surprising calm, "You know this to be true—that Dantine killed your father? You know it is true?"

He too had lost his exuberance. He said quietly, "I saw it," and reached up his hand to her. "He hurt me once—and took my father from me. Don't let him take my sweet Devon . . ."

She was infinitely touched by his voice, his words, his need of her. She bent over him and as he raised his head, she kissed him gently. "I won't let him hurt you."

She knew in this minute that she must marry Denis. It was meant to be. Anything else, any other dream was nightmarish. False.

She and Denis must get away from his brother as fast as possible after the wedding.

At eight o'clock, when Kate came to share her breakfast, she made her wait in the corridor until she had stuffed her ruined clothes under the bed and was bringing out a white summer dimity dress instead.

The hours hastened. Once or twice she had a notion of running away. She did not want to marry that stranger. She belonged to Dantine, mad and violent as he was. But Dantine was beyond her help and her love. She went on calmly with her preparations until, at high noon, she was standing beside

Denis, her eyes upon the pastor of Bruton Parish, and thinking: *It is too late now. No use in looking back. You've done it. Your life is bound to the Varneys.*

The ceremony was like a scene from one of the lesser Dantine plays. It went smoothly, unexcitingly, with Devon and Denis well rehearsed and letter perfect. Bob Traver, whose quiet, unobtrusive appearance was the handsomest in the main parlour of the inn, served as best man when de Guiche did not appear, and Dantine was not present until the last benediction, when Devon, raising her face to Denis for his kiss, saw him across the room, with an inscrutable look on his face. She was icy with fear that he would expose her before the other wedding guests. He said nothing, nor did he move forward with the others to kiss the bride. She lost the cold shroud that wrapped her tight, and found comfort in the anxious touch of Denis Varney's hand now and then, when the press of laughing guests made it possible for them to be together a moment.

"Sweetheart," he whispered at one point. "I'm off to Yorktown tonight to make a report on the swamp murder of the half-breed courier. You must promise to be faithful. I'll be home to my bride before dawn."

It was a piece of bad luck! Yet in her present state of nerves, Devon was relieved, and ashamed that it was so.

There was a great dinner for the newlyweds and Kate whispered in her very public and voluble way: "What excitement, Sweet! While you were being married today, the lads on the Yorktown Road discovered the half-breed courier had been tortured before he died. No one will say why, but I've a notion he was carrying something that would betray the patriots. Gad's my life! Think what damage those papers would do to the rebel cause if our dear Governor Dunmore got hold of them!"

Somebody, overhearing Kate, put in, "Why would anyone want to slice up the courier just for a few rebel letters?"

Devon guessed that this must be the business which would take Denis to Yorktown, and when she charged her husband with putting politics before all else, he admitted it freely. "I want to get permission to search for those papers. They'll make our fortune, Sweetheart. Say nothing to the others."

Bob Traver had slipped away during the noisy table talk. Devon suspected this had also to do with the missing rebel papers. But Kate was vastly upset. Bob might have amused her for several hours. The wedding had put her in a romantic mood, unlike Floss who seemed crushed, embittered, and not her usual shouting, screaming self. Every time Devon saw her that day, she was closeted with de Guiche, whispering, her face paler than usual. The very absence of her normal, sputtering temper troubled Devon. What was Floss planning? And why did de Guiche lend himself to her schemes?

Well, no matter, Devon sighed. She must finish dinner and go and dress for *Othello,* the most difficult play in the Dantine repertory, and on this night in particular, the play frightened her.

She felt the dramatic tension even before the curtains of the first act closed. She knew it was nonsense, but in some subtle way the Varney brothers had taken on the aspects of Othello and that devil's disciple, Iago. As a result, her own Desdemona, with no need for playacting, shrank from the touch of her black master's hand. How overpowering he was in his attraction! Beside him, in the scenes shared between Othello and Iago, Denis was a witty rogue in his crimson tunic and hose, a mere charmer, normal and human. Across the stage, from the wings, Devon looked at him and tried to remind herself of her own luck in winning so fine a cavalier.

Busy with her troublesome thoughts, she was startled when Denis appeared before her, demanding that she mend a torn triangle in his fifth act half cloak. When he joked too loudly and quarrelled too cuttingly with Kate's "Emilia," she suspected he had been celebrating the wedding and his planned financial trip to Yorktown rather too strenuously.

"Kate, my wench, you've trod on my lines for the last time, and that I promise you! Next time, I'll have your scalp."

Dantine was passing at that moment, an overpowering elemental force, Devon thought, drawing as far away from him as possible in the tiny space of the dressing room.

He collared Denis. "And if I catch you nipping one more drop of Blue Ruin before the final curtain, I'll strangle you with these hands. Am I understood?"

Kate seized on Denis and pulled him away. "I'll mend for you. Come along, troublesome rogue."

Before being led off, Denis whispered in Devon's ear, "Take care, my bride. Dantine's not satisfied he's lost you. He's in a killing rage—looked like that the night he killed father."

She tried not to hear him, and it only made the next minutes more painful.

Dantine said abruptly, "You little fool! Do you really believe that play actor's wedding solved what is between us?"

She tried being gentle, to hide the indecision, the anguish she was beginning to feel. "Please, can we not be friends? Can I not love—love you as I love Bob, and the others of my friends?"

He started to speak, something furious, she was sure, but Kate Merilee looked back and called in great alarm, "Curtain, Dantine!"

He looked at Devon, saw her averted face and left without speaking again. She followed slowly into the wings, feeling that a part of her world had ended.

The theatre hushed. The scene had opened and the act went with supreme success. Devon moved through her role, remembering nothing of it. She could think only of Denis's warning. She could not take her eyes from Othello. It seemed to her that a curious metamorphosis took place in Dantine as he began his role. The distinctions between the actor and his part grew fainter. She wondered if he had really looked like this the night his father died and she wondered why she could not stop loving him nor stop the pain inside her at the tortured darkness of his eyes.

It was just at the curtain of act four that Denis caught her as she left the stage. He was pale with excitement. "He's mad. He hasn't said anything that isn't Othello since we started. He will give himself away. I needn't have fretted. Dantine will destroy himself before them all. I heard them muttering a few minutes ago. They suspect already that he *is* the strangler Othello!"

Devon went icy with this reiteration of her own fears. In his present state of mind, he would betray himself and his crime to the entire audience. She was still in this state between scenes when Dantine, coming past her in a great flurry of black and silver robes, stopped to reprimand her. "You give nothing tonight. There is an audience out there. They have paid to see passion in tatters. You are in love—Show it!"

"I can't," she murmured desperately. "I don't feel anything."

"Liar. You love me. You never stopped loving me. He never won you. I know that."

"You are mad! Think what you like, but you are mad to think so."

"Oh, yes. You would like to prove me mad. Then you would be free of your memories, wouldn't you? I knew that when I saw you turn away from me tonight."

She said wearily, "It is no use. I belong to him now."

"I don't think so, my dear. I don't think so at all." He spoke with that dark, sardonic humor she knew so well. She felt his thumbs play along the sides of her throat and the heavy pressure through flesh to the bone. "Very well. You persist in painting me as a madman. There is so little force necessary to play being mad. You see how little? Then, one sharp twist. One twist just under the jawbone. Just about —here. Your neck would snap. Now, what do you say?"

She whispered hoarsely, "This is Othello. This isn't Dantine."

He pulled her head close and kissed her on the mouth and pushed her away roughly. "Go on. There is your cue."

She stopped a moment in the wings, taking a long breath, and went to her death couch. The snuffer clipped the candle at the head of her bed, so that the scene following might be played in the faint gleam of one low-burning candle. She had been half convinced that, in Dantine's playacting, she herself was his next victim, and all the time she knew he loved her. She must not let herself think these things or she would be mad as the Varneys.

Ominous drumming announced the opening of the fifth-act curtain. She lay quiet. Floss Roy stood in the wings, fingering the flat sets that Denis had painted long ago. Her petulant features showed strain. As the curtains parted, she and Denis were thrust aside by the black and silver figure of Othello entering upon the stage.

Devon stared into the eyes, saw the hands, and wondered if her life and Dantine's sanity would end here tonight, together on this stage.

His voice was magnificent as ever; only the throbbing beneath the voice showed his rising agitation.

"I'll not shed her blood nor scar that whiter skin of hers than snow. . . . Yet she must die, else she'll betray more men. Put out the light, and then put out thy light. . . ."

She felt his warm lips upon her brow. How tenderly! Never had he been more tender. Beneath tenderness was the man who had warned her that he would strangle her if she resolved to leave him.

"One more." A kiss. *"One more . . ."* Had she imagined that there was a stir in the wings where Denis and Floss Roy

234

stood? Yes. They were listening closely. Would they understand her if she tried to warn them?

"Be thus when thou art dead, and I will kill thee . . . and love thee after."

She spoke her waking lines without remembering one word before the other, yet all flowed serenely, through long experience.

"Talk you of killing?"

His voice. Something had happened to his voice. It was not muted, as in rehearsal, but hoarse, unlike himself. Or was he only acting? Superbly, but acting. He was trying to tell her something.

"Ay, I do . . . Think on thy sins."

"They are loves I bear to you." Dear God! It is true!

His dilated eyes never left her face. She cried,

"Oh, banish me, my lord, but kill me not . . ." Nor banish me. I love you. I want to be with you. How can you think I would ever leave my love?

"Down, strumpet!"

"Kill me tomorrow; let me live tonight!" She screamed the words. There was still time. He must believe her. He must know. Bob! De Guiche! There were hundreds of sane men listening just below the footlight candles. They must understand. They would not let her die. They would not let Dantine destroy himself in this last madness.

"But half an hour . . . But while I say one Prayer!"

The words were gone. The last words of her role and there were no others. Her mind was blank of words to say. She moved stealthily across the bed. The shadow of his hands came over her face. His warm, large hands that even now had the power of rousing fiery emotions within her. She screamed. Unwillingly, her eyes closed.

Covered by the silk sheets of the death couch she heard the poignant, terrible scene of Iago's capture, the proof of her innocence, and Othello's suicide.

For a breathless time the applause at the play's end was delayed. Then it came in wave upon wave. She stepped forward, trailing her death gown across the floor between Othello and Iago. As Dantine turned to escort her to the smoking footlights, Denis took her hand in his and bowed over it gallantly before bringing her fingers to his lips.

"Damned fine pair, and so we shall always be," he whispered and she pressed his hand while smiling graciously at the audience. She had not exchanged a glance or a word with Michael Dantine. But she was sensitive to his nearness as she had never been to another human being.

She moved closer to her husband. They must leave soon. She would not spend her life in the presence and under the eyes of Michael Dantine.

The starring performers bowed again, three handsome actors who had achieved a pretty success playing at jealousy and murder.

Chapter
Twenty-three

DEVON WAS packing a saddlebag for Denis's overnight trip to Yorktown when one of Governor Dunmore's aides called to see him. They were in Devon's chamber and she watched curiously as he stepped over to the door and carried on a whispered conversation. Whatever the aide's news, it was good, for Denis said, "Many thanks. I accept His Excellency's offer for myself and my wife. If only it were not tonight. But, by Gad, yes! I accept."

When the Redcoat was gone, Denis slipped on his travelling coat under his wife's startled eyes.

"You haven't told me—what did you accept for yourself and your wife?"

He pulled his shirt collar out over his coat, still the dandy, as he came toward her. His face was alight with excitement.

"Darling, our fortune is made. You know, I must see Dunmore in Yorktown harbor tonight. It's about that little shipping affair of mine. But now, His Ignoble Excellency has made me an offer to serve him. An offer we cannot turn aside."

Bewildered, she asked "What kind of an offer? Is it honorable?"

"Naturally, sweet. Would I dream of accepting otherwise?"

"You mean we are to leave the Troupe—now?"

He looked at her, one eyebrow raised. He was smiling, but she was aware of a certain distance, a coldness in that smile. "Now, but a married female accompanies her husband. That's my good girl." He squeezed her by the shoulders, trying to instill in her his own enthusiasm. "Think of it! I shall be in very good odor with the most powerful man in the Crown Colony. Once this idiot rebellion is blown away, who is to say? There may be a governorship for me. . . . Governor's Lady. What will you say to that?"

When she could not answer, he wheedled her with the charm she had once found so irresistible. "Now come, kiss me. We'll be rich and famous and you'll have a new gown every day. Pack a few things in that funny little bandbox with the blue ribbons."

She worked silently, knowing this was the best possible solution. Leave the Dantine Troupe forever. Leave Kate and Bob and the theatre that had become her life. Above all, leave Dantine, that great storm of a man who filled all her thoughts, her heart, and her body.

When the packing was done, with the greater part of her possessions left in a portmanteau to be sent along later, she momentarily expected Denis to say their farewells to the special members of the Troupe. In the end, it became clear that there were to be no farewells. He had no intention of telling any of them.

"Ready, Governor's Lady?"

She smiled with an effort. He was so like a child, mischievous and charming and never quite adult, she thought. "Denis, why don't you go down and arrange with the ostler about the horse and a gig, or whatever. I'll meet you in the stable."

"Just so. But be still as a mouse. We don't want my beastly

brother causing a fuss. And he is sure to, when he knows I've stolen his prize away from him."

She said impatiently, "I know. I know!" and watched him leave, jaunty in his spotless new fawn-colored wedding suit and tricorne hat.

The evening wind had slackened and nothing broke the autumn calm. Devon went to the window and opened the shutters to look out upon the boxwood and snapdragons and the luminous heads of the late roses. She watched Denis as he left the inn by the garden gate. He paused under the tulip tree to adjust his cravat.

She closed her eyes. ". . . Dantine . . . Dantine . . ."

But Dantine had committed the ultimate horror. Dantine had murdered his father. The old nightmare came back while she stood there. She was struggling for breath in a sea of dark waters and a hand suddenly materialized above her. Was it a hand bringing death, or life? She could not know, but she understood at last that it was Dantine's hand.

She roused herself, shook off the black mood, and went over to the little gaming table in the corner. Her script for the new production of *King Lear* was there. She tore off the blank page at the end. Using a pen whose quill needed sharpening, and watered ink which spattered badly, she wrote:

DEAREST FRIEND KATE:
PLEASE TELL DANTINE I
MUST LEAVE WITH DENIS.
GIVE MY LOVE—

Then she crossed out the last word and added:

MY AFFECTION TO ALL.
FORGIVE ME.

And she signed her name: Devon Howard.

It was not until she was leaving through the quiet garden in the rising moonlight that she looked back up at the windows of the inn and remembered that her signature had been a lie. She was no longer Devon Howard but Devon Varney. She laughed, without humor.

She heard Denis calling her and finding it too painful to think about what was past, she went on across the dew-covered kitchen garden to the stables.

The sleepy young ostler hitched up a mare to the ancient gig and with Denis handling the reins, they clattered out of town under the cool autumn starlight. They cut across town and into Yorktown High Road in a bustle that left Devon breathlessly hanging onto her uncertain seat.

There was a rich, golden-harvest look to the landscape. The fields on the west were piled with corn shucks and the swampy woods lay eerie as another planet under the late-rising moon.

Devon was silent, hearing under the clip-clop of hoof-beats and the harness jingle, the soughing of wind in the thick, virgin forest that encroached on the road. No rider, no carriage had passed them for a considerable time.

Denis muttered, "Do you hear anything?"

Devon looked out at the strange landscape. "A night bird, probably. Or some small animal, trapped in the swamp. Hateful place!" She shivered and pulled her cloak more closely around her. But it was merely a gesture. She was chilled to the bone and knew its cause was further to seek than the dismal fringes of a swamp.

"No, no . . ." Denis burst nervously into her thoughts. "On the road. Riders. Don't you hear them?"

"Very likely Governor Dunmore's soldiers, but they needn't concern us . . ." She glanced at him, suddenly alarmed. "Or are you afraid of the other side. The patriots?"

She remembered suddenly the torture and murder of the Indian on this road only last night. "Denis, what of the papers taken from the half-breed who was killed here? What were those papers?"

There was a distinct smugness to his answer: "Merely a

listing of the Committees of Correspondence, and as many of the Sons of Liberty as are known."

"But—but Denis, that list could hang scores of good men, loyal patriots."

"Loyal? Crown traitors, belike! Don't be sentimental, my sweet."

While he went on making political judgments, she looked again at the thick woods enclosing the road. In the back of her brain small hints and growing doubts gathered. She did not voice her fears. They were too terrible. She thought she would rather not know. Yet . . . the half-breed tortured, murdered in the swamp, somewhere near this very spot. The stolen rebel papers that had not been recovered. But, of course, they had been recovered—by his murderer!

"It *is* riders!" Denis exclaimed and suddenly reined in. He sent such erratic signals along the reins that Devon, like the unfortunate mare, was confused over his intent. He was trying to turn the gig but a murky stream bordered the road at this point before it emptied into the woods to the west and fed the swampy regions. The mare trod on the stream bed, slipped, and carried the turning left wheel with her. The gig did not quite overturn, but Devon on her side was thrown far over and had to leap from the vehicle, tearing skirts and petticoats in the effort.

Denis was still scrambling to get the mare back on an even footing when Devon saw the heavy mass of shadow across the road ahead break into moving parts. Denis saw her face in the patch of moonlight, heard her sharp intake of breath, and raised his head.

There were five figures, four men, the fifth smaller, a youth or even a woman in a boy's three-caped driving coat. Two of the riders now cantered slowly toward the trapped gig and its frantic driver, and passed him so that he was surrounded.

"Get down!" said one of the three facing Denis, with just the quiet note of command that permitted no question.

Devon started forward, thinking, as always, to protect him as one protects a headstrong child, but she found her way barred by one of the mounted men. He was unknown to her, which relieved her first horrified fear that he might be Dantine, ready to play Cain to his brother's Abel.

Meanwhile, the other men were dismounting. One carried a lantern whose flickering fire he turned up, showing Denis Varney's pale face as they urged him ahead of them, off the road along a narrow, spongy shelf above the dark mass that was the river swamp.

All of his captors were wearing wide-brimmed hats. It was difficult for Devon to make out their identities, but it was clear to her that they must be men whose names were on the list Denis was apparently going to sell to the British Governor.

When Devon brushed past her guard, suspecting they meant to do murder, the man followed, took her arm, but did not resort to force. "Mistress, this man is an assassin, a torturer," he said, with the kind of dreadful finality of a judge about to put on the black bonnet and pronounce the death sentence. "He has it in his power to hang half a hundred patriots."

The other silent four, single file, were marching Denis toward a glade illuminated by the moon overhead but surrounded by the Stygian black of the woods and the swamp.

Devon tried to run but was restrained by her companion. "A trial!" she cried. "He must have a fair trial. Anything else is barbarous."

"A fair trial?" her companion echoed, heavy with irony. "Before Lord Dunmore? The man he serves?"

She stumbled on across the spongy ground, wondering desperately if Denis might make a bold break for freedom if she could distract them in some way. Her loathing of his crime, her disgust with herself for having been goaded into marrying him, were all swept aside. He was that eternal child, born without conscience, and no more responsible for his actions than if he were raving mad and chained to a wall in Bedlam.

If Dantine were only here! But no! Dantine had committed the greater crime of parricide.

"Please . . . please . . . allow him a trial. Only that!" Her agonized cry seemed to hover on the air, and Denis, stopped now in the glade and surrounded by his judges and executioners, took up her cry.

His face caught the moonlight which glinted off his hair like a golden nimbus. "Ay! That should satisfy you—a trial. I'll abide by it. Let me be taken before a judge—"

"A Crown Judge?" asked a harsh female voice with the well-remembered accents of Cheapside London.

Devon stared at the smallest of Denis's shadowy captors. The woman removed her concealing planter's hat and shook out her yellow hair. It was Floss Roy.

Though Devon gasped as she realized Floss's long pent-up hatred, Denis seized on what he considered a lucky development. "Floss! I got you the post with the Troupe. I loved you. Remember the good days?"

"I remember they were good only because I knew the truth about you. Because I was there when your father died," the woman said hoarsely. "I remember because I found you all those years after, and made my knowledge pay. If it hadn't been for me, you'd never even have known how to reach Dantine or his players. I'd have had nothing. But neither would you. It was I who did everything to help you and me —it was I!"

"Be silent!" one of the men warned them. "Hoofbeats."

"Soldiers?" Denis cried loudly, full of eternal hope. "From Yorktown?"

Devon started to scream for help but the first sounds were snapped off by a gloved hand pressed hard over her mouth. She choked at the salt taste of sweat and leather, her eyes wide and staring over the hand of her captor.

But it was not the soldiers Denis hoped for. It was a single horseman who came from Williamsburg-way and dismounted by the half-turned gig, looped the reins over a tree branch and came striding toward the glade. Devon knew that stride as she knew the great figure in the heavy travelling cloak that billowed around him in the faint breeze soughing through the foliage of the woods and swamp.

She prayed that Dantine, whatever his wrongs, would not be the man who sent his brother to his death.

One of the group around Denis moved violently and Devon caught the glitter of a wide-mouthed carbine. Struggling vainly to warn Dantine, she heard another of Denis's captors speak. It was the low, firm voice of Bob Traver.

Not gentle, loving Bob among these killers!

But in his hand too, was a weapon, a tiny derringer. "No! It is a friend. No one has a better right to judge this man."

Devon moaned and subsided. Her captor took his hand from her mouth and as Dantine came on directly to her, ignoring the others, she murmured brokenly, as she went into his arms, and felt his warmth, his all-encompassing love, "Don't let them goad you to it! My darling . . . my darling, help him. He is such a child!"

"An evil, corrupt child," Bob Traver said.

Denis burst out eagerly, "She is right. I did not think. It was all an accident." His tawny eyes searched each blank face for support. "One thing grew out of another. I did not intend to torture the fellow. Besides, he was only a half-breed. You do see? Look! Here is the list of names. Take them, Bob. You are fair. You won't let them harm me."

"Don't listen! Don't trust him!" Floss screamed.

Bob Traver moved into the moonlight. He wore an army sword slung from a crossed leather bandolier. The steel glittered like a mirror, but no one except Devon noted it. They were all intent upon the derringer he held in his fingers with an ease amounting to carelessness.

"You admit you tortured and murdered the half-breed?" He had not yet taken the small rolled sheaf of dark-stained papers Denis drew out of his waistcoat.

"I admit anything. Anything to oblige you, one and all."

Over Devon's head Dantine said calmly, "Take him back to Williamsburg. Let the House of Burgesses be convened and decide what is to be done with him."

"No!" Floss screamed as the others exchanged undecided glances. "They will give him to the governor. He'll go free. Dantine, you are a fool. All these years he has blackmailed you. Now is your chance to pay old scores. I know the truth. I've always known the truth about your father!"

Devon could feel the stiffening of Dantine's body. She looked up and stared at Floss as they all did.

Dantine said, *"What do you know?"*

Floss pointed a pale, shaking hand at Denis who cowered suddenly, stepping backward, the heel of his boot sinking into the slime at the edge of the swamp.

"I worked there at his father's fine house in London. I saw the quarrel that night Dantine came to claim his father's protection."

"Take care, Floss," Denis called to her, whether threat or bribe, no one could be sure.

But she ignored him, her face swollen and passionate as she spat out his retribution. "On the steps his father struck out at Dantine, and the boy ducked aside. His father over-balanced himself and went hurtling down the steps and into the wrought-iron gate. It impaled him. But who would believe it if Denis and me—we said different? And then Denis screamed, 'You've killed him . . . *You'll pay! You will pay!'* And long after, when we all met again, we made him pay, Denis and me. It was our word against his. And who would believe a workhouse brat when there was this fine, silken little boy that said it was murder? Denis was a liar even then, and he made me one, with a kiss and a promise. God forgive me!"

. . . Even in this, Denis lied to me, Devon thought *. . . Even in this, I was unjust to Dantine. . . .*

In the silence that followed, the sucking of mud in the

swamp was clearly audible, and the darting of a flat-headed snake after a trapped insect. Behind Denis's slim body the reeds shivered in the October night, and the scurrying of other swamp creatures could be heard through the glade.

"He is a monster, this Varney," muttered one of the men.

But Dantine, looking into Devon's eyes, waved aside Floss's bitter testimony. "It was long ago," he said. "And I think" as Devon smiled at him tremulously—"it no longer matters. Bundle him up and take him in to Williamsburg Gaol."

"Always the Noble Moor," Denis jeered bitterly, unable to silence himself. "Leave the villains, the slime, the Iagos to me. But for you, in life as on the stage, it is always the grand role. If I could destroy that crushing black force that has hung over me forever, I would not care if I died for it. Your very existence has ruined my life!"

One of the men said calmly to Dantine, "You are aware, Sir, that he would be freed if word reaches the Governor? And that he must have committed to memory many of the names on that list?"

Dantine said impatiently, "Yet you cannot hang him high and dry without a trial. If so, we are no better than this jackal himself."

As if impelled by some emotion which Devon supposed must be pity, Bob Traver moved close beside Denis who began to brush his fawn-colored breeches fastidiously. His hand was close to Bob's and Devon started to cry out but her voice was drowned by Denis's loud, triumphant shout as he snatched Bob's little pistol.

"Jackal, is it? This to me, from a bastard who let his own father die! Who comes galloping now to steal his brother's wife! Jackal, you say?"

The little pearl-handled derringer in Denis's fingers was pointed directly at Dantine, who had raised his arm at the same time, thrusting Devon from him, out of range.

There was a muffled commotion among the witnesses. Only Dantine and Denis seemed to matter—Denis with his back to the swamp, and his face, with its grinning "Iago" look in the bright moonlight; Dantine gazing at him, as if daring him to shoot.

Something, some tiny movement seen out of the corner of her eye, made Devon look away from the two leading actors in the melodrama. Bob Traver, too, was smiling, a smile that made Devon shudder, it was so unlike his gentle self. She saw then what it was that had caught her eye. The rapier was free, in his hand, the point downward, but the wrist hard, the muscles ready.

In that moment as Devon turned from Bob and reached out to Denis crying, "Denis, no!" it was too late. His fingers had already tightened. The trigger moved and Denis fired at his brother. Devon screamed, conscious of heavy hands struggling to drag her from Dantine. There was an odd, empty click.

Denis turned the little pistol over in his palm, dumbfounded.

In the grim silence Bob moved his sword hand unobtrusively, saying, "Did you imagine I would give you a loaded pistol? Dantine! Are you satisfied? He is no better than a swamp moccasin."

Denis groped for him. "You! It was you, always, who were my worst enemy. And I never knew. You lying, foul cheat!" He flung himself at Bob and in the second's time that the sword was between them, Denis gave a throat-tearing scream, swaying there on the swamp's crumbling bank.

"*Be thus when you art dead,*" Bob quoted with terrible irony. . . . "*And I will kill thee . . . and love thee after.*"

Then, as Denis's tawny eyes emptied of malice and of all else, he screamed, "Michael! Brother!"

Dantine reached him as his fine, polished top boots sank below the scummed surface of the swampy waters. He was struggling horribly, in panic, while Dantine grasped and then lost his wet, slippery hands. Dantine was on his knees on the edge of the bank as Devon and Floss joined him, struggling to save the man Floss had condemned only minutes before.

"He is too far out," Dantine whispered hoarsely, extending himself, his long arms stretching, his powerful fingers reaching out vainly. "God! Too far . . ."

Denis sank beneath the muddy water, then came struggling to the surface. His hair was unqueued and floated eerily. The bright tendrils tied themselves around the reeds. A widening circle spread over the waters and the moonlight gleamed on the swamp creatures beneath. Then all was still.

Three of those who had condemned Denis were gone now. Bob Traver said only, "I will explain to the authorities in Williamsburg. Goodbye, Dantine." He only looked at Devon, saying nothing. But the hand he had extended was not taken: Dantine was still staring at the now-shadowed waters. Bob took the weeping Floss, and they silently left.

Dantine had poled the river to the opposite wooded shore with an itinerant fisherman and found no trace of his brother's body, and still he stood, staring at the secret waters.

Presently he said to Devon, "It is over."

They left the glade just as false dawn had deceptively lightened the sky on the eastern horizon. Dantine tethered his horse to the back of the gig, pulled the vehicle out of the little gulley with surprising ease. Lifting Devon onto the seat, he got in beside her and took the reins.

As the good-natured mare trotted back toward Williamsburg, Devon reached across the reins and clasped his right hand. "Michael," she said, finding a sweetness in saying that name at last, "you did all that could be done."

He put his free hand over hers. "I think, I pray—for one very short moment at the end—we were brothers."

"I am sure of it. Oh, Michael, thank God you came after us!"

"Did you think I would not? It was Kate, of course who

gave me your little note. I would have killed him if he had hurt you. And yet, and yet . . ."

"I know."

When Michael drew her to him, she knew she had never been so loved and so loving. And she understood at last how he needed her, far, far more than Denis had needed her.

At dawn, they reached the outskirts of Williamsburg. The town had just awakened. The crier was on his way home, yawning. The local farmers were beginning to drift in with their autumn produce. And suddenly, as Michael signaled the mare to turn off the wide street toward the stables, a placard on a red brick wall caught the light and seemed to blaze in the sunrise. Devon looked at it once, and resolutely, did not look back again.

THE DANTINE PLAYERS
PRESENT
at the Palace Green Theatre
for the first time in
The Crown Colony of Virginia

The Tragedy of
O T H E L L O
by
William Shakespeare

Othello, the Moor .Mr. Dantine
Cassio, his lieutenant .Mr. Traver
Iago, his ancient . . . . .Mr. Varney
Desdemona, wife to Othello . . . . .Mistress Howard
Emilia, wife to Iago . . . . .Mistress Merilee
Bianca, mistress to Cassio . . . . .Mistress Roy

on October 7, 1775

One Performance Only